GUITAR BOY

GUITAR BOY

MJ AUCH

SQUARE
FISH

Henry Holt and Company
NEW YORK

This is a work of fiction. All characters, locations, and events
are either products of the author's imagination or are used fictitiously.

The author thanks Bernie Lehmann
for permission to use his poem "Sotto Voce."

Thanks to Allen Hopkins, http://www.allenhopkins.org/,
for his help in finding traditional songs.

**SQUARE
FISH**

An Imprint of Macmillan

Square Fish and the Square Fish logo are trademarks of Macmillan and
are used by Henry Holt and Company under license from Macmillan.

Library of Congress Cataloging-in-Publication Data
Auch, Mary Jane.
Guitar boy / MJ Auch.
p.   cm.
"Christy Ottaviano Books."
Summary: After his mother is severely injured in an accident and his father kicks
him out of the house, fourteen-year-old Travis attempts to survive on his own until
he meets a guitar maker and some musicians who take him in and help him regain
his confidence so that he can try to patch his family back together.
ISBN 978-0-312-64124-5
[1. Brain damage—Fiction.   2. Guitar—Fiction.   3. Guitar makers—Fiction.
4. Musicians—Fiction.   5. Family life—New York (State)—Adirondack
Mountains—Fiction.   6. Adirondack Mountains (N.Y.)—Fiction.]   I. Title.
PZ7.A898Gu 2010   [Fic]—dc22   2009050782

Originally published in the United States by
Christy Ottaviano Books/Henry Holt and Company
First Square Fish Edition: November 2012
Square Fish logo designed by Filomena Tuosto
Book designed by Patrick Collins
mackids.com

1 3 5 7 9 10 8 6 4 2

AR: 4.0 / LEXILE: 700L

*This book is inspired by and dedicated
to luthier Bernie Lehmann. When I watch Bernie coaxing
the voice from a piece of wood as he builds one of his exquisite
guitars, it is obvious that he finds pure joy in the process.
Bernie is an offstage character in this book as the
author of the poem "Sotto Voce."*

CHAPTER 1

Travis barely got his long legs folded into the front seat and the passenger-side door closed before his father slammed the gears into reverse and jolted them all out of the driveway. He glanced into the rearview mirror at his older sister, June. She had baby Lester on her lap, his clean Sunday shirt already streaked with some mud he must have kept hidden in his little fist. Travis knew that June hadn't noticed it or she would be working on cleaning him up. The day after their mother's accident, Dad had made June drop out of her junior year of high school to take care of Lester, Earleen, and Roy.

Now the whole family was on the way to see Mom for the first time, and Travis had a sour-note feeling about it. Travis thought either he or June should have gone first, before bringing all the little ones along. They were too young to understand what had happened. Travis looked over his shoulder at Roy, who was nervously running one of Travis's hand-carved cars along the ridge below the car window. Even though Roy was only a second-grader, he hadn't cried since Mom's accident. Travis could tell from the way he kept his lips folded under that he was holding his fears and sadness inside.

"Let's sing a song," Earleen said. "We always sing when we're in the car with Mommy." When Travis didn't respond right away, Earleen's foot hit the back of his seat hard enough to make him lurch forward—an amazingly strong kick for a four year old.

"Okay, Earleen, okay!" Travis launched into the first verse of "John Henry" to stave off another boot in the rear. He deliberately picked a song that could last long enough for the whole trip to the hospital. Travis knew "John Henry" by heart, so he went on automatic pilot and the words continued to spin out of his mouth, no matter what thoughts were running through his head. He stared out the side window, watching telephone poles glide by, their wires dipping, then swooping up in the same rhythm as the music. June joined in with a clear soprano harmony, reminding Travis of Mom singing and playing all the old songs on her guitar. He had to drop out for a couple of bars because he couldn't sing around the lump in his throat.

Just as they finished the last verse, the hospital sign came into view, and Dad pulled into the parking lot. He looked over his shoulder. "I want you kids to act normal when you see your mother, hear?"

Travis thought *normal* was a strange word to describe his family, but he nodded. Checking the rearview mirror again, Travis saw June fish a tissue out of her pocket and wipe some snot off Lester's upper lip and chin. It was hard to make that kid look presentable, but she did her best. "Mom's okay, though, isn't she, Dad?" June asked. "You said she didn't have any broken bones."

"That's right, not one broken bone," Dad said. "Only a bump on her head."

"How bad a bump?" Travis asked. Dad had been pretty vague about that. Why would they keep somebody in a hospital for two weeks because of a bump on the head? Travis hadn't pressed Dad for more information, but now that they were down to zero hour, he wanted to know what they were going to find up in that hospital room.

"She's not perfect," Dad said. "But she's coming along. This hospital is the newest and the best. It has more computers than you've ever seen." Dad was busy maneuvering around the parking lot, trying to find a space as close to the entrance as possible. He spotted a lady who was getting into a car just beyond the handicapped spaces. He started his turn signal and waited while she kept talking on her cell phone before starting the car. Dad's thumb drummed against the steering wheel on the off beat to the blinkers.

Not perfect? What did Dad mean by that? Travis bled off a little of his uneasiness by tapping a riff of his own on his knee, then jumped when Dad laid on the horn and yelled, "Okay, lady, get a move on! Other people need to get into the hospital." The lady gave him a dirty look and backed out. Dad pulled in, overshooting the space so they were halfway onto the sidewalk. Another ten feet would have parked them inside the building.

◆ ✦ ◆

They all piled out and headed for the entrance. Travis tugged at the cuffs of his dress shirt to make them reach his wrists, but they only stayed there if he kept his arms hunched up inside the sleeves. The shirt was new for his sixth-grade graduation two years ago, and Travis had grown a lot since then. Dad had insisted that visiting Mom for the first time was a special occasion and one of his old worn-out T-shirts wouldn't do. When Travis reached out to steer Earleen through a big lobby with a lot of couches, his wrists poked out again, so he unbuttoned the cuffs and rolled up the sleeves.

"Mom is on the third floor," Dad said. "I'll go up to her room and make sure she's ready to see you. You kids wait here until I come get you." He turned and headed for the elevator.

June was trying to carry a squirming Lester. He had learned to walk a few weeks ago, so he wanted to get free and practice his new skill. As soon as she set him down, Lester careened around the empty lobby, ran into a stuffed chair, and plopped down on his diaper-padded rear. Travis started to retrieve him.

"Let him be," June said. "There's nobody here he can bother. Besides, he needs to burn off a little energy before we go up to Mom's room." June settled into a couch and Earleen snuggled in close to her side, sucking her thumb. Roy was running his car around the magazines on a coffee table.

Travis sat on the other side of June. "Maybe I should go up first and check things out," he whispered. "In case Mom looks too scary for the kids to see her."

June kept her eyes on Lester, who had blasted off across the lobby again. "It's been almost two weeks since the accident. If Mom had any bruises they'd be faded away by now."

Travis leaned close to June, speaking softly so Earleen couldn't hear. "But the pickup truck rolled over three times, June. That's no fender bender. What if her head injury is really bad? What if she's acting weird? Dad never could look trouble in the face. This might be a lot worse than he's let on."

"We're here now," June said. "We'll have to make the best of it." She leaped to her feet to retrieve Lester, who had latched on to a small potted tree and was about to bring it down, pot and all.

Travis saw a guy in a bright green uniform wheel a bed out of the elevator. The man lying in it was all hooked up to tubes, with a plastic bag of liquid swinging from a bracket over his head and another bag that Travis figured was filled with piss slapping against the side rail.

Travis felt a wave of nausea roll over him. The smell here brought back a sharp memory of his only other time in a hospital. When he was Roy's age, he had fallen out of a tree. The emergency room doctor had poked around his arm and asked where it hurt. Dad always said that a boy shouldn't be a wimp, so Travis told the doctor it didn't hurt and used every bit of strength he had to hold back his tears. Then the doctor bent Travis's arm, and a searing pain came from all directions, pulling a black curtain behind it until all that remained was a pinpoint of light that flicked out, leaving only a roaring in the darkness.

Later, Mom told Travis that he had passed out without a whimper. An X-ray showed that his arm was broken in three places. Dad had carried that X-ray around for ages, bragging about his brave son. Travis had never again been able to measure up to the image of that tough little kid. Now if he threw up in the hospital at the age of fourteen, it would only confirm Dad's opinion that he couldn't do anything right.

"Okay, Mom's all set and can't wait to see you kids." Dad's words brought Travis back to the present. He glanced over at Roy, who had ducked down behind the coffee table, only the hand running the car still visible.

"How about I go up with you first, Dad?" Travis said. "Maybe this is too much for the little kids. They could wait in the lobby with June."

Dad shook his head. "Nobody's waiting in the lobby. The doctor said it would do your mother a world of good to see you kids, so we're all going in. Come on."

June swooped up Lester, Travis coaxed Roy out from behind the coffee table, and they all followed their father down the hall.

Earleen was afraid to step over the crack in front of the elevator door when it opened, so Travis had to pull her by the hand to get on. It was the first time any of them had been in an elevator, and Travis was surprised that his knees buckled under him when they started going up.

Earleen had the same trouble getting over the crack when they got out on Mom's floor, but Roy loved it. "I want to ride some more. Can we see how far up it goes?" It was the first time Travis had seen Roy smile since the accident.

"This is the top floor," Dad said. "You can ride back down after our visit. Now you all act natural when you see your mother—like everything's the same as it was before." Dad flashed a wide grin that showed all of his teeth. He took a deep breath and led the way down a long hall.

A tune shot through Travis's mind—*Smile, though your heart is breaking.* It caused the hairs on the back of his neck to prickle.

They stopped outside a double door labeled NEUROLOGY. Dad checked each one of them over, wiping the drool from Lester's chin and using the goo to plaster down Roy's cowlick. Something was always dripping out of Lester. Dad scowled at Travis's rolled-up sleeves, then straightened his own skinny shoulders and tuned up his smile a few notes. "Okay, let's go in there and bring some Tacey family cheer to your mother."

They walked into a huge room with a full circle of counters and desks. Computers and monitors flashed jagged heartbeat lines. Dad led the way past the smaller rooms that ringed the outside. He had his arms folded, hugging himself, so his bony shoulder blades poked out against his brand new T-shirt like sprouting wings. He stopped by one of the doors, shot them what Travis thought was a phony, cheerful thumbs-up, and went into the room.

June and Travis looked at each other and paused by the door. There were two beds. The closest one held a little old lady who was leaning way over to one side with her mouth hanging open. Her snoring sounded like Mom's ancient Ford pickup when she tried to coax it into starting every night to drive to work.

A curtain was drawn just far enough to hide Mom's face, but Travis saw Dad reach out and gently take her hand. "Your babies are here to see you, Geneva." He leaned in. "What's that? No, you're fine. You look beautiful, sweetheart." He motioned for them to come into the room.

When Travis got beyond the curtain, all he could see was a fat bald woman with tubes and wires coming out of her. His mind couldn't make sense of what he was seeing. Was Dad making a stupid joke?

"Travis, June, bring the little ones over to see your mother." Dad patted the bald lady's hand, then he came around to the other side of the bed and pulled back the curtain. "You kids, say hello to your mother."

They all stood there frozen, as if they had been playing a game of statues. Even Lester was dead still.

"Come on now." Dad's voice was soft and pleading. He had tears in his eyes.

Travis was numb. No way that bald fat thing in the bed was Mom. Mom was slim and beautiful with long reddish brown hair—chestnut, she called it.

Earleen broke the spell and ran to the bed. "Mommy! Are you coming home with us?" Dad scooped her up. Earleen must have been too short to see before, because as soon as she got a good look at the person in the bed, she stopped reaching out and pressed her little fists to her mouth.

Oh, Lord, please don't let this be Mom, Travis prayed silently.

The woman tried to reach for Earleen, but only her left arm worked. The fingers of her right hand curled up, then the wrist pulled down and the elbow bent, as if the arm had a mind of its own and was doing the exact opposite of what the woman wanted. Her mouth twisted and she let out a weird sound—"Eeeeerrrrrrr."

Earleen buried her head in Dad's neck. "I want my mommy."

Dad rubbed her back. "Mommy's right here, Earleen. Look, sweetie."

Earleen peeked at the woman again, her eyes hopeful, then turned away and sobbed.

The voice in Travis's head had stopped praying and started screaming. *This is not our mother!* He had to get out of there. He backed away from the bed, knocking into the nightstand. Suddenly a piercing beep filled the room. Had he caused that? A nurse came out from behind the circle of desks in the outer room but went to the other bed. "Now, Mrs. Strawderman, remember not to bend your elbow, because it puts a kink in your IV and the alarm goes off." The nurse adjusted a tube, pushed a button on a machine by the bed, and the noise stopped. Mrs. Strawderman never missed a beat of her snoring.

"Travis? Come see your mother." In spite of Earleen's howls, Dad still had the fake smile plastered on his face. Travis forced himself to move closer to the bed. He could see that the woman wasn't fat because the body under the sheet was normal-sized. It was only her face that was all swollen and puffed up. There were three jagged lines of stitches running across her scalp. She wasn't really bald, either. Her hair had been shaved off.

Travis wanted to look away, but he kept searching for signs of Mom. Well, what he really hoped to find was proof that it wasn't her. The bristles of hair trying to grow back sparkled in the sunlight from the window. They were chestnut brown. And worse, when Travis looked into the woman's face for the first time, his mother's eyes looked back at him—light blue like the hunk of beach glass she had saved from a trip to Cape Cod when she was a girl. Nobody but Travis and his mother had that color. The rest of the family had Dad's muddy creek-bottom eyes.

Travis heard someone take a sobbing breath. He wasn't sure if it was June, or if he had done it himself.

Then Roy marched up to the bed, took a close look, and said, "You're not our mother. Where is she?"

The woman . . . Mom . . . stretched out her good hand to Roy, but he yelled, "Don't you touch me!" and ran for the door, dropping his wooden car on the way. Travis saw his chance to escape, but June beat him to it. "I'll get Roy," she said, running out of the room.

"I shouldn't have brought you kids here," Dad said. "How could you do this to your mother? You're breaking her heart." He headed for the door, carrying a screaming Earleen.

Mom moaned, thrashing her head back and forth on her pillow. "Neh, neh, neh," she kept saying in a loud voice. She grabbed Travis's wrist with a surprisingly strong grip. Her eyes locked on his and he tried to think of something to say to make up for what had just happened, but he couldn't breathe. Couldn't utter a sound. Could barely see his mother through his own tears.

Suddenly that mind-numbing alarm went off again. "I gotta go," Travis said, as if the shrill noise was an important phone call he had to answer. He pried Mom's fingers off his wrist one by one. As he ran for the door, his foot kicked Roy's car, sending it skittering into a corner. He didn't stop for it, but kept running. One of Mom's old gospel songs played in his mind.

Run to the city of refuge.
You'd better run, run, run.

CHAPTER 2

he only sounds in the car for the first few miles were Earleen's quiet sobs, punctuated with loud sniffs. Travis held her on his lap, patting her back to comfort her, but she was inconsolable. He had snagged a spot in the backseat of the car, using the excuse that June needed him to help with the smallest kids. No way he was sitting in the front with Dad. He had strapped Roy into that seat. Lester sat on June's lap, looking from face to face in bewilderment. Travis wished he were that young, so he could be clueless about the fact that his family was falling apart. He stared out the side window, burning with the shame of rejecting his mother's silent plea for him to stay with her. But what could he do? He didn't know how to help her. He wasn't sure anybody could.

"There, there, it's okay," he whispered in Earleen's ear the way Mom would have done it if she'd been there. If she'd been herself.

The plan had been that Dad would take them to Carl's Diner for a special meal after the hospital visit. Dad was the main cook there and every once in a while he'd bring the whole family in for a meal. Travis was pretty sure that wasn't going to happen today. Then Dad surprised him by turning toward town instead of going up the mountain road that led to home.

"I should leave you all with empty stomachs for what you did to your mother," Dad said, "but I came in early this morning, special to fix this meal for you, so I'm not letting it go to waste."

Dad was probably one of the best cooks in the Adirondacks. Everybody said his talent was wasted at Carl's and he should be at one of the fancy restored Adirondack lodges, but Dad had never tried to get a job at one of them, even though the money would have been much better.

"You're here earlier than I expected," Carl said, as they went inside. "How did the visit go with Geneva?"

"Don't ask," Dad said, as he forged ahead into the kitchen.

Carl raised his eyebrows at Travis, but he didn't answer, either. This wasn't the time or the place for explanations. "Okay, then," Carl said. "I'll set you up at the table in the corner in case you want some privacy."

While Travis put Lester in a high chair, June settled the other two in chairs—with a booster seat for Earleen. She tucked their napkins under their chins, giving each one a kiss on the top of the head as she did it. June had always helped Mom with the kids, but since she had dropped out of school to take care of them full time, she seemed more like their mother than sister. Lester was certainly starting to think of her that way. Travis doubted that Lester had even

13

recognized Mom at the hospital. Carl seated two couples up front—tourists, Travis figured. One of the men held his cell phone close to the window. "Where can you get reception around here? I only have one bar."

"Reception is spotty here in the mountains," Carl said. "Some folks have luck out by the flagpole in the parking lot." Travis liked the idea of having a cell phone. A few kids at school had them. Mom had once said she'd feel safer driving to and from her job at the prison at night if she had a phone. But Dad had used the excuse of bad reception, and of course the expense. Would a phone have helped Mom the night of the accident? Could it have brought help sooner? Could she have dialed 911 even if she couldn't speak, or was she unconscious as soon as the truck rolled over? Nobody knew.

Dad came in with a big tray of serving dishes. He was smiling, which made Travis feel that they were forgiven for what happened at the hospital. "Okay, kids. I made all of your favorites—meat loaf, mashed potatoes, and peas." He started dishing up the meal family style.

"I'm not hungry," Earleen said.

Dad put a slice of meat loaf on her plate. "Sure you are, Earleen. You hardly ate any breakfast."

"That's because I was excited. You said we were going to see Mommy."

Travis saw Earleen's lower lip start to tremble, so he grabbed the mashed potatoes and put a scoop on her plate. "Here ya go, Earleen. Want me to make a gravy volcano for you?"

14

She shook her head. "Who was that lady in the hospital? It wasn't Mommy."

Dad kept serving up full plates and sliding them across the table to them. His smile had faded and Travis could see the muscle by the angle of his jaw tighten and release as he dished out the food.

"Well?" Earleen persisted. "Who was she?" Earleen was the one who had inherited the biggest lump of Dad's stubbornness.

Dad spoke through clenched teeth. "Hush, Earleen, you know that was your mother. You don't need to be telling stories to the whole world." He cut his eyes sideways to the table behind him.

Travis looked over his shoulder and saw their neighbors, Smoke and Nazerine Feaster, at the next table. Smoke Feaster was stone deaf, but his wife, Nazerine, had ears like a fox and was always poking her snout into other people's business and blabbing about it. Anything she heard here might as well be published in tomorrow's *Intermountain Gazette*. Travis figured old Smoke probably went deaf in self-defense so he wouldn't have to listen to her.

Travis speared a forkful of his meat loaf. He hadn't realized how hungry he was. With his other hand, he kept Earleen entertained with the gravy volcano with peas for rocks.

Then Roy started in. "It was not our mother in the hospital. That old bald lady didn't look nothing like her." He stood up, yanking the napkin out of his neckband. "You know what I think? I think our mom is dead. That's what I think."

Dad had been eating his own meal, but he stood up and grabbed Roy's plate. "Roy Tacey, are you going to say you're sorry or should I take your lunch away from you?"

Roy folded his arms and slumped down in his seat. "I'm not sorry, and I'm not eating nothing until our real mother comes home."

Travis wondered how Roy thought Mom was dead one second and expected her to come home the next, but then realized he had almost the same feeling. Mom might be alive, but he wasn't sure she'd ever be herself again, let alone come home. The mother they had known might as well be dead.

Travis looked around the table, watching for whoever was going to erupt next. He never expected it to be June. She was a lot like Mom, and usually stayed strong for the rest of them, but she had reached her breaking point. She buried her face in her hands, then excused herself and ran for the ladies' room. Of course Lester started to cry the second she left the table.

"That does it." Dad grabbed a bussing tub and started tossing their half-eaten meals into it. "I try to give you kids a treat, take you to visit your mother, take you out for a nice meal afterward, and what do I get for it? Nothing but whining and complaining." He put Travis's almost full plate on top of Roy's, the mashed potatoes oozing out between them like mortar in a rock wall. Travis couldn't believe he was throwing away a perfectly good meal. They never wasted food at home—couldn't afford it.

"You know who has a right to complain?" Dad went on. "Your mother, that's who. But she's taking this like a soldier."

"Dad, you should have warned us," Travis said. "You should have told us what to expect, what she looked like— that they shaved all her hair off."

Dad slammed the serving dishes into the tub and Travis heard at least one of them break. That would come out of his pay, for sure. Then Dad stormed out the front door. Travis jumped up and followed him into the parking lot.

"Dad! Wait!"

Travis's father turned on him. "If I had told you what your mother looked like, not one of you kids would have come to see her."

"Yes, we would have. I would have. And if June could have explained things to the young ones, they would have been okay. They were confused and scared."

"How do you think I feel? Your mother is my whole life." Dad had tears in his eyes, but then he jutted out his chin. "But I'm not letting you hurt your mother again because I'm never taking you kids back there." He got into the station wagon and spun his wheels going out of the parking lot.

When Travis went back inside, Nazerine Feaster was clucking over Earleen and Lester like a broody hen. "It's such a shame about your mother's accident. So she's not looking like herself? She's in a pretty bad way? Did you say she's bald? All that beautiful hair of hers gone? Geneva was known for that glorious hair."

Carl must have heard the ruckus because he came out of the kitchen and saw the mess in the bussing tub. "What the . . . where's your father?"

"He went off in a huff," Nazerine said. "Left these poor

little ones to fend for themselves. We'd be happy to give you all a ride home. I'd love to hear more about your mother. Geneva is such a saintly woman."

Travis glared at her. "We're fine. We don't need a ride." Then, realizing how rude that sounded, he mumbled, "Thanks just the same."

Mrs. Feaster's eyes grew wide. "But I'm sure I saw your father drive off without you."

Carl stepped in. "Everything's all arranged, Mrs. Feaster. They're riding home with me as soon as they finish their meal."

"Well, I think their meal was finished when their father threw it in the—"

"You have a good day, Mr. and Mrs. Feaster." He hustled them toward the door, then came back to the table. "Sit down, kids. I'll fix you up with some food here."

"Thanks," Travis said. "I'm sorry about Dad."

"Your father has a lot more than he can handle right now, Travis. I understand how that can be. Sometimes life piles too much on a man."

Carl gave them a good meal, calmed down Earleen and Roy, and delivered them all home afterward. Travis was glad to see that Dad's car wasn't there yet.

While June put Lester down for a nap, Travis pulled out Mom's old guitar to take Earleen's and Roy's minds off what had happened. He picked funny songs with lots of verses. Hearing his own fingers on the guitar strings made him miss Mom more than ever, especially now that he wasn't sure she'd ever be able to play or sing again.

The guitar had always seemed magical to Travis. It had been built by their great-great-great-grandpa Eli Dunning. They called him 3-G Eli for short. They'd heard stories about him all their lives from their mother—about how he came here back in the eighteen hundreds, set claim to the land, and built the little log cabin that still stood up in the woods. He was long dead before Mom was born.

3-G Eli had been a singer and earned his money by making musical instruments—lutes, dulcimers, guitars, and even a violin or two. They were all gone now except for 3-G Eli's old guitar. It had been played so long and hard there was a big spot on the top that was worn thin from four generations of strumming. Travis had watched his mother coax music out of that guitar right up to the day of the accident. She sang with a voice so sweet and pure it squeezed his chest tight every time he remembered.

"How about 'The Fox'?" June said, coming back into the room. Travis, June, and Mom used to do three-part harmony on that one, and it sounded empty with only two voices. It was an old song, going back for generations, but Mom often added her own line here and there to make the kids laugh. They had gotten to their favorite verse—*old mother slip-slapper swooped out of bed*—when Travis heard Dad's station wagon come to a screeching stop in the driveway.

"Come on, kids," June said. "Let's go out and take a walk." She hustled Roy and Earleen out the back way seconds before Dad came crashing through the front door. He was carrying a six-pack of beer with two missing. That must have been enough to get Dad drunk because he wasn't normally a drinker. He stood there for a minute, staring at Travis, swaying a little. Then he grabbed the guitar by the neck and yanked it so hard that the leather strap broke and snapped against Travis's cheek. "Might as well use this old thing for kindling," he said.

Travis jumped to his feet and tried to take the guitar away from him. "Mom loves this guitar. She's gonna want to play it when she's better."

"You saw your mother. She won't be playing or singing, or even talking. Nobody around here needs a broken-down old guitar to bring up hurtful memories." He raised it over his head, ready to smash it against the wall. Travis lunged for it, knocking Dad off balance enough that he loosened his grip. Travis snatched the guitar out of Dad's hands and ran for the back door.

Travis heard Dad roar, "Come back here!" but he kept running, and didn't stop until he reached 3-G Eli's old cabin. This was Travis's safe harbor—always had been, from the time he was little. Whenever he was in trouble, he would run to the woods, even though he knew hiding out would bring on another scolding from Dad when he got back, usually worse than the first. How many times had these old red spruce trees watched Travis come out here? And his mother before him, and generations of her family before that?

Travis pushed the cabin door open and was hit by the familiar musty smell of the small closed-in space. This was the first building on the land, and the only home until Mom's grandpa bought the trailer that was part of the house they lived in now. The cabin had no windows, so it took a few minutes for Travis's eyes to adjust to the dim light. He settled in on the cot with his back against the wall and ran his hand over the guitar, checking to make sure nothing broke when his father had ripped it from his hands. It seemed to be fine. Travis plucked the strings with his thumb, finding a couple had gone out of tune with all the banging around. He twisted the tuners until each string sounded the perfect note. His mother had taught him how to do that and told him that his ears had the same perfect pitch as hers. The thick bottom strings made his chest vibrate and the upper strings rang like bells. It was an ugly old guitar, but it sounded magical—like an angel choir.

Travis's heart and mind eased as he played a few of his mother's favorite songs. It was as if the guitar strings connected him to her. Now he wished he'd paid more attention when she tried to teach him. Oh, he knew enough chords to play most any song, but he never did master the way Mom picked the strings, making the notes tumble out one after another like the call of a brown veery bird.

Travis's fingers were finding their own music now, and the words came out before he knew what he was singing.

> Sometimes I feel like a motherless child.
> Sometimes I feel like a motherless child.
> Sometimes I feel like a motherless child.
> A long way from home.
> A long way from home.

CHAPTER 3

Things had been going downhill ever since that day Dad took the family to the hospital two weeks ago, and he had been true to his word about not taking any of them back again. When Travis reached for a second helping of mashed potatoes, Dad's fingers shot out and closed around his wrist. "There won't be enough to go around if you shove half of it into your belly, Travis. Serve up more to your sister."

Earleen pushed her plate away. "I don't want any more. It doesn't taste like the way Mommy makes it."

"Eat some to keep peace," Travis whispered to Earleen. It had been a month today since the accident, and she wasn't getting used to the idea of Mom being away. Every time she got upset, it set Dad off. Earleen stabbed her fork into the little dab of potatoes Travis had plopped on her plate.

He gave the last serving in the bowl to Roy because he looked like he might cry from the mention of Mom. Most of the time Roy acted angry, but Travis could tell he was still raw with hurt, and nobody could do or say anything to cheer him up. Roy was old enough to remember Mom, so he knew what was missing. Earleen remembered Mom, too, but she was young enough to crave a mother, and June filled that empty place for her. Travis was so busy trying to soothe all the jagged nerves in the family, he barely had time to think about how much he missed his mother.

When Travis looked over at their big old Kenmore electric stove, he could picture Mom stirring a pot of steaming soup on one of the two good burners that were left. She'd be singing "She'll be coming round the mountain" to the little ones, who stuck to her legs like iron filings on a magnet. Nowadays, Dad had the opposite effect, scattering his offspring to the far corners when he entered a room.

"You been listening to me, boy?" Dad thundered. Baby Lester started to wail, June picked him up and spirited him outside. Dad used to be a patient father, but now nothing set him off faster than what he called "a howling brat." Losing Mom had changed him.

"I heard you, Dad," Travis lied.

"I talked to Verl and you can start tomorrow."

"Tomorrow?" Travis stalled, hoping to pick up another clue about what his father had been saying to him.

"He'll be by in the morning to pick you up about eight."

"But I have school tomorrow," Travis said. Who was this Verl person Dad was talking about? Verl, the dishwasher at the diner? No, his name was Vern.

"You think you're going to be wasting your time with school when there's a family to support? You'll take the job Verl Bickley is offering and be glad for it."

23

That explained it. Verl Bickley of Bickley Used Furniture and Appliances. In other words, the junk man. Exactly the kind of job Travis's ninth-grade computer science teacher, Mrs. Robbins, said education could save him from.

"It's only a month until my final exams, Dad. I can't drop out now. The exams count half of my final grades. Besides, the state doesn't let you quit school until you're sixteen."

"The state doesn't give two hoots about the likes of you. You didn't see the state dragging June off to school, did you? She's been home more'n a month now. Nobody's asked a thing about her."

Travis couldn't argue with Dad's reasoning. Maybe the state did see to the kids in the city when they quit school—try to get them back in line. But out here in the middle of nowhere, if a kid was needed at home and didn't go to school anymore, that was pretty much his family's business and nobody else's. And if he came to no good later in life because of a lack of education? Well, that was just one more hunk of trash to be hauled off by the junk man.

Travis finished his potatoes, then rubbed a piece of pork chop across the plate to pick up the last scrapings. What the heck was in those potatoes anyway? Garlic? With a dab of horseradish? Earleen liked Mom's cooking better than Dad's, but Travis couldn't agree with her on that. Oh, Mom had been a good enough cook, maybe even a little above average, but Dad had crazy mad skills in the kitchen.

Before Dad got fired from being the cook at Carl's Diner, Travis swore he could have whipped up roadkill with skunk juice gravy and people would have lined up around the block to eat it. Dad used to be known for his sense of humor. It wouldn't surprise Travis to learn his father had slipped an occasional hunk of slow-crossing possum into one of his famous beef potpies just to watch some poor fool tourist gulp it down. But since Mom's accident, Dad's sense of humor had disappeared. He started mixing up orders and hurling insults at the customers who complained. Carl had given Dad the benefit of the doubt for a couple of weeks because he felt sorry for him. Then when Dad purposely dumped a pot of chili in the middle of a table of gray-haired lady tourists, Carl told him to get out and never come back. Now Dad was meaner than a badger in a trap, and lazy to boot. But the man could still cook. Travis had to give him that.

Travis put his dish in the sink, then wet a corner of the dish towel to wipe Earleen's hands and face. Roy was still sitting at the table, his hands gripping the chair seat, his bony shoulders hunched over. "Come on outside, Roy," Travis said. "I'll finish whittling that truck you wanted."

"You make sure you're out by the road before eight tomorrow morning," Dad said. "And you do your share of the work, hear? Verl thought you were too skinny to be much help lifting the old refrigerators and such. I told him you're strong as an ox."

"Okay, Dad." Travis's back was aching already just thinking about it.

"And look here, boy."

Travis stopped in the doorway.

"You're tall for your age, so as far as Verl Bickley is concerned, you're finished with school and sixteen, hear?" He stabbed the air twice with his fork when he said "sixteen" to make sure Travis's new age got pierced into his brain.

Travis nodded instead of arguing, but how did his father expect him to pass for somebody two years older than his real age? He skipped every other porch step, taking in a big breath of sweet-smelling spruce as he bounded into the backyard. In the past few months he felt his lungs needed fresh air after being cooped up with Dad. Probably because he was holding his breath the whole time he was with the man, afraid something he'd say would set Dad off.

June was sitting in the tree swing, holding Lester. "You get out of there without a fight?"

"Yup. Kept my mouth shut mostly. Works every time. Well, most times." Travis sat at the base of the swing tree and pulled out his knife and the wooden truck.

Roy sat next to him, leaning over his arm to watch him carve. "Can you make the wheels move on this one?"

"I haven't figured out how to do that, Roy. Wheels wouldn't work in the dirt pile anyway."

Roy nodded. "Okay. I want fenders, though." Travis could feel Roy relaxing beside him. Since Roy had been old enough to crawl, Travis had taught him how to form roads in their backyard dirt pile, pretending it was an Adirondack mountain. Travis had always thought their pile was better than the sandbox at the primary school because the dirt held the shape of the roads better than shifting sand. Roy had one store-bought dump truck, but he seemed to prefer the ones Travis carved for him. Earleen settled on the other side of

26

Travis, picking up the curl of wood that he had peeled off the side of the truck. She put it on her finger like a ring.

June walked her feet in a few circles, then picked them up to let the swing unwind. Lester squealed, loving it. "More!" he cried as they stopped twirling.

June slid him off her lap and onto the ground. "That's enough for right after eating or you'll be puking up your dinner." Lester tugged at June's sneaker laces for a minute, then forgot what he was teasing for and crawled off.

"Was Dad talking about a job for you, Travis? He's not going to make you quit school, is he?"

Travis skimmed another curl of wood from the truck. "Looks that way, unless I can think of how to get out of it. He wants me to go around with Verl Bickley looking for junk."

"You can't let that happen. It doesn't matter so much that I left school. I never had the brains for learning anyway. But you're different. You could make something of yourself, if you had half a chance."

Travis pushed too hard on the knife, almost slicing off the fender. "That's what I had, June. Half a chance. And now it's over and I'm Travis Tacey, Junk King."

"Mom won't let that happen. She's always told us how important it is to get a good education."

"Who knows what Mom thinks, June? Or if she thinks at all. Dad is the only one making decisions around here now."

"We don't have a mom no more," Roy said, and his shoulders hunched tight again. June caught Travis's eye. They had given up trying to convince Roy that he had seen his mother in the hospital. He wasn't having any of it.

June got up and went after Lester, who had discovered some deer droppings and was scowling in concentration as he slowly zeroed in on one of the pellets with his thumb and index finger. Before she got to him, he managed to grasp it. He brought it to his mouth, delighted with himself.

"No! Yucky!" June shook Lester's hand until he relaxed his pinch, losing the prize. He howled in protest.

"Let him eat one and he won't want any more," Travis said. "Mom always says you gotta eat a peck of dirt before you die."

"A peck of dirt isn't the same thing as a peck of poop. Same as me quitting school isn't the same thing as you dropping out." She looked him straight in the eye. "Face it, Travis, I'm slow. S-L-O." She grinned at him, making sure he got her joke, then became serious again. "All the book learning in the world wouldn't fit me for anything more than taking care of babies, which is exactly what I'm needed for right now. But you understand computers and all kinds of things that I can't even imagine. And you're musical, like Mom. You can be anything you want."

"You shouldn't put yourself down, June. You're smarter than you think. And you can sing harmony better'n anybody I know."

She shook her head. "It makes me mad that Dad wants to yank you out of school. It's such a waste. If Dad would get off his sorry bee-hind and get a job again, we wouldn't need you to replace the money Mom made at the prison."

Travis looked up from his carving. "You want to talk about a waste? Mom was wasted being a night-shift cleaning lady at the prison."

"I miss Mommy," Earleen said. "When is she coming home?"

June squatted down and smoothed Earleen's hair. "Soon, baby. Soon as she's all better. Go watch Lester now and make sure he doesn't eat any deer poop." Earleen brightened up a bit as she ran to her brother. Keeping her busy seemed to be the best medicine for her. June gave Roy a one-armed hug. "You go look after the two of them, will you, Roy? Be a big boy for me." Roy got up to follow Earleen.

Travis chipped away at a truck tire, trying to make it round. "You shouldn't keep telling Earleen that Mom's going to get all better. What's going to happen when she finds out the truth?"

June sat down beside him. "Listen, I almost forgot to tell you, Creola Hawkins stopped by today. She visited her mother at a nursing home last week and said Mom was a patient there."

"Mom's at a nursing home now? When was Dad going to tell us that? Did Creola say how Mom is doing? Can she talk yet?"

"I don't know. I couldn't ask many questions. You know how upset Dad gets when anybody mentions Mom. Creola only stopped by because she had some of her daughter's old clothes for Earleen. She did say that Mom is getting around now."

"You mean she can walk?"

"No, but Creola said she pushed Mom outside for a walk in a wheelchair."

"That's not a walk," Travis said. "She should be doing exercises to get her on her feet. I want her out of that place."

"If she was well enough, they'd have let her come home by now," June said. "Mom needs to be with people who know how to help her."

"That's the problem!" Travis flung down the truck. It tumbled end over end across the ground and Earleen scrambled after it, giving up on her babysitting duties. Roy had abandoned both kids and was playing in his dirt pile. "I bet Mom's only in a nursing home because there's no money or insurance to send her someplace where she'll get treatment," Travis said. "I bet she's the only person there who's younger than eighty. Nursing homes are where they store old people until they're ready for the funeral home."

Earleen was back with the truck. June put her finger to her lips. "This isn't talk for small ears."

"Will you carve a bird for me when you finish this, Travis?" Earleen asked.

"Oh, Lester!" June jumped up and swept the toddler off the ground as he reached for another pile of deer droppings.

"Will you, Travis?" Earleen persisted. "Carve me a birdie?" Distracted, Travis pushed too hard on the knife and sliced off the bottom of the tire he was working on. "Now you broke the truck," Earleen whined.

Roy came over to look. "You gave it a flat tire. You can't drive a truck with a flat tire."

Travis folded his knife and pocketed it. "Look, that's the best I can do. You stay with June. I'll see you all later."

"Aw, don't leave me with all of it, Travis." June was bouncing a howling Lester on her hip. "I can't clean up from dinner and get the kids all calmed down and off to bed by myself."

"Leave me be for a little bit, June. I gotta get my head cleared out. Leave the dishes. I'll get them later." He turned away from her and started walking.

Travis felt bad for not helping June, for wrecking the tire on the truck, and for not being able to ease Roy's sadness. Most of all he felt terrible for not knowing how to rescue his mother.

By the time Travis had gone fifty feet into the woods, the tightness started to slip away from his shoulders, as if he were taking off a jacket that was three sizes too small. The cool, shaded air slid down his cheeks, easing the burning, and the ground under his feet changed from dry hard clay to the deep cushion of fallen spruce needles. He ran to his hiding place and pulled 3-G Eli's guitar out from under the cot.

He played through several of Mom's songs. Whenever he was feeling sad or lonesome, strumming that guitar was like holding a living thing. Mom's fingers had run up and down this fret board a thousand times. Like following in her fingerprints, he played exactly the way she had taught him, making the same chords ring out into the woods.

The last song he played was one of Mom's old favorites— "I Know Where I'm Going," but instead of feeling the joy and freedom of the music, a heavy yoke fell on him. Travis knew where he was going, all right—straight down the path to oblivion, with a big old refrigerator on his back. He let the last chord shimmer itself into silence, then tucked the guitar under the cot and headed for the house. He had to get a good night's sleep so he'd be bright-eyed and bushy-tailed when he started his new junk man career in the morning.

CHAPTER 4

Travis went out to the road plenty early the next morning, which meant he was there when the school bus came. He tried to duck behind a tree, but not before his driver spotted him. She opened the door. "I don't have time for playing games, Travis. You getting on or not?"

"Sorry to make you stop, Mrs. Bland. I'm not going to school today."

"And that would be why?" She glared at Travis, her hand still on the door-opening lever.

"I have something . . . I need to do something today."

"Something more important than your education?" Mrs. Philberta Bland had strong feelings about school. More than once she'd been known to leave her driver's seat and storm down a driveway to drag out some late-sleeping kid. If you arrived at school in your pajamas, everybody knew you were on bus #47, and you never overslept again in your whole entire school career.

Travis was sure that Mrs. Bland could be his salvation if

he told her about Dad making him get a job. She'd march right into their house, talk some sense into Dad, and that would be the end of the job. But Travis couldn't say anything with a whole busload of kids watching. Around here, you didn't broadcast your family's faults, no matter how bad things were.

"I have an appointment, ma'am. Somebody's picking me up."

She considered that for a few seconds. Travis felt her eyes boring into his brain, deciding if he was telling the truth or not. He must have passed her test. "All right then. See you tomorrow." She yanked on the door lever and took off. Travis was surprised she couldn't tell he was lying, but then he realized that his words were true, so he had flown under her radar.

As Travis watched the bus waddle down the rutted road, he wanted to run after it and get on when it stopped at the next house down the valley. He might have tried that, but a horn blast made him turn around. Verl Bickley motioned for Travis to get in his truck.

It took three hard yanks to get the rusty door open, and the bottom of Travis's jeans caught on a loose strip of metal as he pulled himself up into the cab.

Verl Bickley looked over at him. "You're the oldest Tacey boy?"

"Yes, sir. I'm Travis."

He ground the truck into gear. "Call me Verl. Ain't you the family where all the kids are named after gee-tar pickers?"

"That's right. My mom likes music. I'm named after Merle Travis."

Verl rolled down the window to spit the juice from his tobacco chaw. "Your older sister is named after June Carter, right? She went to school with my Doris."

"Yep. Then after me comes Roy, for Roy Orbison, then Earleen."

"Never heard of a singer named Earleen."

"For Earl Scruggs. Mom was sure she was going to be a boy, so she didn't have a girl's name ready."

"Ah." He nodded, smiling to show his tobacco-browned teeth.

"The baby is Lester," Travis finished.

"Lester Flatt. Now ain't that something. You got yourself a whole band there. You all pickers?"

"June plays some when she has time. She sings real nice like our mom. I play some and sing a little, too."

Travis usually had his guard up until he knew a person. Why was he blabbing about his family to a complete stranger? He stole a quick look at Verl. He was skinny with greasy gray hair and a beard and mustache that covered everything but his beady little eyes and a sharp beak nose. He looked like an old crow wearing a baseball cap.

Verl was sizing Travis up, too. "How old are you, boy?" Travis could see him doing the math in his head. If Verl knew June was older than Travis, he could figure out his age.

"Fifteen," Travis said. Was that what Dad told him? Or was it older? "Sixteen," he corrected himself.

A bump made Verl shift his eyes back to the road. "Most folks don't have trouble coming up with their age. Should be an easy question."

"Well, I just had a birthday, so I forgot."

"Forgot you're old enough for a driver's permit? Most boys your age are counting the days until that sixteenth birthday."

Travis let that one pass. No sense getting in any deeper. Verl knew he was lying. If he cared, he'd take Travis back home, which wouldn't be a bad thing, except for Dad getting mad.

Verl didn't say any more about it. They bumped along in silence until they came to a house with a washing machine out by the road. Verl stopped the truck and jerked his thumb toward the back. "Dolly's in the bed."

Travis didn't get what Verl was talking about. He waited to see what was going to happen next. When Travis didn't move, Verl got out. "If I have to show you everything, this is going to be a mighty long day." He stuck his head back inside to say, "Your door handle don't work from the inside. Give it a good shove."

The third time Travis slammed his shoulder into the door, the latch gave and he sprawled out onto the road. He scrambled to his feet, trying to pretend it didn't happen.

Verl rolled his eyes, then pulled down the tailgate and slapped the truck bed. There was a dolly in it. Travis reached over the tailgate and pulled it out. This was going to be a lot easier than carrying everything on his back.

"Set up them two boards as ramps," Verl said.

Travis did what he said, then tilted the washer enough to slide the dolly under it. Piece of cake. He pushed the dolly over to the truck and lined up the tires with the two boards. Travis was about halfway up the ramp when he felt the left wheel slip off the edge of the board. As the washer started to tip, he tried to right it, but it was too late to stop what he'd set in motion. Next thing Travis knew, he was lying in the middle of the road with the washer pinning his left arm to the pavement.

Verl let out a string of cuss words as he ran over to squat beside him. "You've bashed in the whole corner of this thing. If I try to pound it out, I'll crack the enamel."

Travis struggled to get up but he couldn't move. "My arm," he said.

"Yeah, your arm might have broke the fall some, but the washer's still ruined. I could've got top dollar for this thing. Now it's scrap metal. Not worth the gas it'll take to drive it to the dump." He set the washer upright, put it on the dolly, adjusted the boards, and rolled it up onto the truck bed. The man was small but wiry and moved faster than a cat being chased by a pack of hounds.

He looked down at Travis. "You gonna just lie there?"

"No, sir." Travis's elbow throbbed, but he moved it around and nothing was broken. He knew that because the bones didn't grind together like the time he broke his arm for real. Travis got up, climbed into the passenger seat, and slammed the door shut.

Verl didn't yell at him about his accident. Once he even looked over and said, "You all right?"

Travis thought maybe Verl was concerned about him

until he said, "Don't be expecting me to pay any doctor bills because you do something stupid and hurt yourself. You take this job at your own risk, got that?"

"Got it."

"I should take what I would have earned from that washer out of your pay. You know that, don't you?"

Travis nodded. He didn't even know what he was being paid, or what Verl charged for a secondhand washer. Was he working this whole day for nothing? Or worse yet, would he owe Verl money by the time he was dropped off at home?

"Well, seeing as how you're new and all, I'll be nice and let this one pass, but you better learn fast. Let's see what you can do with that stove up ahead."

This time Travis checked and double-checked to make sure the boards were lined up straight and he took his time rolling the dolly up the ramp. He got the stove onto the truck without incident.

As they drove off, Verl said, "You're going to have to speed up, boy. Can't take all day loading up an appliance. I need to cover a lot of ground to make a living."

Travis could see that there was no winning with Verl. Luckily, it was slim pickings along the side of the road for the next couple of hours—only a few odd chairs, which were light enough for Travis to lift over the side of the truck bed. Once they stopped to look at an old refrigerator in front of a trailer, but Verl declared it useless. Travis settled back in his seat to enjoy the ride. They had passed through three or four valleys, then the road took a steep climb. They were way beyond Travis's school bus route, so this was new territory for him. As they started down the other side of the mountain, the road went around a deep bend, and suddenly there were no trees blocking the view. There was a tall peak in the distance, with more mountain ranges one behind the other, fading off in the distance like echoes. It was so beautiful it almost took Travis's breath away.

"Wow!" he said.

"Ain't you never seen that before?" Verl asked.

"No, sir."

"You live in one of the prettiest parts of the country, but you can't see it if you stay stuck back in the woods surrounded by all those dang trees."

As much as Travis loved the forest, he had to admit Verl was right about that. All they ever saw from the school bus were trees. Now he could understand why they had so many tourists in the summer. Oh, he had seen some mountains and a lake or two around here, but nothing like that. Travis couldn't believe he lived so close to that magnificent view and Mom and Dad never thought to show the kids. It made him wonder what else they had been missing out on all those years.

Travis saw a sign saying they had entered a new county. Then another for the town of Volga, which he had heard of but never seen.

"You bring your lunch with you?" Verl asked.

"No, sir. I didn't."

"Well, I'm stopping at the Chicken Diner to eat. You got money?"

Travis shook his head.

"I won't get any work out of a starving kid. I'll buy your food today, but it's coming out of your pay. Tomorrow you either bring food or lunch money, hear?"

Verl pulled his truck into the parking lot of the diner. Carl's Diner where Dad worked looked like a regular restaurant, but the Chicken Diner was an old railroad car raised up on a concrete block foundation. It had a huge statue of a chicken on the roof with plaster showing through where the bright yellow paint had flaked off. The chicken had tilted forward from its base like it was trying to lean over and count the customers coming in and out. It gave Travis a funny feeling to walk under it.

The diner was mostly full of locals, with a bunch of construction workers and some truck drivers—no tourists that Travis could see. Verl strutted past the line of stools, making a big show of calling out guys' names and slapping a couple of them on the back. A few turned around and said hello, but nobody seemed all that pleased to see him. He claimed one of the stools near the end of the counter and Travis slid onto the one next to him.

The waitress glanced up and waved. She had the most amazing color of hair—sort of maroon. And her eyebrows were gone and replaced with arched black ones that she had drawn in higher up her forehead, making her look as if she had just heard something shocking. Travis could see that her real lips were thin under the big red ones she had painted on with lipstick, and he could tell she thought she was pretty because she was acting flirty with a couple of truck drivers at the counter. Travis had to admire somebody like that. She didn't like the face she was given, so she just covered it over with a new one. Made him wish he could paint over his real life and come up with something better.

The waitress came over with a pot of coffee and poured Verl a cup without him having to ask for it. She looked at Travis and smiled. "I didn't know you had a kid, Verl."

Verl ripped open four packages of sugar at once and dumped them into his coffee, spilling half of it on the counter. "He's not kin, Ralphene. He's my new helping hand."

She gave Travis a close look, which made him duck his head. "They're getting younger all the time. What happened to your last helper?"

"He was a lazy bum and thought he should get a raise, so I fired him."

Another guy had come in and sat on the stool next to Travis. "Verl, you go through more helpers than anybody I know," he said.

Verl glowered at the guy. "Can't for the life of me see where that would be any of your business, Scott."

Scott was about the same size as Verl, but they couldn't be more different. First off, Scott was handsome and his beard was close-cropped instead of wild and scraggly like Verl's. And where Verl was wound up like a bundle of bedsprings, this guy had an easy way about him—sort of calm and relaxed. He smelled a whole lot better than Verl, too. Out of the corner of his eye, Travis saw that the cap he wore had the word *guitar* on it. That got his attention, but he couldn't stare at the guy long enough to read the whole thing.

Ralphene handed Travis a menu and poured him some

41

coffee. "You look pretty young for a working man. How old are you, kid?"

"Don't ask him," Verl said. "He don't know how old he is. Dumb as a stump. Ain't never been out of the backwoods until today."

Travis opened his mouth to set him straight, then thought better of it. If he got Verl mad, he might not get any lunch, and his stomach had been growling since they saw the old refrigerator. Travis didn't even know how long his workday would be. Could be hours before Verl dropped him back home.

Ralphene moved over to the guitar-hat guy with her coffee. "Well, if it isn't Scott McKissack. What brings you in for lunch today? Haven't seen you since you came in for Easter dinner."

"I haven't had time to get away from the workshop, Ralphene. I've mostly been eating the fast food Clarence and Buddy have been bringing in."

"Oh, you can't live on that stuff, Scott. Can I get you some real food for lunch?"

"Wish I had time, but I'm here to make sure you and Arno can cater the lunch at the festival again."

Ralphene grabbed a small notebook and took the pencil from behind her ear. "Sure, we can handle that. You want the same as last year—some trays of chicken, potato salad? Maybe some baked beans?"

"That sounds great. And some of your pies for dessert. You decide how much you think we'll need. We're expecting several hundred people to show up this year. We have almost a hundred applications for the picking contest alone."

A picking contest? That caught Travis's attention. Was he talking about guitar picking? Travis didn't even know they had contests for that sort of thing.

"Your festival is good for business, Scott. Last year we had quite a few out-of-towners come in for dinner at the end of the day and breakfast the next morning. 'Course they'd break into song at the drop of a hat, but I kind of enjoyed that."

Scott McKissack laughed. "I hope you got the ones who sang on key. We had some who couldn't carry a tune with a forklift. Funny how the worst ones sing the loudest."

"Oh, we had a few corkers, but that made it interesting," Ralphene said. "So what's the date of the festival? You having it July Fourth weekend like last year?"

"That's right. The contest will run all day on Saturday."

Travis usually didn't butt in to adults' conversations, but now he couldn't help it. "Is your contest for guitar picking, sir?"

Scott McKissack smiled. "It sure is. You play the guitar?"

"Not good enough for a contest. I like guitars is all. I have a real old one that was made by my great-great-great-grandpa."

"No kidding. Is it still in one piece?"

"It's pretty beat up, but it sounds nice."

"I'd like to have a look at that sometime. I'm always interested in handmade instruments to see how people put things together—especially one as old as yours must be." He pulled a business card out of his wallet and handed it to Travis. "Bring that guitar over if you're in my neck of the woods. I'm almost always there."

"Oh, I didn't mean I was looking to sell it."

43

"Of course not. You shouldn't sell a guitar that's been in your family for so long, especially since you know how to play it. Some folks keep instruments hidden away in a closet where nobody can enjoy them."

"We don't do that. This guitar has been played all of its life. My mom played it almost every day."

"The more they're played, the better they sound," Scott said. "You and your mother should come see the contest. You'll hear some really amazing fingerpicking."

"His mother's off in some nursing home," Verl said. "From what I hear, her guitar picking days are over. And she can't talk, so I don't think she'll be doing no singing, neither."

Travis felt his face go red. He couldn't stand hearing a loser like Verl talk about his mother. He had no right saying she wouldn't play the guitar again. He didn't know a thing about it.

Verl stuck his elbow in Travis's ribs. "You gonna keep flapping your lips, boy, or are you gonna order lunch so we can eat and get back to work? Ralphene, I'm having a double cheeseburger and an order of fries."

"I'll have the same," Travis mumbled, ducking his head behind the menu.

Verl yanked the menu out of his hand, causing Scott McKissack's card to fall onto the floor. "You don't need the most expensive thing in the diner. How much do you think I'm paying you anyway?" He turned to Ralphene. "A peanut butter and jelly is plenty good enough for him."

Scott stood up and plunked a five-dollar bill on the counter in front of Travis. "If Verl's not paying you enough to cover a double cheeseburger and fries, you need to be looking for another job. Ralphene, either Clarence or I will come down here in a few days to make final plans about the festival."

Travis handed the five to Scott. "Thanks, but I can't keep this. I'll be okay with the peanut butter. Besides, I don't know when I'd be able to pay you back."

Scott put the bill in front of him again. "It's a gift, not a loan. I'm happy to help out a fellow guitar player."

After Scott left, Travis retrieved his card from the floor. It said "Scott McKissack, maker of fine guitars." And there was a photo of a guitar on it—the prettiest one he had ever seen.

"There's a man who's too big for his britches," Verl said. "Just because he sells his fancy guitars to a bunch of rich folks, he thinks he's a big shot."

Ralphene brought their cheeseburgers and fries. By the time Travis got his burger dressed up right, with ketchup, mustard, onions, and corn relish, Verl had gulped his down. Travis hadn't had any restaurant food since Carl fired Dad. This burger was really good—with the charred lines from being cooked on a grill, and the fries done nice and crispy. Travis was savoring every bite while Verl shoved in food as if he were stoking a furnace with coal. Travis could see that Verl chewed with his mouth open, which made him glad he wasn't sitting across a table from the man.

Verl finished the last of his fries, then swiped his sleeve across his face. "Tarnation, boy, you eat like a little old lady. Speed it up, will you?" He grabbed a handful of Travis's fries.

Ralphene saved Travis with her coffee pot, pouring Verl a refill. "Let the poor kid eat in peace, Verl. You think an extra five minutes at the counter is gonna make you miss out on some fine specimen of junk by the side of the road?"

"That's exactly what I think. There's a guy from over in Moatsville who's been horning in on my territory lately. No telling what he's picked up while granny here has been taking dainty little nibbles of her lunch." He reached over to grab the five-dollar bill, but Ralphene's red-nailed fingers got to it first and slid it into her pocket. "I believe that belongs to . . . what's your name, son?"

"Travis, ma'am. Travis Tacey."

Ralphene smiled. "Now that's got a real nice ring to it. Like one of those country western singers. I'll be back with your change, Mr. Travis Tacey."

Verl threw some bills on the counter and headed for the door. "You ain't getting no tip for that performance, Ralphene. Better learn how to treat your best customers if you want them to come back."

One of the construction workers called over his shoulder, "What makes you think you're one of her best customers, Verl?"

Another yelled, "What makes you think she wants you coming back?"

A lot of guys laughed about that.

Ralphene brought Travis two quarters for his change and he pushed one of them under his plate for her. Dad always said you should be sure to leave a tip for your waitress. When you worked in a restaurant, you knew how important tips were.

Ralphene carefully slid Travis's half cheeseburger and

the rest of his fries into a take-out box. "I hate to see you have to shovel down your food, Travis. This way you can eat it leisurely-like in the truck."

"Verl's not too keen about me being leisurely," Travis said. "But thanks."

She laughed. "He's a grouchy old coot, isn't he? Don't let him get you down. He's not all bad. Just mostly."

As Travis was getting off his stool, Ralphene put her hand on his arm. "Don't you listen to what Verl said about your mother. I'm sure she'll be fine. You wait and see."

Her painted face held such a look of hope and goodwill, it made Travis feel better than he had for days.

CHAPTER 5

Verl was none too pleased about Travis's take-out lunch. He stripped a gear getting back onto the road. "You're gonna get my whole truck stunk up with that food."

Travis thought the food smell was a big improvement over the Verl smell, but he kept that to himself. "I can close it up and eat it when I get home if you want."

"You can't store food in a truck. You gotta eat it now or it's gonna attract all kinds of things, like mice, for instance."

"A mouse would have to be going pretty fast to jump on board at this speed," Travis said. He couldn't believe he had made a smart remark to Verl. Maybe hearing other people speak up to him in the restaurant had given him courage.

"Oh, now you're a comedian, are you? Well, if you drop a French fry behind the seat, and then I park back at the store, you know what that might attract? Flying insects like . . . like flies, that's what. And animals like raccoons. You know how far away a raccoon can smell a French fry?"

"No, how far?"

"A long ways. Couple of miles. They've got good noses, raccoons. And they wash their food before they eat it. Did you know that? No, I didn't think so. They don't teach you kids nothing in school anymore."

Travis had his face toward the window as he popped the last of his cheeseburger into his mouth.

Verl wasn't through with his nature lecture, though. "You know what else will go for a French fry?" He took Travis's silence for ignorance and went on. "Bears, that's what. You know what a bear can do to the inside of a truck? No, 'course not. They don't teach you no practical stuff you might use in real life. Well, I'll tell you what a bear can do to a truck.

"Once, maybe about twenty years ago, a guy parked in front of my old place and left a pack of gum in his Chevy Impala with the window open. Just one little measly pack of Wrigley's spearmint. He went into Thompson's Hardware next door for about fifteen minutes. When he came out, the whole inside of that car was shredded. Little strips of the ceiling cloth hanging down like fringe. Bits of stuffing from the seats were blowing all over the street. Looked like a blizzard in the middle of summer."

"How do you know a bear did it? Did you see him?"

Verl nodded, grinning. "I did. I looked up when he accidentally sat on the horn. The noise brought half the town out to see what was going on."

"So how do you know he was after the gum?"

"I saw him work each piece out of its wrapper and put it in his mouth, and then he sat there chewing the whole wad, real pleased with himself."

"He did not!"

"Were you there?"

"No."

"Well, then you don't know nothing about it, do you?" Verl threw his head back and laughed, showing an unappetizing display of tobacco-stained teeth. "You ask your daddy about it. He'll remember. Everybody for miles around here knows that story."

"What happened to the bear?"

"Well, he sat there for the longest time. Just a-sittin' and a-chewin'. Folks tried to shoo him off because he was causing quite a traffic jam. Then Thrummy Thompson—he owned the hardware—he come out with a twenty-two."

"He shot the bear?" Travis asked.

Verl looked over at Travis. "That purely was his intention, but Thrummy wasn't much of a shot. He put three holes in the windshield and flattened two tires. Scared off the bear, though."

Travis popped a French fry into his mouth, trying not to smile. "That whole thing was a lie, wasn't it?"

"That is what you call a local legend. Some folks think they saw it one way, some think they saw it another."

"But you were really there, so you know what happened."

"Doesn't matter what happened. What matters is you don't leave food in a vee-hickle, which is the whole point of the story. Look lively now. There's a good pile of junk up ahead."

He pulled over. Travis put his box of fries on the seat and got out. There were some broken springs from a bed, a rocking chair with only one rocker, a bent bike frame, a rusty push lawn mower, and an old leaf rake with most of its prongs missing. He went around to Verl's window to give his report.

"Go grab the lawn mower. Some of those fancy e-cology nuts that are moving up here will pay big bucks for them old junkers that don't take no gas."

Travis loaded the mower into the truck and got back into his seat. When he picked up his box of fries, it was empty.

"Did a bear get in here while I was gone?"

Verl looked straight ahead as he pulled back onto the road. "It appears that way, don't it?" When the sunlight hit Verl's face, Travis could see little sparkles of salt glinting on his mouth. "They're fast, them bears," Verl said, then licked his lips to destroy the evidence.

Travis was mad about Verl stealing the fries, but he decided not to say something and put him in a bad mood. But Verl's good spirits started slipping away when pile after pile of junk turned out to be useless. "It's that darn guy from Moatsville. He's picked this whole area clean."

"Maybe there wasn't anything good in the first place," Travis said. "Could be a bad day for junk."

"It's never this bad," Verl said. "This ain't natural." He started getting out to look over the junk piles, to make sure Travis wasn't missing something. He finally found a vacuum cleaner that he liked. "I have two like this in the shop. Should be able to have enough parts for one or two good ones out of the three broken ones."

Travis spotted another bicycle and pulled it out from under some wooden pallets. This one was a mountain bike with a solid frame and it had one good wheel, one bent one, and a brake with a cable. "Can I take this?" he asked.

"Nah, there's no money in bikes. Kids always want them for nothing."

"I didn't mean for the shop. I want it for myself."

Verl squinted at him. "One day doing the rounds with me and now you're gonna start your own business? Bad enough I have Mr. Moatsville out there stealing my stuff, but now you?"

"I need a bike to get around is all. I'll keep watching for parts until I can put one together."

"Well, if you're using my gas to collect your bike parts, then seems to me the bike would belong to me. I'd give you a good deal on it, though."

"So I collect the parts, take them home and build the bike, then I have to pay you for it?"

"Yep. It's only fair."

Travis put the bike down. "Forget it. I don't need a bike that bad."

"Okay, you don't have to pay for it. I'll deduct a little bit every week from your pay."

"You think I'm some dumb hillbilly? That's the same thing."

"No, it ain't the same at all. You'll hardly notice a dollar here or there."

"You're right, because I don't even know how much you're paying me."

Verl picked up a brass floor lamp and put it in the truck.

"Your daddy and I settled that all out. You ask him how much you're making." Verl motioned for him to get into the truck.

Travis stood his ground. So that's how this was going to work. Verl would pay Dad, then Dad would keep most of the money and give him whatever he felt like. Travis could be out all day hauling junk around, and Dad would earn money for sitting on his behind. No way Travis was going to play this game. "I quit," he said. "Just give me the money I earned today."

Verl got into the truck and slammed the door. "I should have known better than to take you on." He threw some bills and change from his window. "Don't be crawling back to me asking for your job back."

"Don't worry. I won't."

Verl peeled out onto the road, sending a shower of gravel behind him. The little stones made pinging noises against Travis's bicycle frame. He scrambled around to pick up the money, hoping one or two of the bills would be fives, but they were all singles. Travis added in the change and came to a grand total of three dollars and sixty-four cents. What a rip-off. He stuffed the money in his pocket and turned his attention to the bike. It was the back wheel that was bent. He straightened it out by pushing it down against the edge of the guardrail across the road. By rotating it as he pushed, Travis finally made the wheel level all the way around. One of the pedals was loose, so he tightened that with the point of his knife. He snugged up the brake cable and secured it by tightening the nut that held it. All he had was a rear brake, but that was better than only having one in front and being thrown over the handlebars.

Travis inspected the rest of the bike. It had everything he needed except for another brake and a chain. He couldn't ride it up hills, but for now he could use it to coast down the hills and walk up the other side. It might take him the better part of the day, but he could get home.

Travis walked the bike up to the top of the hill, proud that his wheel-straightening technique had worked. The rear wheel turned easily with only a hint of a shimmy. At the top of the hill, he checked the seat to make sure it was on tight. Then he swung up into the saddle and started coasting down the hill. It was a gentle slope with a wide curve, so the bike held steady and didn't pick up too much speed.

Travis was halfway down the hill when he realized he didn't know where he was going and had no idea how to get home. But from what little traveling he had done, he knew most of the towns were in the valleys, so there was a good chance that when he got to the bottom of this hill there would be someplace where he could ask for directions home. If not, he'd walk his bike uphill, and hope for a town in the next valley. The sun was still fairly high in the sky, so he had plenty of time before dark. Travis was feeling pretty good about himself. He had stood up to Verl Bickley and had a new bike to get around on—well, at least to coast down hills on. That was half the battle, and when he got home, he'd use his money to buy a bike chain and a second brake. Then he'd have his own transportation and could go see Mom whenever he wanted, whether Dad liked it or not.

When Travis rounded the next curve, the road took a sudden dip, with another, sharper curve ahead. The bike picked up speed, so he squeezed on the brake lever and felt it take hold, slowing him to a safer rate of descent. He was pretty proud of that, too. He had tightened up the brake cable and it worked—not bad for a kid who had never owned a bike before.

Suddenly there was a ping and the bike took off like a whipped racehorse. The brake cable had snapped. He was going too fast to jump off, so he hung on tight and tried to keep following the edge of the road without getting into the gravel on the shoulder, which he knew would put him into a skid. The trees were going by so fast, all Travis could see was a blur of green. If he landed and skidded on the pavement at this speed, he'd probably break every bone in his body, not to mention peeling off most of his skin. He couldn't think of any way to save himself.

Then Travis saw a road up ahead branching off to the right and up a hill. If he could make that turn without wiping out, going uphill could slow him down. The front wheel was starting to shimmy now. It took every bit of strength he had to keep it going straight. He concentrated hard on that curve, trying to judge how far to turn the wheel to hit the road dead center. That's why he never saw the pothole, or whatever it was that stopped his front wheel. His hands were ripped from the handlebars and he was flying through the air. Then everything went into slow motion. Travis was afraid he was going to die. He expected to see his whole life flash before his eyes. But he didn't see his life. He saw his bike down below him flip over a couple of times, then land at the side of the road.

Then he saw water coming at him. He smacked into it so hard, it took his breath away. Then he plunged through water until he hit something soft. Mud! His feet went down into it and stuck there. Travis struggled to pull free, but he was out of air. He took a big gulp of water, then started thrashing like mad. The water turned black. He pulled as hard as he could with his arms. He couldn't tell which way was up until he exploded through the surface of the water. His lungs filled with air again. He was alive!

Travis started swimming for the edge of the pond. It wasn't long before his feet touched bottom. He slogged through a few yards of mud that sucked at his sneakers like quicksand, then pushed through a forest of cattails and found himself on the edge of the road near his bike. His right foot squished as he stepped on it, but he could feel the sole of his left foot hit the pavement. He had lost a sneaker somewhere in the muck. He thought about going back to find it, but the cattails had closed in behind him, obscuring the path he had made. It would be hopeless to try. As Travis walked over to his bike, his jeans were so caked with wet mud, they felt as if they weighed fifty pounds.

The bike was a worse mess than Travis was. Now the front wheel was bent so badly, he wasn't sure he could even walk it the rest of the way down the hill.

Travis was standing there, trying to figure out what to do, when he heard a car. It was coming up the hill, the opposite direction from where he wanted to go, but maybe the driver would stop to help him. It came into sight around the curve. It was a truck, not a car. Maybe the guy would let him put the bike in the back and take him . . . wait . . . he knew that truck. It was Verl Bickley. He pulled onto the shoulder of the road. "What in tarnation happened to you?"

"I'm fine," Travis said. "Leave me alone."

Verl got out, crossed the road, and grabbed Travis's bike. "I am going to leave you alone, as soon as I deposit you and your piece-of-crap bike back home."

"I don't need you. I can get home by myself."

Verl slowly looked him over from head to foot, taking note of his missing sneaker, then shook his head. "I can see that. You and your bike would probably get there in two, maybe three days. A week if your present luck holds out."

Verl tossed the bike onto the truck bed and motioned for Travis to follow.

Travis stood his ground. "No way."

"I'm not doing this out of the kindness of my heart, boy. You work for me, you're my responsibility." He grabbed Travis by the arm.

Travis shook free. "I'm not working for you. I quit, remember?"

"If I leave you out here, you'll probably get your dang fool self killed. And who'll get blamed for that? The last person anybody saw you with. And that would be me. They'd probably say I beat you up, drug you through the mud, and tried to drown you. Now I'm not saying I wouldn't enjoy doing just that, but I'm not going to prison over the likes of you, so shut your yap and get into the truck."

Travis was too tired to argue. Besides, he had no way to get home without help. He went around to the passenger side.

Verl reached over and locked the door. "You're not bringing all that muck onto my seats," he said through the open window. "Get in the back with the rest of the trash."

"Fine," Travis said. "I don't want to listen to you anyway."

Travis was sure Verl aimed for every pothole in the road on the way home, just to knock him around in the truck bed.

Dad came out as soon as he heard Verl's tires hit their gravel driveway. He walked over to Verl's side of the truck. "This is kind of a short workday, isn't it?"

"It was a no work day as far as I'm concerned," Verl said. "That son of yours cost me more money than he earned. I had to fire him. Can't afford to keep him on."

Travis tried to slip quietly out of the truck, but Dad saw him. No way he was getting out of this easy, anyway. He pulled the bike after him.

"What happened to you? And what's this about you not working? You look like you went for a swim. Is that it? You were goofing off?"

"No, Dad, I . . ."

"He was goofing off, all right," Verl interrupted. "He's the laziest kid I ever saw. Stupid, too. He ruined the best find of the day by dropping it off the loading ramp. To top it off, I had to buy lunch for him."

"He's lying, Dad. He didn't buy lunch for me. And I worked hard."

Dad turned on Travis. "You get into the house. I don't want to hear any more of your sass. I'm ashamed of you."

Travis couldn't believe Dad took Verl's side over his. He got out of there and headed for the house. June was washing dishes when he went in. She glanced over her shoulder. "Hi, Travis. How did it go?"

"It didn't. I quit." He went over to the window to eavesdrop on Verl's and Dad's conversation, but they were too far away to hear. He saw Dad take some money out of his pocket and hand it to Verl. "That rotten crook," he mumbled. "He's making Dad pay him."

June dried her soapy hands on the dish towel. "Whatever happened, I'm glad you're done with the job. Now you can go back to school."

Dad heard that as he came in the door. "School? I don't think so. It's hard to imagine how stupid a kid has to be to flunk out as the junk man's assistant. You're too dumb to be going to school."

"That's not true, Dad," June said. "Travis gets good grades. You have to let him go back."

Dad folded his arms and glared at Travis. "I don't have to do anything." He looked down and noticed his one bare foot. "What, you've gone and lost one of your sneakers? You know how much those things cost?"

"Mom got my sneakers at the church rummage sale for a dollar. And as long as we're talking about school, June should go back, too. It was okay for her to take care of the kids right after the accident, but now you should hire somebody to do it."

Dad's eyes blazed. "Oh, now you're telling me what I should do, Mr. Doesn't Know the Value of a Dollar? We were counting on you to bring in a little extra money while I'm looking for a job. But no, you have to goof off and get yourself fired."

"Verl Bickley lied. I wasn't fired. I quit."

Dad poked his finger into Travis's chest. "You deliberately left your job when you knew this family needed help? That's worse."

Travis couldn't stand it another second. "This family needs *you* to get a job. You haven't been out looking for work. You don't even make yourself useful watching the kids. June does everything around here. You hang around feeling sorry for yourself because of Mom. It's not only your loss, you know. We all miss her."

Dad's mouth moved without any words coming out for a few seconds, as if he were trying to get his thoughts together. Then he blurted out, "I've known your mother my whole life. She was everything to me." He slumped down onto the couch and buried his face in his hands.

Instead of making Travis feel sorry for him, that made him even madder. "We've all known Mom our whole lives!" Travis yelled. "So don't be using that as an excuse. And if she was so important to you, why didn't you drive her to work that night? You knew she didn't like driving in bad rainstorms. But you were too lazy."

Dad lifted his head from his hands. Travis noticed he wasn't hiding any tears under there. It was all a big fake. Dad jumped up and grabbed the frying pan from the sink, raising it over his head like a weapon. June screamed, "Dad! Don't!"

Dad got a funny expression on his face and put it down.

60

Then he looked at his hand as if picking up the pan had been the hand's idea, not his.

June and Travis stood frozen in place, waiting to see what he would do next. He turned toward Travis. "Get out." His voice was so low they could barely hear him.

Travis didn't move.

"Please, Dad," June said, her voice catching in her throat. "Mom always says when times get tough, the family has to stick together."

"I said, get out!" Dad roared. "Your mother would be ashamed of you." He lunged toward Travis, who slipped past him and out the door.

As Travis ran for the shelter of the woods, he heard Dad yell, "And don't be going to your cabin hideout. I want you gone from the property. Don't show your face back here again! Ever!"

Travis kept going until he ran out of breath about halfway to 3-G Eli's shack. It's not that he expected Dad to be following him. Dad never came out in the woods—always said he didn't like the bugs. But it bothered Travis that Dad had mentioned the cabin, which was exactly where he was heading—and planning to stay until things calmed down.

Travis had never lipped off to Dad like that before. But Dad made such a big deal about how much Mom's accident had hurt him, and he didn't even notice what it had done to the rest of them. Travis had bit his tongue plenty of times to keep from telling the man off. Now he wasn't sorry for a word he said. June didn't like any kind of conflict, so she'd never speak up. She was a peacekeeper, afraid to ruffle feathers. Not Travis. As far as he was concerned, Dad was to blame for Mom's accident as sure as if he himself had caused the truck to flip over. Travis had been thinking that for a long time. Funny that getting it off his chest didn't make him feel better, though.

When Travis got to the shack, he stripped off his soggy shirt and jeans, wrung them out the best he could, and hung them over a low-hanging branch to dry. He went inside the cabin, pulled 3-G's guitar out from under the cot, and strummed a few chords. He figured he could hide out here until June came to let him know it was okay to go home. Dad never stayed mad very long. He'd hold out long enough to make Travis worry, but Travis figured he'd be sleeping in his own bed by nightfall.

Travis smiled to himself and played the intro to the "Worried Man Blues." The words were perfect.

I'm worried now, but I won't be worried long.

CHAPTER 6

Travis ran through some of the songs he knew—old gospel songs and hymns that had passed down through the generations in his family. He knew modern songs, too, things he'd heard on the radio and TV, but 3-G's guitar didn't seem to like them as well. It always sounded best on old spirituals and folk songs. Travis liked the old songs better, too. They seemed to tell it the way he felt it—straight-out truth.

The light was getting dim in the shack, so he put away the guitar and went outside. He sat on the ground and leaned against the doorjamb watching for June. He wished he knew what time it was. It was hard to tell when the sun set when you were deep in the woods. The main thing was that the light turned orange, with the bugs flitting around near the tops of the trees like flecks of gold dust. Then the birds started talking back and forth to one another more than they did in the middle of the day.

Travis's stomach growled. Maybe Dad was going to punish him by not letting him have dinner. Well, two could play that tune. Maybe he wouldn't go back home tonight after all. Maybe when June came out to get him, Travis would have her tell Dad that he had run away. That would serve him right. Let Dad worry about him for a change.

When Travis stayed out too long in the old days, Mom would come looking for him. Would she ever worry about where he was again? Did she remember him, or any of the kids? Travis had been so busy feeling sorry for himself today, having to work for Verl, he hadn't given Mom a thought except when he talked with the guitar guy in the diner. What was that guy's name anyway?

Travis went over to where his pants were hanging and fished the business card out of his pocket. It was all soggy, and too dark to read it now, but he was glad he hadn't lost it. Maybe after his problems with Dad cleared up, he'd try to put the bike back together and find this guy's workshop.

The mud on his jeans was mostly dried now. Travis whacked them against a tree trunk until the hardened mud cracked and fell away. The jeans were still damp, but he put them on anyway to protect his legs against the mosquitoes that he could hear whining nearby. The shirt was damp, too, making him shiver a little, now that the sun had gone down.

It was getting really hard to see. Inside, the cabin was pitch dark. Travis knew there was a candle and some matches in there but couldn't remember where he had put them last. He felt around until he hit the table, then fumbled in the drawer until he found the matches and candle. He slid his hand across the top of the table, looking for the ancient glass

Coke bottle he had always used as a candleholder. He felt his hand touch the glass, then the clank as it tipped over, and a louder clunk as the bottle hit the floor and rolled away. At least it hadn't broken. He crawled in the direction he thought it had rolled, moving his hands in semicircles against the worn floor until the tips of the fingers of his right hand touched the bottle.

Then he turned and crawled one-handed to locate the table leg in the same way, finding it, and pulling himself up to standing again. He gave up to the darkness, closing his eyes. He found it was easier to visualize the objects on the table instead of struggling to see them. As he grasped the candle and twisted it to push it into the neck of the bottle, he had a clear image in his mind as his fingers told him everything he needed to know. He found the matches and lit the candle. The cabin filled with light. It also filled with every flying insect that had been looking for a cozy place to spend the night and a nice juicy human to chew on.

Where the heck was June? Travis's stomach told him it was way past dinnertime now. He stood at the door looking out into the darkness, then decided she'd show up faster if he wasn't watching constantly, so he checked only every once in a while. It worked. Not long after, he saw a flashlight beam bobbing through the trees. He took the candle to the door so she could find him more easily.

The flashlight kept getting closer, sweeping from side to side to find the path, then lifting to see what was ahead. Most people couldn't find their way through these woods at night even with a light, but June and Travis knew the land-marks by heart. One tree after another lit up as if it had a switch inside, then went dark as the beam moved on.

"Travis!" June called.

"Up here!" he yelled. The beam found his face.

He waved and went inside. Everything was going to be fine now. He couldn't wait to go back and have dinner. Soon June's face appeared in the doorway. "I figured you'd be here." She handed him a sandwich and an orange. "I wanted to bring you a hot dinner, but Dad was right there. I didn't want to give away your hiding place in case he followed." She pulled a couple of cookies out of her pocket and put them on the table. Travis was glad she'd thought to bring food. Now he could eat in peace instead of getting another tongue lashing from Dad tonight before he could eat his dinner. And maybe he'd carry out his plan to make Dad worry through the night and not go home until morning.

"Thanks. I'm practically starved." Travis took a bite of the sandwich—Dad's meat loaf with ketchup and a big slice of onion. That was usually Travis's favorite, but now just knowing Dad had made it turned his stomach. That thought lasted about three seconds as his hunger took over. Travis took another huge bite.

June sat across from him at the table. He could see in the candlelight that her cheeks were shiny with tears. "He's mad, Travis. Madder than I've ever seen him before."

"I can go back by morning, though, right? I mean, I'm mad, too, but I'll get over it." He stuffed a cookie into his mouth. The best thing about eating without a parent around was that you didn't have to finish the meal before dessert. Travis liked to mix it up—sandwich, cookie, back to sandwich. "So how long do you think I'll have to stay out here?"

June stopped him from grabbing the second cookie. "I don't think you can stay in the cabin, Travis. Dad knows this is the first place you'd go, and he threatened to burn it down if he found you hiding out here."

"He wouldn't be stupid enough to do that."

June rubbed her forehead. "Probably not, but Dad isn't thinking clearly right now. He was yelling about how he never wanted to see you again. I tried to reason with him, then pleaded, saying I couldn't manage the kids without you. He's not having any of it. You hit a nerve with him, Travis. Especially when you blamed him for Mom's accident."

"Well, it's the truth, isn't it?"

She didn't answer.

"Come on. You can't tell me you never thought about that before."

She shook her head. "No, I honestly haven't. It was an accident. Dad didn't cause it. And now you've gone and opened a hornet's nest."

Travis felt as if she had kicked him in the stomach. He and June had always agreed about everything. He didn't know what to say. He shoved the second half of the sandwich into his mouth.

She studied his face for a few minutes as he chewed. "Dad must know you're right about him not getting a job, though, and that's why he reacted the way he did. I think part of the problem is that you remind him of Mom. You have those same blue eyes, and you play the guitar almost as well as she does. It all makes you an easy target." She took a deep breath. "I could try to bring out food to you for the next couple of days, but he'd get wise to that pretty fast and we'd have a scene. I think you should try to find a place to live for a while."

Travis's stomach lurched. "A place to live! Where?"

"Maybe one of your friends' families would take you in."

Travis couldn't believe she was saying this. "What friends? My best friend was Dayton Mallow and he moved away to Pennsylvania before Christmas."

"I know, but you have other friends, don't you?"

"Well, sure, but not good enough friends to move in with."

A moth fluttered by June's face, headed for the candle flame. She cupped it in her hands, steering it away from a fiery death. "Well, I'm sorry, but you'll just have to find some-place else to stay and a way to earn some money." She was more concerned about rescuing an insect than saving her own brother.

"You want me to get a job? Yesterday you were giving me a big lecture about staying in school."

"Yesterday was a hundred years ago. Now everything's different. You can go back to school when things straighten out."

Travis slapped his palm on the table, making the candle-light shiver on the log walls. "This is crazy. We should tell somebody what's going on. We should turn Dad in for child neglect. That's what it is, you know, if you don't provide for your family. That's what they did to old man Lender, remember? Put him away in the county jail."

"Maybe you're not as smart as I thought," June said. "When the county found out that Mrs. Lender was too sick to take care of the family alone, they split everybody up. Each of those six kids is in a different foster home now. Can you picture Roy and Earleen farmed out to strangers?"

"No, of course not. But we have to do something. Dad can't kick me out of the house."

"You're about the same age he was when his father threw him out," June said. "It probably seems natural to him."

"I never heard about that. Who told you?"

"Mom did, a couple of years ago when I was mad at Dad for something or other. She said he'd had a tough life and his family didn't want any part of him."

"But that doesn't give him the right—"

June put her hand on Travis's arm, interrupting him. "Hush, and listen, because I don't have much time. I can handle Dad and take care of the kids. I checked the pantry to see what Mom had put away in there. She was always buying extra canned goods on sale. We have enough to keep some sort of food on the table for a month, at least."

"Then what? And how does it help that I'm not there?"

"It's one less mouth to feed, Travis. Besides, Dad really isn't so bad when you're not around. You set him off. You always have. Now that he's upset about Mom, it's worse than ever. If you stay away for a little while, maybe he'll calm down, find a job, and we can get back to normal."

"Normal! How can we be normal? Our mother is rotting away in some nursing home, can't talk, maybe can't even think! If you're holding out for normal, June, you've got a big disappointment ahead."

June stood up so suddenly, she knocked her chair over. "Look, I'm doing everything I can to keep this family together. All you have to do is stay out of Dad's hair. Is that too much to ask?"

Travis was thinking fast, trying to come up with any excuse that could help him stay. "How far do you think I'm going to get with one sneaker?"

June dismissed that with a wave of her hand. "I'll bring out some clothes and supplies for you in the morning. I have to go back now before Dad realizes I'm gone."

With that, she turned and ran out of the cabin. Travis watched her flashlight beam bob through the woods. They had been best friends for as long as he could remember and now she wanted him gone.

For the first time in his life, Travis was going to be on his own. Well, if Dad got kicked out at fourteen and survived, he could manage, too. He wouldn't even wait for June to come out in the morning. He'd catch a few hours' sleep in the cabin and leave before anybody got up. He'd show them all. He'd go and never come back and they'd all be sorry—Dad for kicking him out, and June for letting him do it.

But he stayed awake for a long time. He thought of Mom, regretting every time he had argued with her. He remembered the old nonsense song she always used to tease him out of a bad mood.

Peepin' through the knothole of grandpa's wooden leg,
Who'll wind the clock when I'm gone?
Go get the ax.
There's a flea in Lizzie's ear,
For a boy's best friend is his mother.

The last line brought tears to his eyes.

CHAPTER 7

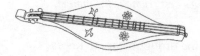

Travis woke when the first shafts of daylight came through the cabin door and fell across his face. He ate the one cookie left from last night, then counted out the money in his pocket. There were three soggy dollar bills but no coins. Thinking they must have fallen out when he was slamming his pants against the tree, he went outside and looked around the ground, scuffing away pine needles with his foot, but he only turned up a nickel and four pennies. There should have been almost a dollar in change, but he decided the rest of it could have been lost when he fell into the pond.

Travis took inventory. He had a pair of jeans, which still showed signs of slogging through the edges of a muddy pond, one T-shirt, three dollars and nine cents, one sneaker, and no food. Not much of a survival kit. As mad as he was at June for writing him off, he decided not to be stupid. He'd wait for his sister to come out with supplies.

He heard the school bus go down the road, then the

squeaky brakes of the mailman's pickup truck, so almost an hour must have gone by before he finally spotted June coming through the woods carrying the backpack he used for school. When she got close, Travis could tell she had been crying, which made some of his anger ease a bit. Maybe she cared about him after all.

"I put some food in here," June said, handing him the backpack. "There's a big hunk of cheddar, most of a loaf of bread, a half jar of peanut butter, and a can of beans. It's not much, but at least you won't starve until you get settled somewhere."

This was like a bad dream. It was one thing to think of stomping off from the family, making them feel sorry that they had driven him away, but another thing altogether to do it.

"What about the kids?" Travis asked, stalling for time. "Don't you think I should say good-bye to them—especially Roy? I mean, if I take off from here, I'll be leaving them exactly like Mom did." He saw June's surprised look. "You know what I mean. Mom went to work and never came back. Never said good-bye. If I leave without seeing them, it's the same thing all over again."

"It's not the same thing at all."

"Yes, it is. Mom didn't want to leave the kids and neither do I."

June grabbed him by the shoulders. "Are you trying to make this as difficult as possible? You can't come back to the house. Roy was crying last night because he heard Dad yelling at you. It took me an hour to calm him down, so don't you go riling him up again." She let go of Travis and opened the backpack. "Here's your other pair of jeans, a T-shirt, and a pair of Dad's shoes."

Travis pushed the shoes away. "I'm not putting on Dad's shoes! Besides, he'll have a fit if he knows I took them."

She shoved them into the backpack. "Well, you won't get very far walking barefoot. These are his dress shoes, so he's not going to miss them. They were tucked way back into the corner of his closet. Last time he wore them was Grandma Warren's funeral, and that was at least five years ago. There's a pair of socks, too."

"What, no underwear?"

She tossed the backpack onto the table. "Oh, for heaven's sakes. The last thing I'm thinking about right now is my brother's ratty underwear. You'll have to make do with what I brought."

"I'm trying to make a joke here, okay?" Travis wanted to see June smile, which had always made him feel better when he was down.

It didn't work. Her face stayed serious. "I have to get back before everybody wakes up and Dad discovers me missing. Oh, and here." She reached in her pocket and handed him some money. "It's not much but it's all I could find. Most of it is in coins from the couch and chair cushions, and a couple bills from Dad's winter jacket pocket."

Travis took the money without saying anything. He realized he had been hoping that when June came out, she would have changed her mind about him leaving. He gave it one more shot. "Look, June, you've always been good at keeping the peace in this family. Couldn't you try reasoning with

Dad? Maybe he's cooled off this morning. And you know you need me to help with the kids."

June rubbed her forehead the same way Mom used to when she had a headache. "What I need is for you to leave so Dad has one less reason to be angry. We've talked this out, Travis. It's not what I want, either, but there's no other way. Be safe. And try to call every now and then to let me know you're okay. If Dad answers, hang up." She gave him a quick hug and ran down the path. He watched her go, raising his hand to wave, but she never looked back.

How did everything get so out of control? If Mom were here, she'd smooth things over with Dad. But then none of this would have happened in the first place if she were still around.

Okay, there was no sense in feeling sorry for himself. Time for a new inventory. He went into the shack and dumped his money on the table, sorting out the coins. Putting together what he had from Verl, his change from lunch, plus what June gave him, he counted out five dollar bills, seven quarters, ten dimes, nine nickels, and seven pennies. It added up to eight dollars and twenty-seven cents—not a lot, but he could make it last.

Travis looked around to see what else he might need. The matches and the candle would come in handy if he had to camp out. There was an old dented tin cup hanging from a hook on the wall. He stuffed everything into the backpack. He thought of all the things at home that would be useful—a flashlight, his scout mess kit, a can opener—how was he supposed to open the beans? With his teeth?—and a rain

75

poncho. If he'd known this was going to happen, he could have stashed them in the cabin for an emergency. But who could have guessed he'd ever need them?

Each time Travis let the full weight of what was happening drop down on him, he felt tears coming to his eyes. No! He wasn't going to do that. Wasn't going to bawl like a baby. He thought about sneaking back to the house to grab the bike, but when he pictured it in his mind, he remembered it wasn't only the front wheel that was bent up. The front forks were twisted, too. There was no way he could force them back into shape. The bike was worthless. He'd have to hoof it.

Except for shoes, he had all the clothes he needed. Of course there was the underwear problem, but nobody ever died from having only one pair of skivvies. He took the scratchy old wool blanket off the cot to use as a bedroll. When Travis was younger, he loved going camping with his scout troop. But there was a big difference between camping for fun and camping because . . . well, because you had no place to live anymore. He felt the tears sting his eyes again. Nope. Not going to give Dad the satisfaction of making him cry. Travis rolled up the blanket as small as he could, then found a piece of rope to tie it to his backpack.

Travis sat on the cot and put on Dad's shoes. They were too big, even pulling the laces as tight as they would go. And they were stiff as a hunk of plastic. When he looked closer, they seemed to be made of some kind of plastic imitation leather.

Travis looked around the cabin to make sure he wasn't leaving anything important. That's when he remembered the guitar. He pulled it out from under the cot. He wished he had some sort of a case to protect it. He'd need to fix the strap that Dad had broken so he could carry the guitar over his shoulder. He took the shoelace out of his orphan sneaker, threaded it through the hole in the end of the leather strap, then coaxed the lace under the strings on the headstock and tied it tight. Perfect.

He put on the backpack, then slipped the guitar strap over his shoulder so the instrument rested safely next to the pack. He was ready. Now he knew how it felt to be one of those tourists who drove through the Adirondacks with everything they needed with them in their camper. He felt strong.

That lasted for about half a minute. Then he remembered that he didn't have anywhere near what he needed, and instead of driving around in a nice cozy camper, he was walking in a pair of shoes that didn't fit, that belonged to a man who had just kicked him out of his home.

Travis started out toward the road, down into a small ravine, then up the other side. Climbing was tricky because the soles of the dress shoes were slippery. When he reached the top, he turned and looked back at the cabin, memorizing the way it looked in the morning sunlight. Then he turned and wound his way through the trees, keeping his distance from the house until he finally came out at the edge of the road. If he headed to the left, he'd have to pass the house, so he went in the opposite direction, away from the familiar route he took every day on the school bus. This was the way he'd gone out with Verl. He remembered there were quite a few houses along the road, maybe some with useful stuff along the way. He wished he could remember how far it was to that town with the diner. He had been pretty hungry by the time they'd stopped for lunch, but Verl hadn't been sticking to the main road. He had driven in and out of hollows, onto some dirt roads and some dead ends. For all Travis knew, they could have been driving in circles.

A melody kept running through Travis's head as he walked. He couldn't name the song, but the rhythm gave him a good pace for hiking. The sun was pretty high in the sky now. He wondered what time it was, then realized it didn't matter. Nobody was waiting for him to show up anywhere.

Travis must have been walking about an hour when he started to feel blisters puffing up on his heels where Dad's shoes rubbed with each step. Darn, that man could get at him without even being here. Travis really needed some sneakers, or better yet, a bike. That's when he saw what Verl would call a likely heap of junk up ahead. It was piled next to a shed at the edge of the road. It was hard to tell whether the owner had set this stuff out to throw away or not. But if he wanted to keep it, wouldn't he have put it on the side of the shed away from the road? Travis decided Verl would consider this pile fair game, so he pulled off the big half-rotted piece of wood paneling that was on top. There was a bicycle wheel in the pile. He gave a yank and freed an old bike from a tangle of chicken wire. The bike was pretty rusted and the chain was missing, but it had the part he needed for the bike at home—a good set of front forks. It would be worth dragging this back home to repair the other bike. The brake cables seemed to be in working order, too. Now if he could only figure out how to get the forks off the—

"Hey! What do you think you're doing?" There was a guy on the porch of a cabin with a big German shepherd that was lunging at the end of a chain.

"Sorry, mister, I thought you were throwing this stuff out."

For some reason, the sound of his voice got the dog really torqued. It did a twisting leap that snapped its chain. Then it headed right for him.

Travis took off like a sprinter, the guitar sounding a chord every time it bounced off his back.

"Karla!" the guy yelled. "Get back here."

But Karla had one thing on her mind, and that was Travis. He only got about twenty strides away before she sunk her teeth into the cuff of his jeans and sent him sprawling. The guitar made a sickening bonk as it hit the pavement. Every string screamed, then quivered into silence. The sound startled Karla long enough for her to let go of Travis and for her owner to grab the end of her chain. "You okay, kid?"

"I guess."

"Stay out of other people's stuff, or you're gonna get hurt, hear?"

Travis got to his feet and started walking away. "If you don't want somebody to take your stuff, don't put it by the road," he mumbled, making sure he wasn't loud enough for the guy to hear. He didn't want to take a chance on tangling with Karla again. The next time she might chomp down on his leg instead of his jeans.

Travis was afraid to look at the guitar. He walked down

the road until he came to a clearing with a fallen log to sit on. Then he gently pulled the guitar around to his lap. The top didn't look any worse than usual, but when he ran a finger around to the back, he felt a crack that started near the heel of the neck and ran almost halfway to the bottom of the guitar. And there was a piece of the side that was dented in. He tried strumming a soft chord. It still had the same sweet sound. He ran through a tune, playing lightly at first, then gradually up to full volume. It seemed okay, although he knew he'd have to find a way to get it fixed. A crack like that could widen and pull the whole guitar apart. Mom always said you had to respect the wood of the guitar because it was like a living thing that gave the guitar its voice. She never would have let this happen.

When Travis started walking again, his blisters had reached a whole new level of agony. The running must have caused them to break, because now he could see bloody pink stains coming through his socks. He took off the shoes and was tempted to fling them into the woods. Instead, he tied the laces together and put them over his shoulder. He could walk in his socks for now, but later there might be a need for shoes—even these stupid ones.

He had to stop quite often to pull the sticky socks away from the raw skin on his heels. It probably would feel better to have the raw skin open to the air instead of rubbing against the socks, yet he knew the soles of his feet were too tender to walk barefoot for very long. When he was little, he went barefoot all summer and most of fall. Later, when he started wearing sneakers all the time, his feet became sissies.

Each hour of the day blended into the next. When Travis got hungry, he stopped and made himself a peanut butter sandwich for lunch. In midafternoon, he had a slice of bread with peanut butter for a snack, then for supper, he made himself a cheese sandwich. He washed all of these meals down with water from streams that he found along the way.

Travis had passed a few houses, but there was no sign of a town, and he didn't even know if he was headed in the right direction to run into one. He could hear thunder in the distance and hoped a storm wasn't coming his way.

When it started getting dark, Travis found a campsite for the night. It was a bunch of small abandoned tourist cabins with an old sign that said SEVEN DWARF COTTAGES IN THE WOODS. There was a new sign that said SIX ACRES FOR SALE. ZONED COMMERCIAL. MAXWELL REALTY with a phone number at the bottom. The driveway was a half circle, with seven pastel-colored cottages lined up like Brownies around a campfire. In the middle of the patch of weeds formed by the circle towered a larger-than-life-sized Snow White made out of cement. Travis could tell she had once been painted with bright colors. Now time had left her faded and flaking. She was looking down, smiling, as if the dwarfs had been around her in the old days. They must have been small enough for people to carry them off. No way anybody was going to lug Snow White out of there without some heavy equipment.

Hoping for shelter, Travis discovered that all of the cottages had their doors locked and windows boarded shut. He went around to the back of each one, trying to find a window he could jimmy open. Whoever had closed up this place had been thorough, nailing everything shut. Each cabin had a small front porch with a roof, so that would give him some protection if it rained. He settled for the cottage labeled DOPEY because he thought it was funny. Who would rent a cottage with a name like that?

Travis gathered up several armloads of pine needles to make a soft bed on the porch, then put the blanket over them. Later, when it got cold and started to rain, he needed to pull the blanket over himself. Then the wind picked up and drove the rain sideways, so the roof was no shelter at all.

Now it was the guitar he had to worry about. He knew the wood could warp if it got wet. He couldn't let that happen, especially with the big crack down the back. He covered the guitar with the blanket, leaned it on its side against the cottage wall, and shielded it from the rain with his body.

CHAPTER 8

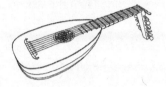

The next morning Travis was freezing because the back of his jeans and T-shirt were soaked through. But when he uncovered the guitar, it was dry. He changed into his other set of clothes, hung the wet jeans and shirt over the porch railing, and pulled out his food for breakfast. He'd have to slow down on the eating. Yesterday he had polished off about a third of the cheese, all but seven pieces of bread, and there were only a couple of inches of peanut butter left in the jar. He had been thinking he had money to buy more. What would he do when he ran out of both money and food?

He packed up his still damp clothes and shouldered the backpack and guitar. He decided to leave the shoes. He was pretty sure they were giving him bad luck because they belonged to Dad. He stopped by Snow White and arranged the shoes so they were sticking out from under her concrete skirt. That would drive Dad nuts if he knew a girl was wearing his best pair of shoes, even if she was only a statue. Travis laughed out loud just thinking about it.

Then he waved good-bye to Snow White and started out. Even with dry socks, the blisters were killing him. He tried to put the pain out of his mind by humming the tune that was in his head. What was that, anyway? It was the same one that had bugged him yesterday. Then the words came to him.

I'm just a poor wayfaring stranger
A-traveling through this world of woe

No! He wasn't going to get sad all over again. Why were so many of those old songs so darn mournful? He wasn't like that. He was strong, and he was going to prove to his father that he didn't need him for anything.

Before long, Travis decided to take off the socks and go barefoot. He thought the blisters might heal faster in the open air, and it did feel better without having the socks rub against the raw flesh. He was coming around a curve when he saw a sign for a garage sale. There was a car just driving off as he went into the yard to investigate. He saw a table with some stacks of dishes and doodads and a bunch of clothes on hangers swinging in the breeze from a line. There were some toys for little kids. The best one was a big red plastic car with a seat—the perfect size for Lester. Travis leaned down to see if the wheels worked. They did. Boy, would Lester love this. Thinking about his baby brother gave Travis a pang.

"That belonged to my grandson, Derek," a lady said. "Rode around in that thing until his tush couldn't fit in the seat anymore. It's still in good shape, though." She was old but had a nice smile, except for not having many teeth on the bottom.

Travis smiled back at her.

"I've got it marked for ten, but I could take less. Maybe eight-fifty."

"What I really need is a bike," Travis said, looking around but not seeing any.

"Got one in the shed I might part with," she said. "Come take a look."

Travis followed her, trying not to get too excited. If she wanted ten for the kid's toy car, she'd probably want more for a bike, especially because she said she "might part with" the bike. That sounded like she'd only sell it if she got a lot of money for it.

She opened the door to the shed. "Pull it out. Give it a try."

It was a good bike—not bent up and no missing parts that he could see.

"How much?" he asked, checking the brake levers.

"Don't you want to try it first before you buy it?"

"I want to know if I have enough money before I try it."

"Fair enough. How does twenty sound?"

"Sorry. Too much." Travis started wheeling it back into the shed.

"Well, don't be a spoilsport. Don't you like to haggle? It's no fun if the price is cut and dried. C'mon. Make me an offer?" She did a stiff little shrug of her bony shoulders.

Travis figured how much money he could possibly spare. "Five bucks?"

"Oh, honey, you don't know how to play this game at all, do you? Ain't you ever been to a garage sale before?"

"Not really."

"Well, it goes like this. I say twenty, then you come back a few dollars below what you think I'll take. Then I come down a couple of bucks, then you go up the same amount, I come down, you go up. Then we meet in the middle and everybody's happy. Okay?"

"Okay." This was more complicated than he thought. So he was supposed to offer her less than he thought she'd take, and raise his price a couple of times. "Two bucks."

"Two? Honey, wasn't you listening to my explanation?"

"Yes, ma'am. I'm doing two bucks, then you could say fifteen, then I'll say three-fifty, and you say ten, then I say five and you say okay."

She laughed. "Well, you have it all figured out, don't you? Me starting at twenty and you starting at two and us ending at five sounds like meeting in the middle to you?"

"Yes, ma'am."

"I swear I'll never understand this new math they're teaching you kids. What makes you think I'd let go of that perfectly good bike for five dollars?"

"Well, because the bike isn't doing you any good in the shed, and I really need a bike. Mostly because that's all I can afford to pay for it."

"Ha!" she said. "Well, that makes some sense. Better than your math, at least. What's that sticking up over your shoulder? A guitar? If you throw that in, we might have a deal."

She went around behind him to look. "Oh, it's in mighty poor shape, but Derek might enjoy thrashing away at it."

Travis turned so she couldn't see the guitar. "It looks bad, but it's a good guitar, not a toy. And I'll never sell it because it belonged to my mom."

Her face softened. "Has your mom passed, honey?"

"No. It still belongs to her. She doesn't play it now because she's . . . she's in the hospital."

"Oh, that's too bad. Well, maybe we can work something out here. You know how to play?"

"Yes, ma'am."

"Sing, too?"

He nodded. His singing was nowhere near as good as Mom's, but he could carry a tune.

The lady settled into a rickety metal lawn chair. "Maybe we have a deal after all. I'll drop the price to ten dollars."

"But I don't have—"

She raised her hand. "You haven't heard the deal. Give me your five dollars."

Travis pulled out five singles and handed them to her.

"Now you're going to play me five songs for one dollar each to make up the other five dollars. But I pick the songs. If I name one you can't play, the deal's off. You have to sing all of the verses, too."

Travis pulled off the backpack and guitar and sat cross-legged on the ground.

The first song she wanted was "The Church in the Wildwood." He knew that one. He checked the back of the guitar to make sure the split hadn't widened. Then he tuned up and cleared his throat. He was nervous because he'd never sung in front of a stranger before, except at church where everybody else was singing, too. His voice cracked a few times on the first verse. Then he looked up at the lady and saw that she had her eyes closed and was rocking her head from side to side to the rhythm. She had a little smile on her face, so Travis took that as an encouraging sign and tackled the next two verses with more gusto. She opened her eyes when he finished. "That was a pretty fair job. Now let's see how you do on 'Ash Grove.'"

Travis got through that one with no problem. The next song was "Black Is the Color of My True Love's Hair." Luckily, she was picking old songs that he had sung with Mom almost his whole life.

"You're not bad," the lady said. "I like to see a kid who's been raised in the old ways, but I'll have to come up with something harder for you." She thought for a minute. "How about 'Gospel Ship'?"

The name sort of rang a bell, but Travis couldn't remember how it went. He strummed some chords, trying to bring it into focus.

"Some people call it 'Sailing Through the Air.' Does that help?"

That was the clue he needed. It was another of the dozens of songs Mom had taught him. "Yes, now I remember it." He played it all the way through and only stumbled over a couple of words. She didn't seem to notice.

A car pulled up, so they had to stop for a minute while she waited on a customer. Travis was one song away from owning his own bike. He couldn't believe his luck. Then the customer spotted the bike. "How much for that?" he asked.

"Fifty dollars."

"Will you take thirty-five?"

Rats! Now she'd say forty-five and he'd say forty, and Travis's bike would be gone. He'd been so close and now he was losing it before he had a chance to sing the last song. It wasn't fair. A deal was a deal. "I'm buying that bike, mister."

The lady raised her eyebrows. "Well, this boy has been *working* on buying the bike. If you can wait a minute, we'll see if he's getting it." She turned to Travis. " 'The Mermaid.' "

His heart dropped. "But that has about a hundred verses."

She waggled her finger at him. "Only fourteen."

"Lady," the guy said, "you want to sell this bike or not?"

"If the kid can play and sing all fourteen verses of 'The Mermaid,' he makes up the balance of what he owes on the bike. If not, I'll let you have it for forty."

The guy seemed annoyed. "Look, I don't have time to stand around—"

She pushed another lawn chair toward him. "Oh, pish posh, take a load off your feet and relax. The kid's not half bad. Certainly better than some of the crap you'll be listening to on your car radio—the likes of that Tiffany what's-her-name who runs around with no underpants. C'mon, kid. Let's hear it."

Travis felt as if he were on a TV quiz show and this was the million-dollar question. He knew the song. When he was little, Mom used to play it almost every night to put him to sleep, which seemed kind of weird, because it was the story of a shipwreck where most of the sailors died. The tune was lively, but it repeated over and over, like a drone, so it gradually lulled him to sleep every time.

Travis had never tried to play the song before. He strummed a few chords and figured out he only needed G, C, and D7. Then he drew a blank on the lyrics and started to panic. He knew that those words had to be buried in his brain somewhere, so he took a deep breath, heard Mom's voice in his head, and put his mind on automatic pilot. All he had to do was tell the story. When sailors saw a mermaid, it was an omen of a shipweck.

> *Last Easter day, in the morning fair,*
> *We was not far from land,*
> *Where we spied a mermaid on the rock,*
> *With comb and glass in hand.*

Travis hadn't understood why the mermaid was holding a glass, so Mom had explained that it was a looking glass—a mirror—and if you looked into it, you would see your truest self. The next few verses were sung by members of the crew, and then the boatswain gave them the bad news.

> *Our gallant ship has gone to wreck*
> *Which was so lately trimmed;*
> *The raging seas has sprung a leak*
> *And the saltwater does run in.*

In verse six, they threw all of their gold and silver overboard. Travis remembered how he used to picture the coins sparkling as they slowly spiraled down into the sea. Following that, there were three verses almost exactly alike as the captain, mate, and boatswain predicted their wives would be widows. The next verse was Travis's favorite because the crew member was a kid.

> *The next bespoke the little cabin boy*
> *And a well be-spoken boy was he;*
> *"I am as sorry for my mother dear*
> *As I am for your wives all three."*

That's when Travis drew a blank. Couldn't remember where the story went from there. Was that where he used to start daydreaming about being the cabin boy on a ship and fell asleep? He kept vamping through the chords, hoping something would come to him.

"Enough with the musical interlude already," the old lady said. "Let's hear the rest of the song."

"The next bespoke the mate of our ship," he sang.

"You did that one."

He scrambled for words. Any words. "The ship it did sink to the floor of the sea."

"You're making that up. That's not in the song."

"Well, the ship did sink," Travis said. "Maybe I know a different version of the song than you."

The lady wasn't buying it. "You already missed three verses, anyway, so the deal is off."

All that singing for nothing. "Okay, mister. I guess the bike is yours." Travis put on the backpack, slung the guitar strap over his shoulder, and headed toward the road. He'd had his heart set on riding away from here, and now he was back to walking on his sore feet.

"Hang on, kid," the guy said. "How much money are you short to buy the bike?"

"Five bucks."

The guy pulled out a five-dollar bill and handed it to the woman.

"That wasn't the deal," she said. "Five songs not five dollars."

"Lady, the kid gave you some good entertainment. When's the last time you went to a live concert? Woodstock? I'm giving you the five bucks. Give him his bike. He earned it."

Travis shook the guy's hand. "Thanks, mister! I really appreciate it!"

He jumped on the bike and took off before the lady could stop him. The guy was right. He had earned the bike. And now he could see that Mom's guitar might give him a way to support himself. As he pedaled down the road, he heard a new song in his head—not a sad one this time—"On the Road Again."

Travis sang that Willie Nelson song at the top of his lungs as the scenery streaked by. He could almost feel Willie's long braids flying out on the wind behind him. He had gotten rid of his dad's evil shoes and his luck was changing already! Oh, Yeah!

CHAPTER 9

The road twisted, dipping lower. Travis remembered from Social Studies that lakes were usually in the valleys and most of the villages grew up around water. If he kept going downhill, he had to run into civilization. He went around a final curve and the road leveled off, but there was no lake, and worse yet, no town—not even a house. Now he'd have to make it up another mountain and down the other side. Why hadn't June thought to bring him the map from Dad's car? Of course a map only helped if you knew where you were, and he didn't remember seeing any route numbers or signs for a long time.

Travis's stomach started growling again, so he sat at the side of the road by a stream and took out his food. Even though he tried not to eat much, he was too hungry to save enough for dinner. He used the tin cup to drink from the stream and polished off the last of the bread and cheese. Now all he had was a little peanut butter in the bottom of the jar and a can of beans that he couldn't open. He needed to find a town where he could buy some more food, and maybe earn some money playing the guitar. Travis remembered his mother telling him that once, when she was young and broke, she sat in the middle of a town square playing her guitar and singing. Some people ignored her, but others had stopped to listen. At the end of the day, enough of them had dropped coins into the glass jar she'd set out to add up to almost ten dollars. That was years ago, before she'd even met Dad, so the going rate was probably twice as much by now.

Encouraged, Travis shouldered his stuff and started riding again, deciding that this must be a wide valley with the lake and town on the other side. After finding nothing for what seemed like miles, he was about to lose hope when a house came into view, then another. He arrived at a fork in the road. The branch to the right seemed to be starting up a hill again, so he took the one on the left to stay in the valley.

Travis rode for at least half an hour without spotting anything but a couple of dirt driveways that probably led into some hunting camps. The road twisted around so much, he couldn't tell what direction he was going in, and the sky was covered with a layer of wet, wool blanket clouds, taking away any clues the position of the sun might have given. There were small stretches where the road went uphill, followed by some downhills, so he had been wrong about being in a valley. He thought about going back the way he had come, but he knew there was nothing behind him for miles.

When he heard a small stream trickling along the side of the road, he stopped to drink, filling the tin cup with water three times. He used his finger to scrape every last bit of the peanut butter from the bottom of the jar and washed it down with more water. Now he was completely out of food, except for a can of beans he couldn't open. He made a mental note to get a water bottle when he finally reached a town. He couldn't rely on always finding a stream when he was thirsty.

He spent the next hour climbing and coasting, having no idea where he was. Lines of old traveling songs kept going through his head and he sang out loud to keep his spirits up—"can't help but wonder where I'm bound"; "been havin' some hard travelin'"—and his favorite, Arlo Guthrie's "I don't want a pickle, just want to ride on my motorsickle," which he changed to *bicycle*.

Travis was starting to worry about food. He knew that there were large stretches of wilderness in the Adirondacks, but he hadn't realized you could ride for mile after mile without seeing anything. Occasionally he passed a cottage that would probably have people in it after school was out and families took their summer vacations.

His family had never taken a vacation, but he knew some kids from school who went away for a week or two in the summer. Dayton Mallow's family even went to Disney World once. Dayton used that for his "what I did on my summer vacation" essay three years in a row. He had plenty of good stories, so the teachers cut him some slack. Travis wondered if the kids who traveled with their folks in the Adirondacks wrote about what they saw here. It seemed weird that the place he'd lived in all his life was a big enough deal for a vacation.

Travis spotted some bushes with berries along the side of the road and stopped to investigate. They looked like small raspberries—most still green, but others had started to ripen. When he reached through the bush to pluck the reddest ones, the thorns scratched his arm, but he was too hungry to care. He popped several berries into his mouth at once. They were bitter and had so many seeds it was like chewing on sand. He forced himself to swallow anyway. Mom had always made a big deal about how nutritious fruits and vegetables were. Maybe these things could keep him from starving until he came to a town.

Then deep in the bush he saw a plumper berry that had turned black. He wove his hand through the brambles to capture it. It was almost sweet, with more fruit pulp than seed. So these were wild blackberries, and that's what they were supposed to taste like. He searched for more ripe berries, but couldn't find a single one. Either it was too early in the year, or something had beaten him to the sweet ripe ones—maybe a bear?

Travis got back on his bike. He needed to find a town where he could sit down and play some music to make his twenty bucks. Then, with the money he had left over after buying food, he should be able to get a place to stay. Not a motel—he knew they were too expensive—but a room somebody had for rent in their house. That's all he'd need. If a guy was smart, he could get along on very little money.

He was beginning to worry, though. He knew people could get lost in these mountains and not be found for days, especially if they were in the heart of the Adirondack wilderness. Why hadn't he paid more attention to the maps they studied in school for local history? But weren't those missing people the ones who climbed the mountains or hiked through the forest? How could he get lost if he stayed on the roads?

It seemed to be getting darker behind the clouds, and Travis hadn't seen any traffic on this road for a long time. Then he saw a dirt driveway and decided to follow it back into the woods. It led to a summer cottage. If somebody was home, he wasn't too proud to ask for something to eat. There was a car off to the side of the driveway—a good sign. He went up to the door and knocked, but nobody answered. Then he walked around the cottage calling, "Hello? Is anybody here?" Still no answer. He peeked in a window and saw a kitchen with cupboards. There must be food in there, or even a can opener so he could get into his useless can of beans. He tried all the doors and windows, but they were locked. The only way he could get in was by breaking a window, and he wasn't desperate enough for that. Maybe he'd resort to stealing a couple of days from now, if he was still lost and really starving to death, but not now.

Travis shouldered his gear, climbed on the bike, and took off again. He hadn't been riding for more than fifteen or twenty minutes when he spotted a sign way up ahead. All right! He must be coming to something. He cranked harder. When he got closer he could see that it was faded—probably some old tourist trap that had closed years ago, but it had to be near something. Then he saw clearly—SEVEN DWARF COTTAGES IN THE WOODS. RUNNING WATER AND ELECTRICITY. JUST AHEAD.

"Nooooooo!" he howled, with nobody to hear him but the trees. How could he have reversed his course without noticing? Could he have been riding all day in a big circle? Sure enough, he rounded a curve and there she was—Snow White—still wearing Dad's shoes.

He threw himself down on the front steps of the "Happy" cabin. If the dwarf signs were going to predict how he felt at the end of the day, the least he could do was pick a good one. He took a stick and drew a map in the dirt—trying to remember the turns he had taken that brought him back to his starting place, but he couldn't figure it out. Then his growling stomach sent him on a search for berries, but he didn't find any. He saw some mushrooms growing at the base of the tree, but he knew they could be poisonous. Besides, he never liked mushrooms in the first place.

Maybe he could get into the can of beans. He found a big rock, turned the can on its side, and started bashing it up near the top, hoping the lid would split off at the seam. Instead, it dented the side of the can without splitting, so he abandoned that plan and hit it with all his strength, over and over. Apparently the beans were soft enough to compress into nothing because the can never burst open. It was killing him, holding food in his hand but not being able to get at it.

Then Travis remembered a weed that Mom used to pick and use in salads. It was called purslane and grew in places where it could get sun, which at their house was only out by the road because the trees shaded their whole yard. He walked along the edge of the road, and sure enough, there was a clump of it, spreading along the ground with red stems and plump green leaves. He pulled up several plants and took them back to the cabin, eating everything but the dirt-covered roots. Purslane was juicy with a slightly sour flavor and would probably be ninety-nine on his list of a hundred favorite things to eat, but it was free and edible, and that's all that mattered right now.

It was getting too dark to keep riding any farther today, so Travis decided to spend a second night with Snow White. He drank a lot of water from the nearby stream, which, with the purslane, helped fill his stomach. Then he settled in to practice singing. He'd have to be good if he expected to get paid for performing. He checked the back of the guitar. He couldn't tell if the crack was getting longer, but it still sounded good. He'd have to get the guitar fixed as soon as he had some money.

He needed to find that guitar guy he met in the diner. He fished around in both pockets to find the business card, but it was gone. He pulled everything out of his backpack, shaking out his extra clothes. The card was lost. How could he be so stupid?

He couldn't even remember the guy's name to look him up in a phone book. Wait—maybe he'd be listed as a guitar maker. Soon as he got to a town, he'd try to find him in the yellow pages. That thought made him feel a little better.

Travis gathered up his pine needles from the Dopey cottage, and used them to make a bed on Happy's porch. He had settled in for the night and was drifting off to sleep, when a woman's voice called. "Hey, kid. Come over here." He scrambled to his feet and slipped around the side of the cabin.

He couldn't believe somebody was in this dump. He was so sure it was deserted. Were they going to make him pay for sleeping on a cabin porch?

"I can seeeee you," she sang in a sugary voice. "Come out, come out, I know where you are."

Travis didn't answer. This was too weird. There hadn't been any signs of life. And why hadn't this woman shown up when he stayed here last night?

"Now, now. Don't be foolish. I know *who* you are, too, Travis Tacey. Might as well come out so we can have a little conversation."

She knew him? Was this somebody the school sends out to find kids who skip school? He'd only missed a few days. He could have been home with a cold, for Pete's sake. Why would they come looking for . . .

"Allrighty now, the last of my patience has seeped away. Get your little butt over here right this second."

Travis moved slowly into the open. Whoever it was wasn't carrying a flashlight and the moon wasn't bright enough to see clearly. He looked for some sign of movement but there wasn't any. His gut told him to run for the woods, but his feet felt like cement.

"Yeah, no fun, is it? Now you know how I feel. The cement feet thing."

Had he said that out loud?

"No, you were thinking it. I also know about the running for the woods thing, so forget about that."

This wasn't somebody from the school. This was some

kind of . . . what? Ghost? Monster? He didn't really believe in that stuff, but there was no other explanation.

"Oh, now you're hurting my feelings. Monster, indeed. Now get over here. That's it. Right foot, left foot."

That's when Travis lost control of his feet, and no matter how hard he tried to go the other way, they were carrying him right toward the Snow White statue.

Suddenly Travis saw a movement—a beckoning finger. No, wait, he had to be going nuts, because the finger belonged to Snow White. He'd heard of people going crazy way back in the wilderness from living all alone, but that was supposed to take years, not days.

Now the statue was pointing to the ground in front of her. "You're not crazy. This is one of those unexplained phenomena. Now sit."

He sat, sort of floating to the ground. And that's when he realized that this was a dream. Now that he knew this wasn't really happening to him, he decided to relax and enjoy whatever came next.

"What are you going to do?" she asked.

"I'm sitting. Just like you said."

"That's not what I'm asking. What are your plans? What are you going to do about your situation?"

"What can I do? I need to find a place to stay and earn some money so I can afford to eat."

"That's it? You're thinking about your own selfish needs? What about your family? Your sister has all those kids to care for, and your poor mother is in a nursing home. Aren't you

101

worried about them?" She waggled her finger at Travis, setting loose a little shower of skin-colored paint flakes.

Sheesh! This was going to be one of those instructional dreams. Bummer. He liked the ones where he got to do something fun. "I know you're a dream," he said, "so how about letting me fly? I can't do anything about my family, okay?"

"No, not okay. You're their only hope. Your father is hopeless. He can't even get a job."

"Hey, I'm just a kid. Kids aren't supposed to be carrying the world on their backs."

"Just a kid, huh? Nice cop-out." She folded her arms, making new cracks on the insides of her elbows. "And June, your sister. Isn't she what some people might call a kid? Seems like she's carrying a lot on her back."

"Look, I wanted to help her. I'd be there now if she hadn't sided with Dad to kick me out."

"Ah, so she deserves to be punished because you're mad at her?"

"Who says I'm mad at her?"

"There's mad all over your brain, Travis. It's orange, you know. The inside of your skull looks like somebody spilled a pail of tangerine paint. So what's your excuse for not helping your mother? Mad at her, too?"

"No! But what's the use? There's nothing I can do for her."

"I'm sure a visit from you would pick up her spirits. You could do that much, couldn't you?"

A picture of Mom in the hospital flashed through Travis's mind. He couldn't stand to see her again like that. This dream had turned bad and he wanted out. "Look, if there isn't going to be any fun stuff like flying, I'll wake up."

"You can't until I'm finished with you." Snow White dropped her arms to her sides and he could see the missing pieces inside her elbows where she had cracked. "Travis, if you had been in a horrible accident, and didn't look like yourself, and couldn't talk, what would your mother do?"

Travis hung his head. "I don't know."

But of course he did know. Mom would be there at his bedside every day. She'd hug him, and talk to him, and sing to him, until he was back to normal.

"Exactly," Snow White said. "Now get up and go visit your mother. You'll know what to do when you get there."

Snow White started to get dim and blurry, as if she were going to disappear.

"Wait! Can you tell me where she is?"

Snow White shook her head, breaking off a chunk of ruffle from her collar. "All I can do is read your thoughts."

"But I wasn't thinking about Mom just now."

"She's stored in the back of your mind, Travis . . . along with some other stuff that you should be ashamed of, but that's a whole different subject."

Snow White started to fade, then came into focus again. "One more thing, Travis."

"What?"

"Your father's shoes are killing me." When she raised one eyebrow, a little plaster flaked off her forehead.

This time she disappeared and Travis was right where he knew he'd be—lying on the porch of the Happy cabin. It

103

was morning, already getting light. He raised himself up on one elbow. The dream had already started to evaporate. He closed his eyes and tried to remember what Snow White had said because it had seemed important. But the dream was getting wispy and floating away before he could grasp at pieces of it. Finally he lost it all. That was the trouble with dreams. The harder you tried to think about them, the fainter they got. He wasn't going to worry about it. Dreams never made sense anyway.

Travis took a leak in the woods, had a breakfast of purslane and water, and gathered up his stuff. Before taking off, he stopped in front of Snow White. She looked the same as before, but he scrutinized her face, half expecting to see a brittle smile or a crunchy wink.

Nothing. Not a twitch. She was just a big hunk of cement.

CHAPTER 10

Travis started riding in the same direction he had gone the day before. This time he'd be watching closely for the fork in the road where he had made the wrong choice. When he saw the garage sale up ahead, he was torn between stopping to ask the lady for something to eat, and the fear that she might want the bike back because he hadn't paid enough. He decided that the bike was more important than food. The lady had her back to the road, rearranging some dishes on a table as he approached. He speeded up and got past the yard before she turned around.

There was a long stretch of nothingness after that. Travis wondered if he had missed the fork and was repeating the endless circle he had pedaled yesterday. Then he went up a hill, coasted down into a valley, and saw it—a road off to the right, going uphill. Sure that this was where he made his mistake before, he took the uphill road. It was hard climbing. At one point he thought he might be going deeper into the wilderness instead of toward a town. He finally had to get off and push the bike. Then, without the wind rushing in his ears, he could hear something—traffic! He climbed back on at the crest and started downhill. He saw a sign for a junction with Route 32. Then the road came into sight and a sign that said POTTSVILLE—1 MI.

Energized with the hope of food, Travis pedaled like mad. Soon he was entering the town. There was only one cross street, where a few stores, a diner, a post office, a church, and a gas station clustered. He was hungry enough to eat right away, but now that he knew he could get food whenever he wanted it, he figured he should try to earn a little money first. He could see a few people going in and out of the hardware store, so that looked like a good spot. He leaned the bike against a tree, sat on the store's front steps, and began playing. He started with the same songs he had sung at the garage sale, since they were fresh in his mind. There was more traffic here than he'd seen for the past two days. It shouldn't take too long to earn extra money for lunch, then he could look for a place he could afford to stay.

An older couple parked in front of the hardware store and walked by him on their way up the steps. The woman smiled and said something to the old guy, but he shook his head and looked grumpy.

Travis realized he should have had his cup out. He was sure the lady would have dropped some change. He pulled it out of the backpack, fished a couple of dimes out of his pocket, and slipped them into the cup so people would know what it was for. He saw a truck coming down the road, so he started playing in case they pulled over to go shopping. They didn't. Neither did the next two cars.

Then a guy came out of the store. "Hey, kid. What do you think you're doing?"

"Playing my guitar."

"Don't be a smart-ass. I don't allow any soliciting in front of my store."

"I'm not soliciting. I just sat down here to play." Travis hoped the man wouldn't notice the cup. "It's a free country. If I want to play in public, nobody has a right to stop me."

"You can play in public all you want. Just not in front of my store."

"I bet I could bring in business for you." Travis launched into a verse of "If I Had a Hammer."

The guy stood there with his arms folded, glaring at him. "My customers don't want to step over a panhandler to get into the store."

"Who's panhandling? I'm giving people some free entertainment."

"Oh, yeah? Free, you say?" The guy was eyeing the cup, so Travis picked it up and pretended to take a sip, catching the dimes against the floor of his mouth with his tongue.

"I don't think I've seen you before. You live around here?"

"A lull ways away," he said. Holding the dimes didn't leave much tongue for talking.

"Do I know your family? What's your last name?"

"Tacey." On the second syllable, his tongue lost the dimes, then took on a life of its own. Before he knew what was happening, the back of his tongue had pushed the coins down his gullet. He started coughing, which brought one dime back up. He shoved it into his cheek with his tongue and clamped his teeth shut to keep it there. Tears came to his eyes as he stifled another cough.

"You okay, kid?"

"Yeah, fine," he said through gritted teeth. He picked up his belongings and headed down the street. When he looked back a couple of times, the hardware store man was still watching him. The man finally went into his store, so Travis retrieved the dime from his cheek. As short as he was on money, he was calling the other dime a lost cause. No way he was going to fish it out of a toilet somewhere. He settled on a picnic table in front of the diner and pulled out the guitar again. He turned it over, running his hand across the back. It might have been his imagination, but the crack seemed to be growing. He had to get it fixed before it broke apart altogether. He didn't see any phone booths around, so he started to go into the diner, but stopped when he saw a sign that said NO BARE FEET.

Now he wished he had saved Dad's shoes. Even the cheapest sneakers would cost much more than the eight dollars and change he had. Then he spotted a general store across the street that had a big SALE sign in the front window. He left the bike and backpack behind a bush and went in. There was a table near the front that had a bunch of things for fifty cents. He found a can opener, which would have come in handy for the beans. He thought about buying it now, but decided to wait, since he didn't have any cans to open at the moment.

There was a dollar table that had all kinds of toys and junk, then a two-dollar table with a pile of clothing. It was mostly little kids' T-shirts and shorts, but buried in a pile at the far end, Travis fished out some rubber flip-flops. Those should count as shoes. The first pair he tried on were too short, so his heels lopped over the backs. Next he pulled out a pair of pink ones for ladies, with a plastic flower at the part that went between your toes. A little more digging produced a decent pair, blue, and just the right size. He took them to the cash register and dug out a single and four quarters. "That's two-sixteen with the tax," the cashier said. Travis fished in his pocket for the extra sixteen cents. He'd forgotten about tax.

He almost stopped the cashier from putting the flip-flops into a bag, then realized a bag might come in handy for something later. As he was going out the door, Travis spotted a can of cherry pie filling, and it gave him such a longing for Mom's pies, he picked it up and went back for the can opener. That cost him an extra three dollars and fourteen cents. Even as he was peeling off the three dollar bills, leaving only one, he thought he might be spending too much money, but the can opener was a good investment, and his pocket was still heavy with change, so there had to be at least a couple of dollars' worth there. He went outside, cut the plastic tie holding the flip-flops together, and put them on. Now he could walk on gravel and sharp stones. He stowed the bag with the can opener and pie filling in his backpack and even kept the plastic tie. It could be useful for something. Then he rode down the street and went into the diner.

This was smaller than the Chicken Diner. A counter ran along the left side of the room, and the right side was crammed with four small square tables. Two men were sitting at the front end of the counter talking and another guy wearing a cowboy hat was on the far end by himself. An older couple sat at one of the tables. They were all locals, not tourists. Travis had spent enough time in Carl's Diner to be pretty good at telling the difference.

There were four ladies at the back table and he figured them to be tourists, maybe just driving through.

A waitress was wiping off the empty tables. She wasn't wearing a uniform like the woman in the Chicken Diner. She had on an apron over jeans and a T-shirt, with a name tag that read HI, MY NAME IS LOIS.

"You want to sit at the counter or a table?" she asked Travis.

"I'm not here to eat. I mean, not yet. Maybe later, for dinner, but I need to see a phone book now, if you have one." The burgers that the cook had going on the grill smelled so good, Travis had to swallow a couple of times to keep from drooling.

"One phone book coming up." Lois got the book from behind the counter and plopped it on the front table. "We're not open for dinner, though. Only breakfast and lunch."

This meant Travis probably wouldn't have time to earn more money for a meal before the diner closed. He was glad he'd bought food at the general store, but he sure would love one of those burgers.

Lois had gone in the back to wait on the table of ladies. Travis carefully set his guitar on its side, leaning against the wall, then sat at the table and began looking through the yellow pages. There was no listing for "guitar maker," or even "guitar" by itself. Then he tried "music" and found "musical instruction," with only one listing—"piano lessons."

If he could remember the guy's name, he could look him up in the white pages. The first name was something like Steve—no, that wasn't right, but he was pretty sure it started with an *S*. And the last name started with a Mc, he was positive about that. Travis traced his finger down the column of "Mc"s. There was a long list of first names beginning with *S*, but no Steves, and nothing else jumped out at him.

Travis put his head in his hands. Why was everything going so wrong?

Lois was giving the tourist ladies a hard time. One of them couldn't make up her mind. Then she finally decided, but kept changing every time somebody else ordered.

"You don't have any idea what you want, do you, honey?" Lois never cracked a smile, but the women all laughed. Lois was kind of mean, but in a funny way, so nobody took offense. Travis saw one of the guys at the counter look over his shoulder and shake his head, grinning, as if he'd seen her routine before.

Travis scanned the room. Above the counter were a couple of signs. One said AROUND HERE, NORMAL IS JUST A CYCLE ON THE WASHING MACHINE. That should be hanging on a wall at his house. The other one said PRICES ARE SET ACCORDING TO THE ATTITUDE OF THE CUSTOMER. That one sounded like something Dad would say.

Lois took a load of food over to the tourists, two plates

111

balanced on each arm. One of them asked, "When you have a chance, could you please bring me a glass of water?"

Even though she had asked politely, Lois shot back, "Do you mind? I have my hands full here."

They all laughed again, and Travis noticed some of the locals smiled and caught each other's glances. Too bad Dad couldn't work in a diner like this, where making nasty remarks was considered a comedy act. Of course dumping a bowl of chili on a tourist's head was probably out of line even in this place.

Lois stopped by Travis's table on the way to the counter. "Sure you don't want something now?"

"No, thanks."

"Glass of water?"

They didn't charge anything for water, did they? He decided it must be free, and it would taste better than the stuff he'd been drinking from streams. "Yes, please."

Lois brought a menu with the glass of water. The burgers were three dollars and seventy-five cents. He hadn't counted his change, but he was pretty sure he didn't have that much.

"There aren't too many places open around here for dinner this time of year—just some taverns, but you'd need to have your parents with you. You're not from around here, are you? You and your folks on vacation?"

"Not exactly."

She pulled out a chair and sat across from him, leaning in so she could talk quietly. "You look like you might need help. Are you in some kind of trouble?"

She seemed friendly. Maybe if he told her his problem,

she could give him some food. But what if she asked a lot of questions and he told her about Dad kicking him out, and Mom being stuck in a nursing home, and June managing all by herself? Adults couldn't keep that sort of thing secret. There was some law that said if they thought a kid was in trouble they had to report it. Then they'd send somebody out to check on them and his brothers and sisters would be sent off to foster homes, exactly like the Lender kids. No, he wasn't going to blab to a complete stranger. Maybe Lois could help him find the guitar guy, though.

Travis tried to force a smile. "No, ma'am, I'm not in any trouble. Well, I might be in trouble with Mom if I don't find the guy who can fix this." He picked up the guitar and showed her the crack on the back.

"That's a mighty old guitar. You sure it's worth fixing? Looks like you could bust that thing just from picking it up."

"I have to get it fixed. Do you know a guy around here who makes guitars? His last name is Mac something or other."

Lois tapped the shoulder of a guy at the counter. "Hey, Jake, who's that guy who runs the picking contest over by Cuyler? He knows about guitars, doesn't he? Think he could fix this for the kid?"

The guy with the cowboy hat must have been eaves-dropping because he came over to the table. "Could I see that guitar for a minute, kid?"

Travis handed it to him and the guy looked it over, then put his foot on the chair to support the guitar and gently played a few chords. It had been a long time since Travis had heard that guitar from the front where the sound came out,

113

instead of playing it himself. The tone was wonderful. Travis thought he saw Cowboy's eyes light up when he heard it, but after playing a minute or two, he shook his head. "The lady is right. This is one mighty old piece of junk you got here." He tapped his thumb on the top of the guitar and all of the strings rang. Travis knew that was a sign of a great guitar but this guy didn't have a clue. He handed the guitar back to Travis.

Lois called over to Jake. "Come on, Jake. You went to that picking contest a couple of times. Can't you remember the guy who runs it?"

Jake nodded. "Oh, yeah. Scott McKissack."

"That's it!" Travis said. "I couldn't find his name in the phone book. Where is his workshop?"

"Over in Cuyler, isn't it?" Lois said.

Jake nodded. "Yep. Just as you're going out the other side of the town."

"Is it far?" Travis asked.

"About a forty-five-minute drive," Jake said. "But if you keep following the highway, you'll come to it."

"Thanks, mister. I'll start out right now."

The ladies in the back had finished and chipped in their money. It was the tall blond one who came to the cash register to pay. She pointed to the sign over the counter. "Just so you know, the tip was set according to the attitude of the waitress."

Everybody laughed.

As they left, Jake called out, "How much does Lois owe ya?"

That got another laugh from both the locals and the tourists.

Travis was over in the corner, gathering up his things, when Lois handed him a paper bag. "I got these doughnuts that'll be too stale to sell in the morning. You want 'em? No charge."

"Sure. Thanks."

She leaned closer and spoke softly. "Look. I wrote my phone numbers on the bag. Top one is the diner. Bottom one is my house. Call if you need help, okay?"

Travis couldn't look at her. She saw right through him.

"Okay," he mumbled as he shoved the door open. "I will."

He was getting his pack and guitar onto his back when Cowboy came out of the restaurant. "You riding your bike over to Cuyler, kid?"

"Yeah."

"That's a pretty long haul on a bike. I can give you a lift if you want. Put the bike in the bed of my pickup."

Travis remembered that Mom always said not to accept rides from strangers, but that was for little kids. He could take care of himself now. Besides, a forty-five-minute drive in a car could take hours on a bike. The guy looked all right. Heck, he liked guitars. How bad could he be?

"Okay, mister. Thanks."

Cowboy lifted the bike into the truck bed. Travis put the backpack and guitar behind the seat and climbed in.

Travis noticed the clock in the hardware store window said 2:15. They could be at Scott McKissack's place by three. He had doughnuts and cherries for dinner and breakfast, and he could camp out somewhere overnight. Even though he didn't have much money, things were starting to look up.

"So, you any good at playing the guitar, kid?"

"I do okay."

"It's hard to play on an old junker like that. Be easier if you had a new guitar. I collect old beat-up instruments— hang them on the wall of my family room. I'd give you maybe twenty for it."

"I couldn't get a new guitar for twenty bucks," Travis said.

"Well, since it's got so much character, I could go up to thirty. You can get a pretty decent guitar for that price."

"I don't want a new guitar. This one's been in my family a long time. I want to get it repaired."

"Yeah, well, wait until you find out how much Scott McKissack is going to charge to fix that thing. He probably can't even save it."

Travis didn't say anything. It didn't matter how much money it cost to fix the guitar. Whatever it was, he'd earn it somehow.

Travis was surprised at how important the guitar had become to him. He had always loved it, but since Mom's accident, it was the only part of her he could hang on to. And now the guitar was an even bigger deal because he was counting on it as a way to earn money, although he could see that wasn't going to be as easy as he had thought. Soon as he got the guitar repaired, he'd have to find a good place to play where people would actually listen and throw money into his cup. Maybe Scott McKissack could give him some advice on that.

They had passed the last of the houses a while back and were way out of town now. Travis was starting to feel uneasy.

Maybe he should have turned down the ride and toughed it out on his bike.

After a long silence, Cowboy turned to him. "Tell you what. I'm in a generous mood. Forty bucks for the guitar. My final offer. What do you say?"

Didn't this guy ever give up? "No! I'm not selling it. Can't you get that through your head, mister? How much farther is it to Cuyler, anyway?"

Cowboy slammed on his brakes and pulled off on the shoulder of the road. "Is that how you talk to somebody who tries to do you a favor? You can get yourself to Cuyler on your own. Get out of my truck."

Travis climbed out. "Fine! I'd rather ride my bike anyway." He threw his backpack on the ground, then pushed the seat forward to get his guitar. That's when Cowboy gunned the engine and took off, knocking Travis into the ditch.

He scrambled to his feet and yelled, "Hey, come back here!" which was useless because Cowboy was already too far away to hear. Travis figured he'd stop as soon as he realized he had Travis's guitar and bike, but the truck kept going. Why hadn't he noticed the license plates? He couldn't even remember what color the truck was, and now it was too far away to tell. Travis shouldered his backpack and ran like crazy. The pack thumped against his back with each step, as if it were calling him stupid, stupid, stupid.

The truck went beyond a curve and was out of sight. Okay, maybe Cowboy left the bike and guitar at the side of the road.

Sure enough, when Travis came around the curve, he saw something glinting in the sunshine on the shoulder of the road. It must be the chrome handlebars. He couldn't see the guitar, though. There was a little ditch running along the edge of the road with a few inches of water in the bottom. Had Cowboy left the guitar down in the water, just to be mean? That guitar had survived for a hundred years. It wasn't going to get wrecked by a little water. Besides, as soon as he reached the town, he'd ask how to get to Scott McKissack's place.

Travis finally reached the spot where the guy dumped his stuff. All that was there was his bike.

3-G Eli's guitar was gone.

CHAPTER 11

Travis sat on the edge of that ditch for a long time, and in spite of his vow not to cry, he sobbed his heart out. He had lost Mom's precious guitar and was left with nothing. How could he possibly survive on his own now?

Finally his hunger pangs made him dig into his backpack for the doughnuts. But he couldn't find them. Then he remembered taking out the bag, offering one to Cowboy, deciding not to eat one himself, and setting the bag on the front seat. Cowboy had his doughnuts. As upset as he was about the guitar, the doughnuts made him mad. He slammed his fist on the ground. "All right, that's it!" he shouted. "That's enough!"

He didn't want to open the pie filling because he needed to save part of that for supper, and the open can would leak all over his backpack. He looked around the shoulder of the road for purslane but didn't find any. So he pressed his cup down into the ditch water and drank it, even though it was muddy. Why hadn't he bought a water bottle in the store? He wondered if he had enough for one now. He pulled the money out of his pocket and counted it. It came to two dollars and eighty-seven cents. How had he gone through so much money in the two days since he left home?

He put on the backpack, jumped on the bike, and started pedaling, but the fender was rubbing against the tire, so he had to stop and fix it. Did Cowboy have to throw the bike in the ditch? Couldn't he have set it down easy?

Travis got the fender bent out, and started off again. He went mile after mile, alternating between feeling sorry for himself and being furious with himself for putting the guitar in that truck so Cowboy could drive off with it. He was in the feeling-sorry-for-himself mode when he spotted a pay phone outside a closed tavern. He pulled out his change, spread it on the little metal shelf, then put in a quarter and dialed his home number.

June answered on the third ring. Then another voice asked Travis for forty cents more. His hand shook as he tried to get another quarter, a nickel, and a dime into the slot. He could hear June saying, "Hello? Hello?"

Travis called back to her, but she couldn't hear him until the dime dropped in. "It's Travis." She didn't say anything. "Can you hear me, June?"

"Yes."

"Can you talk?"

"Um. No, thank you. We don't need any."

"Dad's there, right?"

"Yes."

"Do you think he'd let me come home yet? Because I'm having a hard time out here, June." His voice cracked at the end of that.

He could hear her draw in a sharp breath. "Oh, I don't . . ."

"Who's on the phone?" That was Dad in the background.

"Somebody selling something, Dad," she called out.

"Tell him we don't need anything."

"I'm sorry," June said, into the phone this time.

"June," Travis blurted out. "It's all going wrong. I'm out of money and food and a guy stole Mom's guitar."

"Oh, Travis, that's awful," June whispered. "Things are a little better, but Dad is still unbelievably mad at you."

"Travis?" Dad yelled. "June, are you talking to your brother?"

June must have muffled the phone with her hand, but Travis could still hear. "He needs to come home, Dad. Please?"

It sounded like something scraping against the phone, then Dad's voice, breathing hard. "So you're not doing so well on your own, huh? You're getting a taste of what the real world is like?"

Travis didn't answer.

"Okay, if I let you come back here, you live by my rules, got it? I'll try to get your job back with Verl, if he'll have you. But you're going to pull your weight around here from now on. And there's not going to be any—"

Dad was still spouting off his rules as Travis hung up.

He jumped on the bike and started riding again. Things had changed. He wasn't just on the road until Dad got over

121

being mad. Now Travis was on the road until *he* got over being mad, and that might be forever.

He lost track of time after that. It must have been about an hour later when he came to the outskirts of Cuyler. He rode into the center of town, then stopped at a laundromat to ask directions.

A woman was putting her clothes into a dryer.

"Excuse me. I'm trying to find Scott McKissack's place. Do you know where it is?"

"Doesn't ring a bell," she said. "Sorry."

He asked an older lady who was waiting for her washer to stop. "Excuse me, ma'am, but I'm looking for a guitar maker named Scott McKissack. He runs the picking contest every year."

"Oh, sure. Keep going down this road. Scott's place is a little ways beyond the end of town. He has an old white farmhouse with a brick workshop next to it. I'm not sure he even has a sign, but you can't miss it."

He thanked her and started out again. It seemed stupid to be going to see Scott McKissack when he didn't have a guitar anymore, but he didn't know what else to do. Besides, he was hoping that Cowboy might have taken the guitar to Scott to get it fixed. Where else would he take it? It's not like there were a lot of guitar repairmen around. And it had to be repaired before it fell apart.

Travis rode past a long stretch of woods and thought he might have missed Scott's place. Then he came up over a rise and saw a brick building with a long cement platform that ran across the front with four rocking chairs on it. The mailbox out front said MCKISSACK. He leaned his bike against the side of the building and knocked on the door.

Someone inside called out, "Door's open!"

Travis went in. The crowded shelves around three of the walls were filled with more instruments than Travis had ever seen in one place, only most didn't have all their parts. There were guitars with no necks, necks with no guitars, a mandolin with the top missing, an old banjo with the head bashed in. It looked like a place where old instruments went to die. Travis quickly scanned the shelves. Was 3-G's guitar somewhere in that mess? He didn't see it.

The main worktable in the middle of the room held all kinds of hand tools and other stuff that looked like junk. There were big power tools around the room, too, like a table saw, a band saw, and a drill press. Scott McKissack was at one end of the worktable, sanding a thin piece of guitar-shaped wood. He was just the way Travis remembered him from the diner—even had the same hat and shirt on. He looked up. "Can I help you with something?"

"I'm looking for a guitar."

"Hey, you're the kid I met a few days ago at the Chicken Diner." Scott brushed the sawdust off his arm and reached out to shake Travis's hand. "I was hoping you'd stop by. Did you bring that old guitar with you?"

"No, but I'm hoping a tall skinny guy in a cowboy hat brought it in a couple of hours ago for repair."

Scott came around from behind the workbench. "No, you're the first one in here this afternoon. Something happen to your guitar?"

123

Travis couldn't hide his disappointment, even though he knew he'd been kidding himself about finding the guitar here. "It has a big crack down the back."

Scott looked puzzled. "So who was supposed to bring it in? Some relative of yours?"

"No, the guy that stole it."

Scott let out a low whistle and leaned back against the workbench. "Oh, man, I'm sorry to hear that. Did you report it to the police?"

"No."

"You should do that right away. If it's only been gone a couple of hours, they might have a shot at catching the guy." Scott shuffled through the junk on his workbench and fished out a stubby pencil and an old envelope. "Here, write down your name and phone number. I'll give you a call if the guy brings it in here."

"I, um, we don't have a phone."

"Okay, give me your address and I'll drop by your house."

Travis didn't want to give Scott his home address. He couldn't take a chance on having the police poking around their house. He should never have come in here. He handed back the pencil and envelope. "Forget it. I changed my mind."

Scott shrugged. "Suit yourself," but his expression said he wanted to know more. Travis was tempted to tell Scott about what was going on with his family, but he knew he shouldn't. He had to get out of there.

"Thanks anyway." Travis ran out the door and grabbed his bike. He didn't know which direction to ride in. He'd been stupid to think that Scott McKissack could be the answer to all his problems. Scott was nice enough, but there was nothing he could do to help. There was nothing anybody could do.

Travis looked toward what he thought was the direction of home. Should he go back and take what Dad had to dish out to him? Without food or cash, he wouldn't last long on the road, especially since he had no way to earn money. But would he cause more problems for the whole family if he went back? Travis stood there by the edge of the road, straddling his bike and gripping the handlebars, not knowing which way to turn.

He was clean out of ideas and hope.

CHAPTER 12

Travis thought about the songs Mom used to make up. Most of them were funny songs about each of the kids. But sometimes when she was sad about something, she'd come up with a song to make herself feel better. One was about doors.

> *When you're tired of life's rat race,*
> *And every door slams in your face,*
> *Don't give in. There's hope in store.*
> *Just open up another door.*

Travis wished he had Mom's optimistic spirit. She always believed that things would get better. After what had happened to his family, Travis didn't buy that anymore.

But what if Mom was right? What if he did exactly what that song said—opened up a door for himself?

Travis leaned his bike against the building, turned the doorknob, and went back into the workshop.

Scott looked up. "You forget something?"

Travis was already feeling foolish. Why had he done this? "I, um, was wondering. You have that picking contest coming up."

"Yep. It's two weeks from today. You want to enter?"

"No, I'm not that good." Travis almost added that he had no guitar, but didn't want to bring up that subject again. "I was wondering if you could use some extra help."

"Sure, we can always use an extra volunteer the day of the festival."

This wasn't going the way Travis had hoped. He needed a job now—one that would earn him some money. Okay, he had to come out and say it. "Do you have something I could help you with right away? I'm good with my hands. I'm a hard worker. I can carve things out of wood. Or haul stuff around—like I did with Verl Bickley."

Scott put down the wood he was sanding. "So you're talking about a paid job?"

Travis swallowed. "Yes, sir, I am."

"You're finished with school, right? I saw you working with Bickley in the middle of the day."

"Yeah, I'm done with school. I look young, but I'm . . . I'm sixteen." Travis tried not to let his face give away his lie.

"I know how that goes," Scott said. "I was small for my age, too. So you have working papers for the job with Bickley?"

"Yeah, sure," Travis lied again. He didn't mention that Verl wouldn't bother with legalities like working papers.

Scott looked around the workshop. "Okay. I hadn't thought about hiring an assistant, but there's a lot of work to do in the next two weeks. So, yeah, I could take you on from now until the festival, and maybe a day or two afterward. You'll need to go to the guidance office at the school you went to and get a copy of those papers for me. But since you're not eighteen, I'll also want a note from one of your parents saying they're okay with you working for me. I can use you every weekday, and Saturday, too, when we get to that last week. There's always a lot to do at the end."

"Okay, I'll have my mom write a note."

"I can only give you minimum wage, but the work isn't hard. Since you like guitars, I think you'll enjoy yourself."

Travis couldn't believe he had a real job, even if it was only for a couple of weeks. "I sure will. Thanks, Mr. McKissack."

"Forget the 'mister.' Just call me Scott. Do you have to give Bickley notice that you won't be working for him anymore?"

"No, I quit that job."

Scott laughed. "Can't say I blame you for that."

Travis's spirits soared as he left Scott's shop and rode back toward Cuyler. Mom always said your luck could turn from bad to good in the space of a single minute. Unfortunately, he had learned it could change in the other direction even faster.

Travis needed a piece of paper and a pen to write his note. He remembered passing a library back in town. Libraries always had stuff like that for kids who forgot to bring them. He parked his bike in their rack and went inside.

First thing he noticed was a poster on the bulletin board

about the picking contest. It said the winner would get a guitar made by Scott McKissack. Travis wondered if he'd get to help Scott build it. There were small wooden braces inside a guitar that needed to be whittled to the right shape, and Travis had told Scott he was a carver.

A girl about June's age was pushing a cart full of books. She stopped to slip one into the new books display under the bulletin board. Travis stepped out of her way but kept reading about the contest. It said musicians from all over would be coming. He'd get to hear some really good players. And learning how to build a guitar would be so much fun, he wouldn't care if he got paid or not. Then his stomach growled so loud the girl looked up, and he remembered why getting paid was more important than having fun.

"Are you going to the picking contest?" the girl asked.

Travis nodded.

"I guess that's a silly question. Just about everybody goes. You must be new around here, though. I haven't seen you before."

"I don't spend much time in the library."

She smiled. "Are you working on the final project that Mrs. Randolph assigned? Everybody's been in here complaining about that."

He didn't want to say too much and give away the fact that he was a stranger, so he said, "I forgot to bring paper and a pen."

"No problem," she said. "I'll get them for you."

That's when his stomach let out such a loud noise even

129

the librarian at the checkout desk looked up. The girl said, "If you're hungry, there are some cookies left from the afternoon story hour group in that room over there. Take all you want. If they're still there when I go in to clean up, I'll probably eat them, and I shouldn't."

"Thanks. I guess I should have had a bigger lunch."

Travis went into the story hour room and found a plate with at least a dozen chocolate chip cookies. He stuffed two in his mouth right away, and almost moaned with the pleasure of eating something besides purslane. He forced himself not to eat any more cookies, but filled his jeans pockets with the rest. He didn't know how soon he'd get paid for working, so he'd have to make these last.

When he went back into the main room, the girl met him with the pen and paper. "The books for Randolph's class are over on that far table. I see you found the cookies." She brushed her finger on the corner of her mouth to show him that he had some cookie crumbs on his face.

He ducked his head and wiped them away. "Yeah, they're good. Thanks."

He took the pen and paper over to the table. Two girls were huddled over a book, talking about the project. They ignored Travis, which was fine with him. He opened one of the books and pretended to be reading it. Then he wiped his hand on his jeans and wrote his note, being careful to form the letters to look like Mom's handwriting, even though Scott wouldn't know the difference. It just couldn't look like a kid did it.

Dear Mr. McKissack,
Travis has my permission to be your
helper for the picking contest.

The note looked too short, but he didn't know what else to say. Mom always wrote something chatty in her excuse notes to his teachers, so he added some things that he thought she might say.

Travis has always been interested in
guitars and he's an excellent wood carver, too.
I hope he can be a good help to you.

Did that sound right or would Scott know Travis wrote it? He read it over again and decided it was pretty believable. Then he thought back to when they learned about business letters in English class and finished with "Yours very truly, Geneva Tacey."

He folded the paper in three parts, closed the book, and stood up. One of the girls at the table looked at him and rolled her eyes. "Study much?"

Travis returned the pen to the front desk, stopped in the bathroom to clean up a bit, and used some paper towels to wrap the cookies. They might have to last for a few days so he didn't want to end up with nothing but pockets full of crumbs. He also took some extra paper towels and some toilet paper. He carefully put the note in his backpack and headed out of town in the direction of Scott's shop.

131

Travis didn't have money to rent a room, so he looked for a place to camp out overnight. He found a wooded area near Scott's workshop that had a small creek running through it. Perfect. It was a warm night so he didn't even need to build a shelter, but he put together a temporary lean-to out of broken branches to keep the dew from falling on him after the sun went down. Then he gathered up some spruce needles to make the ground softer to sleep on.

He had a safe place to stay, cookies and water to fill his stomach, and a permission note from his mother. He pulled out the note and read it over, pretending it was really from her, even feeling kind of proud about her calling him an excellent wood carver. As he tucked it away in his backpack, he wondered if she would ever write a note for him again.

CHAPTER 13

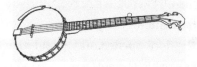

The next morning Travis had been waiting about half an hour before Scott came out from the house to the workshop.

"You're here bright and early," Scott said.

"You didn't say what time, so I didn't want to be late." Travis handed him the note.

Scott stuffed it into his pocket without reading it, then went over to a table against a wall and picked up a coffee maker. "You know how to do this?"

"Make coffee? I'm not sure how this one works. We have a regular old pot at home."

"Yeah, that's what I always had, too—a pot and a hot plate. Then my friends thought I needed to get fancy. Coffee tastes all the same to me. This'll be the first thing you do every morning. Also washing out the mugs. My friends like to come in for coffee, but they're not so good at cleaning up after themselves."

Travis watched how Scott put in the filter, coffee, and

133

water so he'd know how to do it. "Some days we go through two, even three pots, depending on how many people show up."

"Are they all coming in to buy guitars?"

Scott laughed. "Don't I wish. No, all these guys want is coffee and conversation."

Just then the door opened and an old man came in with a big bag. "Breakfast is served!"

"This is Clarence Alcorn, Travis," Scott said. "He's the chief advice-giver around here. Travis is my new assistant."

Travis liked the sound of that—*assistant.*

Clarence was shoving some junk on the worktable aside with his arm to make space for the bag. Whatever was in it was hot and smelled wonderful. "Scott wouldn't get any guitars built without me helping him. I'm the one who keeps him working. Otherwise he'd sit around carving birds or some dang stupid thing."

"You carve birds?" Travis asked. That was another thing he wanted to learn how to do.

"Don't listen to Clarence," Scott said. "You can't believe one word that comes out of that man's mouth."

Clarence laughed. He pulled a small wrapped package out of the bag and tossed it to Travis. "Here, Travis, put some meat on your bones. Scott's going to have you doing some heavy lifting."

"That's okay," Travis said. "I'm pretty strong." He figured there was nothing here that would be heavier than the old appliances Verl had him lugging around.

Scott poured a mug of fresh coffee and handed it to

Clarence. "I told you not to listen to him, Travis. Your job to-day doesn't involve any lifting."

Travis opened the little package. It was a hot sandwich with egg and bacon on a biscuit. Travis had only allowed himself to eat one cookie and a couple of cherries for break-fast, so he was still hungry, and the smell of food drove him crazy. He had to force himself not to swallow the sandwich in one bite. This job was going to work out great if he got to eat here. He'd save the cookies and cherries as a backup, but he sure wasn't going to starve today.

"What's the job you're going to have me do?" Travis asked when he had finished the sandwich. He had seen a little pile of what he figured were roughed-out braces for the inside of a guitar. He was sure Scott would be showing him how to carve them into their final shape, and he couldn't wait to get started. He didn't care if his work was on the inside of the guitar where it wouldn't show. He'd know it was in there. That was the important thing.

"You're working on the cows today," Scott said.

Clarence laughed. "See? What did I tell you? He's going to have you hauling the bovines around. I'd call that some heavy lifting. Yessir. I never met a skinny cow." Clarence stuffed a breakfast sandwich in his mouth, almost swallow-ing it whole. Then he grabbed another one and did the same thing. Travis could see where he got the big belly that strained the buttons on his sweater.

Travis turned to Scott. "So I'm working on cows?"

"Yep. Come over here. I'll show you." Scott pulled out one of the big sheets of corrugated cardboard that were stacked against the wall behind a workbench. They were the sides of old refrigerator cartons, cut apart. "We have a lot of activities to keep the little kids busy while their folks are either watching the contest or playing in it. One of the most popular things is cow painting."

"And tell him who came up with that idea," Clarence said, pouring himself another cup of coffee.

"Yeah, this is one of Clarence's harebrained projects, but I have to admit the kids seem to like it," Scott said. "You can use this cow from last year as a pattern. Trace around it on a new piece of cardboard and cut it out with this craft knife. You can use a knife without cutting yourself, can't you?"

Travis took the knife from him. "Sure. I've been carving stuff since I was a little kid."

"Oh, a whittler, are you?" Clarence said. "Now there's a mountain kid after my own heart. When I was a tyke, my dad had me carving before I could walk."

Scott rolled his eyes. "Well, that explains a lot." He turned to Travis. "I cleared some space for you on the floor."

Travis started tracing a cow. He tried to hide his disappointment about not working on a guitar. Maybe this was a test to make sure he could use a knife without slicing off a finger. Maybe when he finished cutting out the cows, Scott would give him something important to do, like carving braces.

"When you get the cows cut out, you can take them out back to paint them."

"I thought the little kids were going to paint them,"

Travis said. He saw Scott and Clarence grin at each other. Maybe they were just yanking his chain. He thought cow painting had sounded pretty dumb.

Sure enough, Scott gathered up those little pieces of wood and came over to him. He was going to have Travis carve braces after all.

"You're going to paint the cardboard white on each side. Makes the kids' paintings show up better than they would on the brown cardboard. I left a can of paint and a brush out back for you."

Travis still hoped Scott was kidding until he sat at his workbench and started whittling the braces himself. So much for getting to work on a guitar.

He was cutting out his fourth cow when another old guy came in. Scott called him Buddy, but he didn't introduce him to Travis, who was out of sight working behind the big band saw. Buddy and Clarence sat around insulting each other and Scott, but Travis could tell it was good-natured banter among friends.

He peeked around the band saw and caught a glimpse of Buddy, who was the exact opposite of Clarence—tall and skinny. Travis gave his knees a rest from the cement floor and sat, leaning his back against the saw table. He looked around the workshop. The top of every table and machine had wood and hand tools piled on it. In one corner of the room, there was a big heap of scrap wood. Travis thought of asking Scott for a piece to whittle on. That would help him pass the time each evening in his campsite. He missed watching TV and having a guitar to strum, not that he'd had a lot of free time at home, what with doing his homework and helping June with the kids.

Travis went back to cutting and had just finished the horns on cow number five when a little black hound dog appeared out of nowhere, squatted in the middle of his cow, and peed. "Hey!" he yelled. "Stop that!"

"Don't let Buddy's mangy mutt do his business on those cows," Clarence said.

"You're too late with that warning." Travis ran over to the sink, grabbed some paper towels, and took them back to blot up the mess.

"Aw, Shirley can't help herself," Buddy said, scooping her up. "She's only got one bladder and it's old."

"It's her kidney that got taken out," Clarence said. "Nobody's got two bladders, you old coot."

Buddy settled into the rocking chair by the workbench with Shirley on his lap. "Well, whatever she's got don't work right, is all I'm saying." Buddy reached into Clarence's paper bag and pulled out one of the little breakfast sandwiches. He unwrapped it, took a bite, and broke off a piece for Shirley.

"You see anywhere on that wrapper where it says dog food?" Clarence asked. "Because if it don't, you're wasting perfectly good human food on that hound."

Buddy ignored him, giving every other bite to Shirley.

Scott shook his head and smiled. "Travis, this is Buddy Hubert. He's another person who gives me headaches around here. And don't listen to Clarence complain about Shirley. He's an old softie. I can't even count the number of strays he's taken in over the years, canine and human. So how are those cows coming?"

"I've done five, if you count the one that got peed on."

"Good. Why don't you get those painted before you cut out any more."

Travis dragged the cows out behind the workshop, lined them up across the grass, and painted one side of each. By the time he finished the last one, the first one was dry. When all the cows were painted on both sides, he stood them against the back wall of the shop to admire his work. They looked pretty good—almost the size of a real calf. Travis stacked them together and carried them inside. That's when he heard the music. It was Clarence, making sounds Travis had never heard come out of a guitar before. Maybe it was because Mom was the only person he had ever heard play in person. She was good, but she was nothing like Clarence. His fat, knobby fingers moved too fast over the strings for Travis to see which notes he was playing. And the guitar sounded even better than 3-G Eli's. The high notes rang like bells and the low notes were deep and rich, vibrating against the walls of the workshop.

Travis stood, transfixed, until the song ended. "You're the best guitar player I ever heard."

Clarence shook his head. "No, this is the best guitar you've ever heard. A gen-u-wine McKissack. She's a beauty." Clarence turned the guitar so Travis could see it from all angles. The top was honey-colored and the back and sides were a rich, dark brown with thin curving streaks of dark orange. A narrow strip of lighter wood outlined the top, and the whole guitar was covered with a high-gloss finish. The sound hole was surrounded with a dozen narrow rings of black, white, and a wider one in shades of blue and green that sparkled in the shaft of sunlight coming through the window.

"You made this?" Travis asked. He couldn't imagine how it would feel to create something this beautiful.

"Yep," Scott said. "Just strung it up this morning."

"It's real pretty," Travis said. "I like that design around the sound hole."

"That's called the rosette," Scott said.

Travis leaned in for a closer look. "You must have a really fine brush to paint those thin lines."

Scott took the guitar from Clarence and polished the top with a clean rag. "It's not painted. These are all fine strips of wood. I'll show you when I make the guitar for the contest."

"I thought this was the one for the contest," Clarence said.

"No, this is for a customer coming in from Ohio. The contest guitar is over there." Scott pointed to a pile of thin wooden slabs on his workbench.

"You haven't started it yet?" Travis asked. The contest was only two weeks away. How long did it take to make a guitar, anyway?

"No, but here's the sketch." Scott moved some notebooks and uncovered a life-sized pencil drawing of a guitar—a flat view from the top, like a blueprint with measurements on it. "This will be the pattern for shaping the sides. Here's the wood I chose for it. Listen to this." He started to pick up one of the pieces and put it down again. "Wait, you need to hear an ordinary piece of wood first." He grabbed another thin piece of wood from a pile in the corner, held it by the corner, and tapped it with his knuckle. "Hear that?"

"It just sounds like you're tapping on wood," Travis said. "I don't know what I'm listening for."

"Remember what you heard. Now listen to this." He did the same thing with one of the pieces of wood for the new guitar. It made a ringing sound that vibrated for half a minute before fading away.

"Wow! What kind of wood is that?"

"Adirondack spruce," Scott said, "the best wood in the world for the soundboard of an acoustic guitar. It's so strong, you can carve it really thin and use light bracing, so it vibrates freely. That's why the sound is so full." Scott ran his fingers over the wood. "This tree grew right here. There used to be plenty of huge Adirondack spruce trees in these parts before logging wiped out the old-growth trees. The man who owned the property cut this one down about fifty years ago. He made guitars and I was lucky enough to be his apprentice." Travis had noticed that Scott wasn't much of a talker, but he sure could get excited about building guitars.

"Scott's got enough Adirondack for a lot more guitars stacked in his drying shed out back," Buddy said. "At the rate he works, he'll finish up the last of it when he's about a hundred and ten."

Scott was still tapping the piece of Adirondack, smiling at the sound it made. "I'd likely have used it up by now if I didn't have so many distractions around here."

Clarence picked up a pile of papers. "Well, this distraction is getting out of your hair right now. I want to get these flyers in every store window around. I'll take the kid with me. He's so noisy and all. I'll leave you with the old coot and the hound with the leaky bladder. That'll be nice and peaceful for ya."

Travis started to follow Clarence, then hesitated. "But I haven't finished the cows."

Scott waved him away. "Go ahead. The cows will keep for another day."

By the time Travis got outside, Clarence was hefting his bulk up into the driver's seat of an old Ford pickup. Travis climbed in and the truck took off with a jolt. They drove along in silence for a couple of miles with Clarence taking the curves at a fast clip. Travis figured he was mad about Scott calling him a distraction, and if he didn't slow down, they'd end up in a ditch. The third time Travis slid into the car door, he spoke up. "I don't think Scott meant anything by it. He was only joking."

Clarence looked at him. "Oh, you mean us trading insults? That's just the way we talk to each other—all three of us. Don't mean a thing. I even like Shirley, the pee queen. What made you think I was mad?"

He took a curve to the right, almost sending Travis into his lap. "The way you're driving!"

Clarence laughed. "That's a bad habit of mine. I know every bend in the road so I sort of get into the rhythm of the thing, you know? This next section always reminds me of the song 'Comin' 'Round the Mountain.' Watch this." He sang with a surprisingly good voice, the curves landing at the last word of each line.

Clarence glanced over at him. "You're looking a little

peaked there, boy. I'll slow it down. Long as I have some company in the truck, I don't need to keep myself awake by singing."

Oh, man, he was supposed to be keeping Clarence awake? Travis figured he'd better get a conversation going. "You're a good singer," he said. "A really good guitar player, too. Are you entering the picking contest?"

"Me? Nah."

"You mean because you and Scott are friends, so it wouldn't be fair?"

"That wouldn't make any difference. It's a blind contest. The judges can't see the contestants."

"But Scott would know your singing voice, right?"

"Oh, you can't sing in the contest. All you get is three minutes of pure guitar picking. And the reason I don't enter is that the players are way better'n me. I wouldn't stand a chance."

Travis couldn't even imagine how good those players must be. He could see out of the corner of his eye that Clarence was looking at him. He had slowed way down. He seemed to have two speeds—one where the scenery blurred past and the other where you could count the blades of grass along the side of the road. "So are you from around here?"

"Not far away," Travis said, careful not to give away any information.

"What road you live on?"

"It doesn't really have a name. One of those back roads, you know?" Was that vague enough? He hoped Clarence would be satisfied with that.

"Oh, I know every one of those back roads. I've lived around here for nigh onto eighty-one years. What road is it off of? And how come you've never been to the picking contest before if you love guitars so much?"

In the side mirror, Travis could see a car coming fast behind them. The driver had to slam on his brakes until they hit a straight stretch, then laid on his horn as he blew past them. This took Clarence's attention away from Travis while he muttered a few mild cuss words at the other driver.

Travis had to change the subject. He could tell Clarence was suspicious of him. "So are there many guys who make guitars around here?"

"Oh, sure, there are some who dabble in it, but Scott is one of the best luthiers in the country."

That seemed like a weird thing to say. "What does his religion have to do with it?"

Clarence looked at him. "Religion?" Travis wished he'd keep his eyes on the road. "Oh, you mean Lutheran?" He laughed. "That's a good one. I'll have to remember that to tell Scott. You were kidding, right? You know that *luthier* is the name for somebody who makes stringed instruments."

"Sure I know that. I was making a joke," Travis lied, so Clarence wouldn't think he was dumb. *Luthier*—he'd have to remember that.

Clarence chuckled to himself for a while, mumbling, "Lutheran. That's a good one." Then he turned to Travis again. "So are you a runaway?"

"No! Why are you asking me that?" What the heck? First

the waitress, now Clarence. Was he wearing a HELP THIS KID. HE'S IN TROUBLE sign on his forehead?

"You're acting like a runaway because you don't want anybody to know where you live, for starters."

"I'm new here. I don't know the names of all the roads yet."

That seemed to be a good enough answer for Clarence because he stopped with the questions. They came into a town, parked, and Clarence held out some flyers and tape. "You go across the street and I'll take this side. Show them the flyer. Make sure you mention Scott's charity, Adirondack Jam. The money he makes from the festival goes to help disadvantaged kids." He peered at Travis over his glasses. "You wouldn't qualify to be one of them, would you?"

Travis yanked the flyers out of his hand. "You sure get crazy ideas."

"Uh-huh. That's what Scott says. Anyways, be sure you tape the flyer to the window yourself. If you leave it for them to do, it'll end up in the trash."

"Okay." Travis took off, glad to be away from the nosy old man. Telling the truth was easy because there was only one story to remember. Travis could see that once you started lying, you had too many false "facts" to keep track of. He'd have to be on his guard from now on.

CHAPTER 14

Clarence had counted out just enough flyers for all the stores on Travis's side of the street. He was waiting in the truck when Travis came back with three of them still in his hand.

"Who wouldn't let you put the flyers up?" Clarence asked.

"The shoe store was closed, the lady in the gift shop said her boss would have to decide, and the guy in the hardware store said no."

Clarence reached through the window to open the broken door handle from the outside. "Give me those things. I don't know what's the matter with people around here. The main reason Scott puts on this festival is to make money for the kids. He doesn't make a cent off it for himself."

Clarence hitched up his pants and headed across the street. Travis was going to stay by the truck, but the old man called over his shoulder, "Come ahead and see how this is done."

They stopped into the gift shop first. The same girl who had given Travis the brush-off didn't talk back to Clarence.

"Mary Beth, you give this to Aileen when she gets back. Tell her I want to see it in her window when I drive by tomorrow. And take this extra one to Sam next door when he comes back from lunch. Tell him the same thing, hear?"

"Yes, sir, Mr. Alcorn. I sure will."

Clarence headed on down the street. "How hard was that?"

"Well, it's not hard if you know everybody in the whole darn Adirondacks by their first names."

Clarence looked straight ahead, but he was smiling. "That's why it was strange that I didn't know you."

Travis followed him up the steps to Thompson's Hardware. "Thrummy, you old fool. Where are you?" Clarence bellowed. A lady customer turned and waved at him.

"Thrummy?" Travis said. "Thrummy Thompson?"

"That's me, kid." Thrummy had come out of the back room. "Clarence, what are you yelling about? You'll drive away my paying customers."

"You're the guy who shot at the bear?" Travis asked. Thrummy almost looked like a bear himself—big, with hairy arms showing under his rolled-up sleeves.

Clarence gave him a quizzical look. "How did you hear that story?"

Before Travis could answer, Clarence went on with his business. "Thrummy, I'm putting this picking contest flyer in your window and I don't want no arguments."

"Oh, sure. Is that the thing the kid was talking about? I was busy—wasn't paying much attention to him."

"Figures," Clarence said. "And I can't stand here flapping my gums with you. We got more territory to cover."

As Clarence was taping up the flyer, Travis asked Thrummy, "Is it true about the bear chewing the gum?"

"No, of course not. Whoever heard of a bear chewing gum?"

"Ha! I didn't think it was true."

Thrummy leaned against the counter, his hands in his pockets. "No, sir, that old bear never chewed a stick of gum. It was Life Savers. Three whole rolls of Life Savers. He ate everything but the green ones. Those he lined up on the dashboard as neat as you please."

"He did not," Travis said, grinning.

Thrummy raised his shaggy eyebrows, pointing at Travis. "Were you there?"

When they were back in the truck, Clarence reached behind the seat and pulled out another pack of papers. "I want to put out flyers in the next town, too. Make sure you tell people it's for Adirondack Jam."

"What is that, anyway?"

Clarence glanced at Travis. "Didn't Scott tell you? It's the whole reason he does the festival. The schools have cut way back on music budgets, so Scott uses the festival profits to buy instruments for the kids who can't afford them. He buys some new and fixes up old ones."

"What kinds of instruments?"

"Anything with strings—guitars, mandolins, violins, banjos, and even a couple of stand-up basses."

"So Scott teaches the kids to play?"

"Mostly. He goes around to the schools and shows kids

148

the traditional mountain music that used to be played in these parts. Buddy and I help sometimes when he wants them to hear how it's supposed to sound with several kinds of instruments playing together."

Travis would have loved doing that, but he'd never heard about Adirondack Jam. "Nobody comes to my school," he blurted out, then regretted having said it. He was supposed to be out of school. Luckily, Clarence didn't notice.

"Well, Scott hasn't got around to every one of them yet, but he will. The kids from the different schools get together to play in a band called Adirondack Jam. You'll hear them at the festival."

"So this is only for kids who are in trouble?"

"Nope. It's for anybody who wants to be in it. Playing in a band gives kids something to get excited about, so maybe they stay out of trouble." They had reached the next town, and Clarence pulled into a parking spot, switched off the engine, and turned to look nose-to-nose at Travis. "Which brings me back to you. Why can't you go home?"

"Who says I can't?" Travis shot back, opening the car door.

"Okay, if that's the way you wanna be." Clarence seemed content for now, but Travis knew he wasn't through asking questions.

Now that Travis could talk about Adirondack Jam, he had much better luck. People just assumed he was in the band. The lady in the antiques shop said, "Wait a minute, honey. I've been saving something for you Jam kids." Travis didn't try to set her straight. Hey, he played the guitar and he was disadvantaged. What more did she want?

The lady went into the back room and came out with an old beat-up guitar. Travis's heart stopped for a second, until he realized it wasn't 3-G's. "It's kind of a mess," she said, "but I know Scott can work miracles with these old instruments."

"Sure," Travis said. "Thanks a lot."

Travis's last stop was the barbershop. He started his Adirondack Jam Spiel, but the guy already knew about it. "My nephew was in a bad crowd, but now all he can think about is his music. His grades have even gone up." He went to the cash register and came back with a fifty-dollar bill. "Tell Scott that Hal Otis says thanks." When he got outside, Travis studied the picture of Ulysses S. Grant on the bill. He'd never seen anything bigger than a ten.

Clarence was pleased with the guitar and the money. "That's more like it. I think we've earned ourselves a lunch."

They stopped at a fast food joint where Clarence picked up hamburgers for everybody, even one for Shirley the pee queen.

"Lunch is served," Clarence said, when they got back to the shop.

"You all go ahead and eat," Scott said. "I've got my hands full here. Gotta finish bending the sides of this guitar while the pipe is hot."

"Can I watch?" Travis asked. "I've always wondered how a flat piece of wood gets to be curved like that."

"Sure. Just don't touch the pipe. It'll give you a pretty bad burn." Scott spritzed something from a spray bottle on the wood, then pressed the thin board against a pipe that was clamped to his worktable. There was a sizzle, followed by the smell of scorched wood.

Travis saw that Scott had a gas torch shooting a flame up into the pipe. "What's in the spray bottle?"

"Plain old water." Scott took the curved piece over to the pattern on the table and lined it up on the pencil outline. Travis could see that this was only one side of the guitar. "Not enough bend to it yet," Scott said. He gave the wood another spray, then rocked it gently against the pipe, making the curve deeper. Clarence and Buddy were eating. Travis figured they'd seen Scott do this dozens of times before. Travis was hungry, but too fascinated to stop watching. He couldn't imagine ever being bored by watching a guitar take shape. Each time Scott took the wood away from the pipe, it held the curved shape he had formed. "So do you spray the wood with water to soften it up?"

Scott was lining up the wood on the drawing again. "Nope. The heat melts the resins in the wood to allow it to bend. The water keeps it from burning on the hot pipe. Some guys put the wood in a steamer to make it soft, then clamp it into a mold. I like hot pipe bending better."

"Scott enjoys doing things the hard way," Clarence said.

Buddy laughed. "Ain't that the truth."

Scott was curving the wood against the pipe in the opposite direction now, forming the narrower waist part of the guitar. It was like magic, the way the wood took on an *S* shape and held it. "This is how they made guitars in the old days. It's the way I was taught. Still seems like a good method.

151

I like feeling the wood give way under my hands with the heat."

"You think that's how 3-G Eli made his guitar?" Travis asked.

"Who?" Clarence asked, with his mouth full.

"That's the nickname we have for my great-great-great-grandfather," Travis said. "He made violins and guitars."

Clarence brushed some crumbs off his belly. "Did he make the one that got stolen?" It surprised Travis that Scott had told Clarence about the robbery. He hadn't taken Scott for a blabbermouth.

"I'd like to get my hands on that guy," Buddy said. "I'd show him what's what." So Buddy knew, too. If Travis let anything slip about his family in front of these guys, it would be all over town in a heartbeat.

Scott checked the wood shape against the pattern again and, satisfied, turned off the torch. He took a burger out of the bag and tossed one to Travis. "How old do you figure your guitar was?"

"Mom told me it probably was made sometime in the late eighteen hundreds."

Scott shook his head. "Sure wish I could have seen that guitar. I'd love to know how it was put together. They wouldn't have had propane torches back then. They used to make a metal box with an oval pipe like a chimney. Then they'd fill the box with hot charcoal and when the chimney heated up enough, they'd press the wetted wood around it, just like I did here."

Clarence reached in the bag, tossed another burger to Travis, and took the last one—probably Shirley's—for himself.

Travis slipped outside and tucked it into his backpack. Now he had supper for tonight.

When he went back in, Buddy was playing the banjo. He was as good on the banjo as Clarence was on the guitar—maybe better. The fingers of his right hand moved so fast plucking the strings, they looked blurry.

"Did you finish repairing that old mandolin you were working on the other day?" Clarence asked.

Scott looked up from sanding the second side piece. "Yep. It's over on the top shelf. It's not tuned, though."

Clarence found the mandolin and twisted the tuners, plucking the strings to test the notes as he walked over to take a seat on the old rocking chair next to Buddy. He vamped for a few minutes while Buddy did some fancy stuff, then Buddy nodded and Clarence started in playing notes all up and down the neck of the mandolin. Travis couldn't believe how fast these old geezers could play, especially since both of them had fingers that were gnarled knobby from arthritis. He sat on the floor in front of them and stared.

Scott's foot was tapping as he sanded. "Darn you guys," he said. "How's a person supposed to get any work done when his fingers are itching to play?" He grabbed a guitar from one of the worktables and joined them. The whole room seemed to explode with the music. They were all so good, Travis laughed right out loud from the pure joy of it.

He didn't know the first song they were playing, but when they switched into "The Fox," he joined in, singing harmony, slapping the rhythm out on his knees. Scott grinned and handed him the guitar. "Go for it, Travis."

"I can't play like you guys. I only do chords."

"So you're playing backup. Nothing wrong with that."

Travis took the guitar. "I can't tell what key you're in," he said, trying to read the flying fingers.

"Key of G," Clarence yelled over the music.

Without even thinking about it, Travis's fingers found the chords and he strummed in their rhythm, filling out the sound. This must be what it felt like to play in a real band. They went through three more verses, with Buddy and Clarence taking turns doing fancy riffs.

Then Buddy said, "Take a verse, Travis."

He shook his head. "I'm not good enough."

"What are you worried about?" Buddy said. "Don't matter if you goof up. Nobody paid to see this performance."

"Heck," Clarence said, "we've goofed up when people *have* paid to see us perform."

So Travis took a deep breath and jumped in. It was his favorite verse. As he strummed, he sang out his mother's words loud and clear all by himself, with Clarence and Buddy playing the backup.

> *Old mother slip-slapper swooped out of bed.*
> *Her eyes were blue and her nose was red,*
> *She cried, "Roy! Roy! Come be a big boy*
> *And chase that fox from our town-o."*

Then Clarence took the next verse, Buddy the one after that, and they finished in three-part harmony, with Clarence yelling, "Yee haw!" at the end.

Scott applauded from over by the workbench where he had gone back to bend the second side of the guitar. "That was some fine strumming, Travis. I liked that verse of yours, too. Never heard it before."

"Mom used to make up verses about all of us kids," Travis said. He strummed a chord, then broke it up into individual notes. "I wish I could learn how to do that finger picking you guys do."

"I can show you a little bit right now"—Clarence raised his voice—"unless Scott has some work for you to do."

"Go ahead," Scott said. "Can't let work get in the way of a guitar lesson."

"I still haven't finished the cows," Travis admitted.

"They're not gonna stampede off anywhere," Clarence said. He rummaged around the shelves in the back of the room and found a guitar. "This one doesn't belong to anybody, does it, Scott? Can Travis use it to practice?"

Scott looked up. "Sure. It's a spare Adirondack Jam guitar."

Travis could smell the toasting wood and was torn between wanting to watch Scott bend another side and getting a lesson from Clarence. He decided on the free lesson, because who knew when Clarence would be in the mood to teach him again?

Clarence spent the next hour showing Travis how to take the chords he had been strumming and break them into patterns of separate notes. They started out slowly, with Clarence calling out which order the fingers should go in, "Thumb, index, middle, ring." Then he had Travis gradually

155

speed up until it felt natural. The first pattern had the fingers picking in order, but when Travis had that under control, Clarence started mixing it up. "Okay, now try this. Thumb, middle, index, ring."

Travis's fingers wouldn't cooperate with that one. They'd start out okay with the first couple of repetitions, then get all mixed up when he tried to increase his speed.

"Don't worry about it," Clarence said. "You have to keep going over it until it becomes automatic. You don't even need a guitar. You can practice the patterns on a table, or scratch them out on your knee. I do that all the time when I'm driving around."

Travis shuddered at that thought. Clarence didn't need anything extra to distract him from his driving.

"When you're sitting around at night, watching TV," Clarence continued, "just run through the strums. Pretty soon you won't even have to think about it. 'Course it's better if you have a guitar." He looked over at Scott. "You don't mind if he takes this ax home to practice with, do you, Scott?"

"Be my guest," Scott said.

"Thanks anyway, but I can't take it home on my bike." When Clarence had tuned into *News at Noon* on the truck radio, the weatherman had predicted heavy storms for tonight. Travis sure didn't want to chance having Scott's guitar out in the rain.

"No problem," Clarence said. "I'll give you a lift home." This was like a game of chess. Travis would make a move, then Clarence would trap him.

"I can't have the guitar at my house," Travis countered.

"We have little kids running around and they might hurt it." He thought that was a pretty good move on his part.

"What do you live in—a one-room cabin? There's no safe place to put the guitar?"

"No, it's a regular house—living room, dining room, bedrooms for everybody." Travis pictured their patched-together house that started as a trailer, with extra rooms cobbled onto the sides and back over the years. But he had to make Clarence think they lived in a normal house so he wouldn't decide the family was "disadvantaged" and start snooping.

"Well, where did you keep that old guitar? The kids didn't beat up on that, did they?"

Travis had run out of arguments, but Scott saved him. "Leave the kid alone, Clarence. Not everybody wants to play guitars every waking minute like you. Why don't you take off for home, Travis? There's nothing for you to do until morning."

"Okay," Travis said, heading for the door. "Thanks for the lesson, Clarence."

"Sure you don't want a lift?"

"No, I'm good." Travis shouldered his backpack, grabbed the bike, and took off before Clarence could come outside.

It didn't take long to get to the campsite. Travis ate his hamburger, drank a few cups of water from the stream, and ate a cookie with cherry pie filling on top for dessert. The pie filling had been a big disappointment—not at all like the pies that Mom had made from her own fresh-canned cherries, but it tasted okay if he used a cookie for a crust.

Travis had thrown together a quick lean-to as a shelter last night. Now he went around collecting fallen spruce branches that still held their needles and wove them into the branches he had set up before. Evergreen boughs were good at shedding water, so he should be prepared for tonight's storm. Then he gathered extra armloads of needles for a softer mattress, covered them with the wool blanket, and filled the plastic bag with more needles to make a pillow. He used his extra T-shirt for a pillowcase, propped the pillow on top of his backpack, and tested out the whole arrangement for comfort.

This was almost as good as his room at home—maybe better because he didn't have to share it with Roy and Lester. Most of all, he didn't have to put up with Dad. Travis relaxed, let out a deep breath, and settled in to think about his amazing day. He concentrated on his new fingerpicking patterns, scratching them out against the leg of his jeans, which was probably why he never heard someone coming slowly through the woods to his campsite.

CHAPTER 15

"**N**ice home you got here," a voice said. "So is this your living room or dining room?" Travis looked up to see Clarence Alcorn staring at him with his hands on his hips.

Travis's mind was racing. He couldn't think of a way to lie himself out of this situation.

"You mind telling me what you're doing out here?" Clarence asked, not moving.

"I was too tired to ride all the way home on my bike."

"I offered to drive you home. Why didn't you take me up on it?" They were going to play another chess game. Why did Clarence care about him, anyway? They only met this morning and already Clarence was thinking everything Travis did was his business—as if he were some kind of relative.

"It's fine with my parents that I camp out. I do it all the time. When I told my mom where I was working, she said that I should camp over here instead of riding back and forth every night."

Clarence walked in front of him and eased himself down on a fallen log. "You know, for a young kid, you have an unusually large dose of baloney in you." He looked hard at Travis for a minute. "So why didn't your mother mention the camping in her permission note?"

"How do you know what she wrote? That was private."

"It was sitting on the desk where Scott keeps his orders so my eyes happened to fall on it. I thought it was odd that your mother could write a note, seeing as how it was less than a week ago that she was in a nursing home and couldn't talk."

"You know where she is?" Travis blurted out.

"No, but it wouldn't be hard to find out."

"But where did you hear . . . how did you know . . . ?"

"Scott came back from the Chicken Diner last week and said he met a kid who had a real old family guitar and that his mother played it every day until she was in an accident. And now she was in a nursing home and couldn't talk."

Travis stood up. "Sheesh! Don't you guys have anything better to do than gossip? You and Buddy and Scott are like an old ladies' quilting society, spreading other people's business around. Where my mother is and what she can or can't do is none of your business. Just leave me alone!" Travis wanted to storm out of there, but Clarence was blocking his way toward the road and there was nowhere else to go, unless he splashed through the creek.

Clarence sat on the log with his arms resting on his knees. He didn't look like he was planning to take off, either.

The sun was setting beyond the trees, making his fluffy white hair turn pink, like a circus clown. But Clarence wasn't clowning around. He was dead serious. "You finished having your little tantrum now? Because I'll tell you one thing straight out. Scott McKissack doesn't go messing in anybody's business just for gossip. He was interested in what you said about the guitar. And he felt bad that your mother had played it and sang every day and now she couldn't play and couldn't even talk. Buddy and I agreed that it was a darn shame, and that's all the discussion we had about it."

"But now Scott knows my note was phony."

Clarence shrugged. "I don't believe he made the connection. That man has so much on his mind with the festival, the last thing he's thinking about is you."

"But you're going to tell him about the fake note, right?"

"Can't see as I have a reason to, as long as you answer a few questions . . . like why you're a runaway."

"I told you, I'm not."

Clarence leaned way forward to get himself off the log, rubbing his knees all the way up to the standing position. "Suit yourself."

Travis watched him head for the road, disappearing through the trees.

He didn't know whether to run after Clarence and spill his guts so he wouldn't tell Scott, or stay put and hope he'd keep quiet. Just as he decided to stop him, he heard Clarence's truck motor kick in. He had waited too long.

✦ ✦ ✦

161

Travis was sitting on the front steps the next morning when Scott came out. "You sure are an early bird. What time do you have to start out to ride over here?"

"It's not so bad. Our whole family gets up early. I wanted to finish up those cows this morning."

When Scott unlocked the door, Travis went right to the sink to get the coffee maker going. Before he finished with the coffee, Travis heard the door bang open. "Breakfast is served," Clarence said, but he didn't have his usual cheerful smile.

Travis mumbled a hello, but avoided looking at him. Was Clarence going to give away his secret?

Clarence held the bag out to Travis, shaking it by one corner until Travis reached in and took a breakfast sandwich.

"Thanks," Travis mumbled.

"Don't mention it."

Travis glanced at Scott. He had glued the two pieces of the guitar top together and was pushing them in place with a series of clamps. He seemed oblivious to anything else that was going on in the room.

"I had an interesting conversation with Ralphene last night," Clarence said.

Scott didn't look up. "Oh?"

"Yep. I figured she might know somebody who could help with our problem."

Scott nodded and kept working. There was silence after that, which seemed odd—not for Scott, who wasn't much of a talker, but for Clarence, who never shut up. Travis was suspicious that the problem Clarence mentioned might have something to do with him. He tried to work on cutting out the remaining cows, but the suspense of wondering when the ax would fall was too much for him. He might as well get out of the workshop and let Clarence blab everything to Scott. He picked up the rest of the cardboard and the cow pattern. "I'm going to finish these out back. It's too crowded in here."

Travis spent the next couple of hours cutting out the rest of the cows and painting them. At one point he heard Buddy's truck tires crunch in the gravel driveway. Then Shirley came out to see him, sniffing at the cow he was painting.

"Pee on this and you're dead meat," he said. She raised her head, a little dab of white paint on the tip of her black nose, then disappeared around the front of the building. Travis sat back and looked around. He felt so much at home in this place already. Was it all about to end?

He was checking to see if the last cow was dry when Clarence came out. "Get in the truck. We have an errand to run."

"Okay. Let me put the cows away first." Travis took the cows into the workshop, then climbed into the truck, where Clarence was waiting for him. Clarence slid the fast-food bag across the seat. "There's one left. Saved it for you."

As they took off, Travis didn't say a word—just chewed on the cold breakfast sandwich. He wasn't about to give Clarence any more information. But oddly enough, Clarence wasn't prodding him with questions. They got past the "Comin' 'Round the Mountain" curves without any singing,

163

either. As much as Travis hated to be grilled by Clarence, this silence seemed ominous. Was Clarence taking him somewhere to turn him in as a runaway?

Travis considered saying something, but thought better of it. Maybe he was letting his imagination get the better of him. Maybe everything was fine and they were just going out to do an errand for the festival.

Travis was starting to let his guard down, when Clarence said, "So, you were about to tell me why you left home."

"No I wasn't."

"Well, you are now."

Things were back to normal. Every time Clarence had Travis trapped in the truck, he'd start in with the third degree. Travis figured he might as well tell him something, then maybe the old man would lay off. "I had a fight with my dad and he kicked me out. It's no big deal. His dad booted him out at my age, so it's sort of an old family tradition."

"Does he know where you are?"

"He doesn't care. The family's better off without me. I've always rubbed Dad the wrong way."

"How about your mother? Does she know you left home?"

"I don't want to talk about her." Travis pictured Mom the way he had seen her last. Right away, his eyes stung with tears. He turned his head away from Clarence and pressed his forehead against the window to keep from crying.

That's when Clarence pulled into a driveway. "Well, if you don't want to talk *about* her, maybe you'd better talk *to* her." There was a big sign in front of the building. It said PEACEFUL MOUNTAIN NURSING HOME.

"This is where your mother is, Travis."

"How do you know?" Travis couldn't move. He was stalling for time. There was no way he could make himself go in there.

Clarence got out of the truck. "I had Ralphene check around for me. She learns a lot from people who come into the diner."

This was all happening too fast. Travis couldn't get his thoughts together. He was torn between wanting to see Mom and being terrified of what he would find. He got out and leaned on the hood of the truck. "Wait. I can't go in there."

Clarence came around the truck and put his hand on Travis's shoulder. "Let's just see where she is. You don't have to talk with her if you don't want to. But you've been worried about her, right?"

"Yeah, sure, I've been worried." The words caught in his throat.

"Well, things are rarely as bad as what you conjure up in your head. You'll feel better when you see her. If you want to, you can go up to her, say hi, maybe tell her about the festival. She'd like to hear about that, don't you think? She loves music, right?"

He droned on in a low voice, all the time gently but firmly steering Travis toward the nursing home entrance with that hand on his shoulder. Before Travis knew what was happening, they had set off whatever automatically opens the door, and Clarence pushed him across a small lobby to the front desk.

The receptionist was filing her fingernails. She looked up. "May I help you?"

"No," Travis said, turning away, but Clarence's grip held him there.

"We've come to see Geneva Tacey," Clarence said.

"Most of our residents are in the sunroom now. It's the second door on the left."

"Thank you." Clarence aimed him down the hall. Travis was numb, so he let himself be steered to the door of the sunroom. Clarence had both hands on his shoulders now. They paused at the entrance to the room, then Clarence nudged him inside.

Travis's senses came back to him one at a time. The first thing was the smell—a combination of disinfectant, the faint scent of urine, and food cooking somewhere nearby. His stomach lurched with that. Then the blurry shapes around the room became people—old people, mostly women, all in wheelchairs. Then sound—a nagging buzz coming from a TV with no picture. Some of the people were staring at the snowy screen, and some were sleeping, slumped in their wheelchairs, held from falling out by wide cloth bands around their waists that fastened them to the backs of their chairs.

A woman in a pink uniform with a nurse's aide name tag came over to them. "Are you looking for someone?"

Travis shook his head, but Clarence said, "Geneva Tacey."

The aide looked blank for a second. "Oh, you mean Jennifer Tacey. Well, isn't this nice. I don't think Jennifer has had a visitor since she came here."

"It's 'Geneva,'" Travis said. "Her name is Geneva." What kind of a place didn't bother to keep the patients' names straight?

166

"And you are—what? Relatives?" She seemed annoyed that he had corrected her.

"This is *Geneva's* son, Travis," Clarence said, with an edge to his voice that showed he didn't think much of this place, either.

Travis kept his eyes on the floor. He was terrified that he'd look up and discover that his mother had turned into one of these creepy old people. The aide led them over to the far corner of the room. She started talking in a high sing-songy voice, the kind you'd use with a baby. "Look what a nice surprise we have for you, Jennif . . . Geneva. It's your son Travis and his grandpa. Can you say hello? Hel-lo? Can you try that, Geneva? Say hel-lo?" She turned to them. "We're not sure if she understands anything. You can talk to her, but don't expect a response." She turned and left them with Mom.

This was worse than anything that Travis's imagination could have dreamed up. Clarence was crazy to bring him here. "Let's go. You said I could leave if I wanted to."

"Just look at your mother, Travis."

"I can't."

The hand was on his shoulder again. "Yes, you can." To keep Clarence from making a scene, Travis gathered his courage and raised his eyes. It was his mother this time, not the puffy, bald lady from the hospital. Mom's face was back to normal size and her chestnut-colored hair had grown in a little, making a wavy halo around her head. Her right hand and arm were curled up much worse than they had been in the hospital, though, and her eyes didn't seem normal, ei-ther. They were dull and not really looking at anything. But she was definitely Mom, and that gave Travis a little jolt of hope.

He cleared his throat. "Mom? It's Travis. And this is my friend Clarence."

She didn't show any signs of having heard him, or even sensing that somebody was talking to her. He looked to Clarence for support. "She doesn't know me."

"Now don't jump to conclusions," Clarence said. "Let's bring a couple of those folding chairs over here and sit for a spell. They probably have her on some pills that make her sleepy. We need to give her some time to wake up."

Travis helped with the chairs, but he didn't believe that Mom was going to wake up, no matter how long they stayed here.

Clarence put the chairs right in front of Mom and motioned for Travis to sit down. Then Clarence took Mom's good left hand and patted it. "Geneva?" he said in a loud voice. "Geneva, your son Travis is here."

Mom scowled and pulled her hand away.

Travis started to get up. He couldn't take this.

"Tell her about the festival," Clarence said, grabbing his arm, pulling him down into the chair again. "Even if it doesn't seem like she's listening, give it a try."

Travis took a deep breath and started in. "I'm helping out with a music festival, Mom. Clarence works on it too. This guy named Scott McKissack runs it."

She kept staring at something beyond him, as if she could see right through his head. "Scott makes guitars." When he mentioned the word *guitar* she blinked.

"Did you see that?" Travis asked.

"I sure did. Keep talking."

He leaned in closer. "Mom, do you remember when you used to play the guitar? When we used to sing together?"

There was no reaction this time. Travis had a sudden pang about 3-G's guitar. If only Mom could hold that guitar in her hands again, would that help bring her back? Would strumming her fingers across the strings make some connection in her memory? But there was no hope for that. The guitar was broken and lost, just like Mom. Still, he could try to reach her without the guitar.

"Remember my favorite song? It's the first one you taught me. 'The fox slipped out on a frosty night,'" he sang softly. "'Hoped for the moon to show some light.' Remember, Mom? You know the words. You made some of them up yourself."

Still nothing. He looked at Clarence, who made a circling motion with his hand, urging him to keep going.

"'He'd run and run with all his might before he'd get to town-o, town-o . . .'"

Mom started to nod her head in time to the music. When he sang the third *town-o*, Mom's eyes suddenly came to life and locked on his. He was so startled, he stopped singing and missed a few beats. The next time he got to the *town-o* part, he wasn't alone. Mom was trying to sing with him. She sort of hummed at first, her mouth working for a few bars before any real sound came out, and when it did, it sounded thin and husky. First, she was singing, "ah-oh," then "ahn-oh," but by the last couple of verses, it sounded like "town-o." She wasn't exactly on the right notes and it was far from the rich voice she used to have, but every time Travis got to the repeating words at the end of a verse, Mom joined in.

And even though she could smile with only one side of her face, she looked more beautiful to Travis than he had ever seen her before.

CHAPTER 16

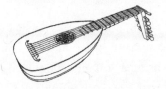

Travis only got to stay with his mother for about half an hour because the aide said she was getting too tired. When they got up to leave, Mom grabbed his hand, but he didn't pry her fingers loose the way he had in the hospital. This time he squeezed her hand, hugged her, told her he loved her and that he'd come back soon. He knew she understood because he could see tears in the corners of her eyes.

When they got in the truck, Travis could hardly contain himself. "Did you see that, Clarence—how she tried to sing? That aide was dead wrong about Mom not responding. We have to get her out of there. They're not doing anything for her. I bet she sits there staring into space when nobody's around."

"You're probably right about that, but getting her moved somewhere else might not be easy. I think your father has to be the one to request it. And even then, it might not be possible. There's a lot of red tape."

"But Dad isn't even visiting her, Clarence. He's given up. Can we keep going to see her? You think Scott would mind?"

Clarence fumbled for his keys, finally dumping the contents of his pocket onto the seat before he found them. "Not as long as we keep getting things ready for the festival. I'm sure we can handle both. Buddy can pick up more of the work, too."

Things were racing through Travis's head. All of a sudden Mom was a real person again, and he could help her get better. "I want to bring a guitar next time we go to the nursing home. I bet she'd really perk up with that, don't you think?"

"Yep, I think she might. I know you did her a lot of good today." Clarence backed slowly out of the parking space, then took off down the road. He kept his eyes straight ahead, but he was smiling. "You can practice tonight, too, because you're going to stay at my house until we get your home situation straightened out. No more camping out in the woods, hear?"

The thought of sleeping indoors in a real bed appealed to Travis. "Okay, thanks." They rode along in silence for a few miles. Travis couldn't figure out why Clarence was being nice to him, especially since Travis had told him off last night. But Scott had said that Clarence took in strays—even human ones. Maybe that's how Clarence thought of him—a stray who needed a place to stay. Probably wasn't too far from the truth. "I guess I've been kind of a jerk. I'm sorry about that."

"You've had a lot on your mind," Clarence said. "Too much for a kid to handle by himself."

When they got back to the workshop, Travis told Scott about his mother's reaction to his singing. "That's good, Travis. I play in nursing homes sometimes. Music helps people come

172

out of their shells. You and Clarence should try to visit your mother for a little while every day."

"But I'll still do my job," Travis said. "I finished the cows. What do you want me to do next?"

Scott took a piece of paper off his desk. "Here's a list of phone numbers for the schools I'm working with on the Adirondack Jam project. Call all of the contact people and remind them that we have a rehearsal tomorrow at Groveland Central. Give them the names of the kids from their school and tell them I've arranged for a bus to pick them up sometime between two thirty and three and drop them at their homes after the rehearsal. Can you handle that?"

"Sure." Travis took the list and found the phone buried under some papers on Scott's cluttered desk. How could that man organize so many projects in the middle of this mess?

Travis wrote himself a note so he'd remember what to say, but when he made the first call, and the woman's voice on the other end answered, "Arden Middle School," he got scared. Could she tell that he was a fourteen-year-old kid who should be in school himself? Then he came to his senses, asked for the guy on the list, and read him the message about the rehearsal and the bus.

Travis put a check next to the name of that school and phoned the other four.

"Okay, I'm done," he called, finally.

Clarence made a motion for him to be quiet and pointed over to Scott.

"That's all right," Scott said. "Travis, come here and see how this is done. I'm putting the rosette together." He was

173

holding a bunch of long, thin strips of wood that looked like uncooked spaghetti—the flat kind that Mom called linguini—only some were black and some were white. There was also a thicker coiled strip of blue plastic.

"These wood strips are called purfling," Scott said. "I'm alternating black and white rings on the outside of the circle, then a strip of abalone, then black, white, black again on the inside. I've made a round groove that's just wide enough for me to press all these glued strips into it."

Travis leaned in close to see better. "Is that curled-up strip the abalone?"

"No, that's a piece of Teflon. It's a placeholder. The glue doesn't stick to it, so when I pull it out, it leaves exactly the right-sized groove for the abalone."

"Is abalone that sparkly green stuff you have on the other guitar?"

The coil of Teflon suddenly twisted in Scott's hand, shifting the black-and-white strips out of order. Travis saw Scott's jaw clench, the way Dad's always did when he was ready to blow his top. Travis got out of Scott's way fast. "Did I mess him up by asking questions?" he whispered to Clarence.

"Don't worry about it. He invited you to watch him."

Travis observed from a distance as Scott patiently untwisted the strips, putting them back in order. The glue made them stick to his fingers. Then, when he started pressing them into the groove again, the Teflon sprang loose, making the purfling strips fan out across the top of the guitar. Clarence grabbed Travis's arm and headed for the door.

They sat in the rocking chairs on the front porch.

"Is he going to have to make a whole new top now?" Travis still felt guilty for distracting Scott with that question.

"No, he'll work it out. Anybody else would have been filling that room with cuss words, but Scott takes most things in his stride. He usually keeps to himself when he's doing rosettes. It's like wrestling with skinny snakes. Scott let me help build some parts of my guitar when he was making it, but he didn't want me even trying to do the rosette with these big, clumsy mitts of mine."

About fifteen minutes later, Scott came out. "I'm going to call it a day. Lock up for me when you head out, Clarence?"

"Will do."

Travis watched Scott walk over to his house. "Do you think he ruined the whole thing?"

"Probably not. Let's go see."

Travis was almost afraid to look, but when he did, he saw a perfect design of black-and-white rings with an empty groove waiting for the abalone.

"The man is good," Clarence said. "Gotta give him that."

After that, Clarence took Travis home with him. Well, at least when they drove past his house, Clarence pointed it out to him. "We're going to the Chicken Diner first," he said. "I always eat dinner there. I used to cook some when my wife was ailing, but now that she's gone, I sit back and let Ralphene wait on me."

When they went inside, Clarence headed for a table by the front window. "This is my regular spot."

Ralphene saw them and came over. "Hey, Travis Tacey. I see you're keeping better company than Verl Bickley now. I heard you were working on the festival."

Clarence tucked a paper napkin under his chin. "Travis is staying with me until after the festival, Ralphene. We'll take two specials." He looked at Travis. "Meat loaf okay with you?"

"Yeah, sure, but I don't have any money yet."

"Don't worry about it," Ralphene said. "Since Clarence is our next-door neighbor, we have a special deal going with him." She headed back for the kitchen.

"You eat here every single night?" Travis asked. "Don't you get tired of having the same thing all the time?"

Clarence leaned back and smiled. "Nope. It gives a nice rhythm to my life. Monday—country fried steak, Tuesday—meat loaf, Wednesday—chicken potpie, Thursday—spaghetti and meatballs, Friday—fish fry, Saturday—sirloin steak, and Sunday—pot roast. If I forget what day it is when I get home, I just burp and it all comes back to me." He laughed at his joke.

"Did you ever go to Carl's Diner over in Mansfield?" Travis asked to keep Clarence from coming up with more corny jokes.

"Yes, I've been there a couple of times. Mighty good food as I remember, but I don't get over that way very often."

"My dad used to work there. His meat loaf was their most popular dish."

Clarence raised his eyebrows. "Really. He must be a good cook. I'm surprised he hasn't been able to find another job."

"I don't think he's trying very hard," Travis said. He looked out the window to cut off the conversation about Dad. He shouldn't have brought him up in the first place.

"Anybody else at home?" Clarence asked. "Brothers or sisters?"

"An older sister, a younger sister, and two younger brothers."

"So your sister takes care of the kids? She's out of school?"

Travis just nodded. He wasn't going to say any more. If he slipped and told Clarence that June was only sixteen, he'd be giving a hint to his own age, and that was the one secret he'd managed to keep.

Luckily, Ralphene interrupted the conversation. "Two specials. Watch out. They're hot." Ralphene set down their plates.

Travis could tell just by looking that this meat loaf wasn't as good as Dad's. He had a way of making it dark and crusty on the outside while the inside stayed soft and juicy. This meat looked soft all the way through with no crunchy edges. He took a bite. It was okay, but he missed the wild flavor of Dad's meat loaf.

"What's the verdict?" Clarence asked. "As good as your father's?"

"It's good," Travis said, without looking up.

"But your dad's is better."

Travis wasn't going to lie about it. "Yeah, Dad's is a little better."

Clarence tore a roll in half and sopped up his gravy with it. "Well, he must be some cook, if you can still give him a compliment after he kicked you out of the house."

"I'm just telling the truth. I can be mad at him and still like his meat loaf."

When they got back to the house, Clarence showed Travis where he'd be staying. "This room used to belong to my son, Jeff. You remind me of him when he was a kid."

"Does he live around here?"

"No, he's . . . well, we lost him in the war. That was a long time ago."

Travis wanted to say he was sorry and ask which war Clarence meant, but before he could say anything, the old man turned away. "There are some clean sheets you can put on the bed, and the blue towel in the bathroom is for you."

"Okay. Thanks."

Clarence stopped at the door and looked back. "I usually watch TV for a while after dinner, but if you want to practice the guitar, the screened porch out back of the kitchen is a nice place to do it."

After he left, Travis looked around the room. There were half a dozen sports trophies on the shelves—mostly baseball—and a framed family picture. It was Clarence when he was a young guy, with a pretty woman and one kid—a boy. It seemed weird to think of Clarence having a family. And sad that they were both gone.

Travis took the guitar out of the case. He strummed a couple of chords. Even though it was bigger, the sound wasn't anywhere near as loud or as good as 3-G's guitar. He still couldn't believe he had been stupid enough to let it get stolen. But there was no sense in dwelling on that now. He was going to practice a song to sing to Mom, and this guitar would be fine.

When Travis walked through the kitchen to get to the porch, Clarence had *Jeopardy!* blasting in the living room. The house was high up with no trees in the sloping backyard, so Travis could see the mountain ridges that followed one another off into the distance—each one fainter than the last, like echoes. He watched as the sun dropped behind a massive bank of purple clouds, turning their top edges first pink, then orange. Clarence was right, this was a nice place to play the guitar.

Travis sat and strummed through the chords of "Flow Gently Sweet Afton," one of Mom's favorite songs. Then he started breaking the chords into finger-picking patterns. He did the easier ones first, repeating them until it felt easy. Then he did the complicated pattern slowly so he could make every note ring. He did it over and over, gradually building up speed.

"Now you're getting the hang of it." Clarence was in the doorway. "I think we can turn you into a pretty decent player if you stick around long enough. Which reminds me, your folks don't know where you are, do they?"

"I told you. Dad doesn't care."

"Well, what about your sister? She must be worried about you."

"My sister wanted me out of there, too. She said Dad is worse when I'm around." Travis put the guitar back in the case. If Clarence was going to bug him about his family, he might as well go back to his room.

Clarence kept at him. "People say things when they're mad or confused. That doesn't mean they don't care about you. I'd feel better if you gave your family a call to let them know you're okay. I wrote down my address and telephone number so you can tell them how to contact you."

"I called my sister last week. Then Dad grabbed the phone and yelled at me."

Clarence set the phone on the end table next to Travis's chair. "If your father does that again, give me the phone and I'll calm him down. Tell your sister about the nursing home. She probably doesn't even know where your mother is."

That made sense. Travis knew he should let June know about Mom. "Okay, I'll call." Travis dialed his home number. When Clarence started to leave the room, Travis panicked. "No, wait. Stay in case Dad is there."

"I'll give you some privacy. If you need me, I'll be in the next room."

Travis held his breath, hoping Dad wasn't home. Each ring made him jump.

"Hello?" It was June. He could breathe again.

"Hi, June."

"Travis? I've been so worried about you."

"I'm fine."

"Mrs. Bland wondered where you were. She parked the school bus out front and marched right up to the door last week. I told her you went to live with relatives out of state so she's left us alone. School's out soon anyway. But where have you been staying? Are you all alone?"

"No, I'm helping with a music festival. A guy named

Scott McKissack builds guitars and his friend, an old guy named Clarence Alcorn, is letting me stay at his house."

"You haven't told them anything about the family, have you? If these guys find out about Mom and Dad, they could report us."

"Clarence knows that Dad kicked me out and that Mom is in a nursing home. He won't report us. And the best thing is that he found Mom for me. I saw her today. She's in the Peaceful Mountain Nursing Home."

He heard June take in a sharp breath, then Earleen's voice whining in the background. It made him homesick. "You saw Mom? How could you stand it? Dad told us that she's . . . well, he said she's a vegetable now. I can't bear to think about her."

Travis felt a flash of anger. "That's not true, June. They have her on some medicine that makes her sleepy. But when I tried singing to her, she sang along a little. We can help her, June. Clarence and I are going to see her every day from now on. You all need to go visit her, too."

"That's not going to happen, Travis. Dad told me Mom wouldn't ever get any better than she was in the hospital. I don't want to see her like that again. And the little kids were scared of her. There's no way we're going to that nursing home. Dad won't even talk about her anymore, so that's the end of it."

They were writing Mom off without even seeing her. Travis had to knock some sense into their heads. "Haven't you been listening, June? She's still Mom. Don't go by what Dad says. He hasn't seen her since they sent her to the nursing home."

Earleen was crying in the background now. "Wait a minute, Earleen," June said. "Look, Travis, I'm doing the best I can here, but my hands are full. I don't have time to be worrying about Mom."

She was going to hang up and leave him to handle everything. It wasn't fair. They all needed to be involved. "No. Wait! Where is Dad? Is he home?"

"Yes. He's outside, working on the car. It barely runs anymore."

"Let me talk to him."

"Oh, Travis, I don't think—"

"Just quit whining and go get him."

June sighed. "All right, but he's been more like himself lately, so try not to rile him up. He got a part-time job, working at a hot dog stand."

"So he deserves a medal for slinging hot dogs?" June must have missed that comment. Travis heard the whack of the screen door, then June calling Dad. His throat closed up. What was he thinking, asking to talk to Dad? He'd gotten mad and made a stupid decision. The door slammed again and he heard footsteps coming toward the phone. Travis almost hung up, then heard a gruff, "Yeah? Who's this?" and he got steamed all over again.

He took a deep breath. "It's Travis, Dad. Listen to me before you start yelling."

"What do you want? You in some kind of trouble?"

Travis saw Clarence appear in the doorway, waiting, in case he was needed. "I went to visit Mom in the nursing home."

"Oh, yeah? Well, then you know what shape she's in. She might as well be dead."

"That's not true! She's getting better. She sang with me today." There was silence at the other end of the line. "She's lonely, Dad. You gotta go see her and take June and the kids. She needs to have visitors. Clarence and I are going back every day from now on."

"Who in Sam Hill is Clarence?"

"He's a guy who's helping me. I'm doing fine." When Travis said that, he realized Dad hadn't bothered to ask him how he was doing.

"Oh, yeah? Helping you, huh? We'll see about that. Put him on."

Travis held out the phone to Clarence. "He wants to talk with you."

He couldn't hear what Dad was saying to Clarence, but whatever it was, he was yelling. Clarence could hardly get a word in edgewise. "Mr. Tacey, let me explain . . . Travis is fine, he . . . no, if you'd calm down . . . No, I did not kidnap your son! You threw him out." Clarence was red in the face and yelling. "You go right ahead and call the police. . . . No, I'm not the one who's in hot water here." Dad must have gone ballistic at that point because Clarence didn't get to say anything for at least a full minute. Then Clarence drew himself up tall. "Listen, you dang fool, you're talking to a retired state trooper. . . . Yes, that's what I said, and I think my friends over at headquarters would be real interested in a father who threw his son out of the house with no place to live." Clarence hung up on Dad.

"Wow, I never guessed that you were a retired trooper." Travis wondered if that made Clarence a danger? Would he be obligated to turn Travis in to Social Services?

Clarence shrugged one shoulder, looking sheepish. "Well, I never was a state trooper, but I didn't think your father would be scared off by a retired bait shop owner."

Travis grinned and breathed a sigh of relief.

CHAPTER 17

S cott was already at work, carving away at the neck of the guitar, by the time they arrived with the breakfast sandwiches the next morning. He looked up. "I'm glad you guys are here early. There's a lot to do today. I'll need both of you to help me with the Adirondack Jam rehearsal at three thirty."

"You must have stayed up all night," Clarence said. "I told you I'd rough out the shape of that neck on the belt sander to save you some time."

"I got too far behind yesterday," Scott said. "So I came back after dinner and worked till about three, then went back and slept until seven. A couple cups of coffee got me going again this morning."

Travis moved in close to see how Scott was carving the guitar neck. He had clamped a long, narrow block of wood in a vise and held a knife with handles at each end. As he pulled the knife down the length of the neck, paper-thin curls of wood peeled off and dropped to the floor.

"What kind of wood is that?" Travis asked.

"Mahogany," Scott said. "I have to take just a little wood at a time with this draw knife and make sure the two sides stay even with each other. When it gets closer to the right shape, I'll switch to a scraper. It's slow work, but carving the neck is one of my favorite steps in guitar building."

Travis's fingers itched to pull that draw knife across the wood, but Scott didn't offer. He must have read Travis's mind, though. "Someday when we have more time, I'll let you try your hand at this." He put down the knife. "Right now, we have to get ready for the Adirondack Jam rehearsal. Your biggest job will be helping to get everybody in tune. We taught all the kids how to tune their instruments, but some of them have a tin ear so they can't tell when they're off. The second biggest problem is broken strings. You know how to replace a string on a guitar?"

"No, Mom always did it."

"Okay, Clarence can give you a crash course on that. Now, about the tuning—you know the names of the guitar strings, right?"

Travis knew the names of chords, but not the individual strings. "I tune by matching each string to the one above it by fretting at the fifth fret—except the second to last one is the fourth fret."

"Okay," Scott said. "If you can do that, you must have a good ear. Besides, I could tell that from the harmony you were singing the other day." He rummaged around on the worktable and pulled out a small black device with a window on the top and a big clip on the back. "You can't tune by ear in a noisy room, so Clarence will show you how to use this electronic tuner. When we get to the rehearsal, you, Clarence, and Buddy will help the kids who can't tune up. Travis, don't mess with the mandolins, fiddles, or banjos. Don't replace strings on them, either. Your job is the guitars."

"Okay," Clarence said. "Let's work on replacing strings first." He walked to the back of the room and pulled a guitar off the shelf, making space for it on a worktable. "This one is strung with nylon. The strings, starting from the lowest, are E, A, D, G, B, E." He plucked the strings as he named them, except for the broken D. Clarence pulled a couple of boxes off the shelf—one labeled STEEL STRINGS, and the other NYLON. "So for this one, you look through the nylon strings for a package that says D."

Travis watched intently as Clarence removed the old string, then threaded the new one through the bridge. He pulled it up through the hole in the tuner, then turned the knob until the string was taut. Then he twisted it tighter, constantly plucking the string as the note got higher and higher. "When it sounds about right to me, I check it with the electronic tuner." He clipped the tuner to the headstock, then flipped the switch so the window lit up. "Watch the needle now."

Travis leaned in to see. "It says D, so it's tuned, right?"

"Nope, that needle's got to be dead center on the scale." He tightened it a little more, continuously plucking the string until the needle hit the middle of the dial. "There you go."

He moved so Travis could be directly in front of the guitar. "A new string will stretch and go out of tune at first, so

187

I like to help that stretch along." He hooked his finger under the string and gave it a few gentle tugs. When he plucked the string, the tuner registered C sharp. "You're a half step flat now, so tune it up again. Then repeat the same thing, stretching and tuning until the needle says right on target."

After that, Travis spent the rest of the morning tuning and changing strings. This was the first time he felt he was really earning his pay. The cow painting and taking flyers around had seemed like busywork, but now he had his hands on the guitars and he loved every minute of it.

Buddy came in around one o'clock with lunch for everybody. Then it was time to pack up and head for the rehearsal.

This was the first time Travis had walked into a school since dropping out. Even though it was barely a week ago, Travis felt as if he were entering alien territory. Mr. Elkins, the music teacher, met them at the front office and took them to what used to be the band room. "The kids from our school left their instruments in here this morning so I could check them over. We have a few broken strings and the mandolin is totally out of tune. I left that for you guys. Figured I'd mess it up."

"I'll fix that," Buddy said.

Scott introduced Travis as his assistant, then set him to work on the guitars. He was working close enough to Scott to hear the conversation between him and Mr. Elkins.

"We sure appreciate what you do here, Scott," the teacher said. "I can't do anything but chorus work in the school now that the music budget is slashed. You don't know how much it means to these kids to have instruments they can learn to play and actually take home."

Scott was tightening the drumhead on a banjo, working his way around the top, snugging up each nut with a tiny wrench. "Oh, I know exactly what it means to these kids. If it hadn't been for my music teacher showing me how to play the guitar, I'd probably be in prison by now."

Mr. Elkins laughed. "Oh, come on. That's hard to picture."

When Scott looked up, he wasn't smiling. "I'm not kidding. I didn't have a thing in the world that meant anything to me. I'd gone from one foster home to another and was heading for no good. Music gave me one decent thing to care about."

Travis hadn't taken Scott for someone who'd had a tough life, but he understood the music part. Music had been the one thing that had kept him going when life at home got rough. Well, two things had kept him going—music and Mom. He felt bad that he and Clarence hadn't had time to visit her today. But he'd practice tonight so he'd be able to play even better tomorrow. He couldn't wait to see how she reacted to hearing the guitar.

When the buses arrived and students started coming into the room, Travis didn't have a moment to think about anything. The kids found their seats and Scott started the tune-up. He plucked a low E, and all of the guitar players tried to match it. Scott had told him in the car, "Wander around the room during the tune-up and if you hear somebody who's off-key, tune him up with the electronic tuner."

Travis heard a clunker right away. But it was a big kid, and he looked kind of tough. Still, Travis went up to him. "Want me to get that tuned for you?"

The kid handed him the guitar. "Yeah, sure. I can play pretty good, but I can't hear whether it's in tune or not."

"Me neither," Travis lied. "I use a cheater."

Even with all the noise in the room, Travis could easily see when the strings were tuned by watching the needle.

He found a few more kids with tin ears and tuned up their guitars. He looked across the room and saw Clarence tuning a fiddle. Then Clarence knocked off a few bars of "Soldiers Joy" like a pro. Was there any instrument that man couldn't play?

Finally everybody was ready and Scott picked up his own guitar. "Listen up, kids. We're going to do 'Turkey in the Straw.' Remember, everybody plays the chorus, then guitars take the first verse, mandolins the second, banjos the third, and Joe Butler solos the fourth verse on his fiddle. Now, do we have the guitar and mandolin soloists here?" Two kids raised their hands. The one with the guitar looked to be about Travis's age.

When the band started playing, Travis was blown away. The kids seemed to range from about seventh or eighth grade up through high school seniors, both boys and girls. And he could tell that some of them were struggling to keep up, while others were practically pros. But the main thing was that all together, they sounded great, and he could see from the expressions on their faces that they were proud to be in the band. It made him wish he could be a part of it.

✦ ✦ ✦

Travis practiced hard that night, putting the new picking pattern into the chords of "Flow Gently Sweet Afton." He worked some of the tricky parts over and over until it started sounding really good. He even tried a verse of "Turkey in the Straw," adding his own embellishments.

Clarence called out to the porch from the living room, "If you stay up any later practicing, you won't be able to get up in the morning." What he didn't know was that Travis was so excited about seeing Mom again, he wouldn't be able to sleep anyway.

The next morning, Scott had Travis cleaning up the workshop, in case people from the festival came over to see where he made the guitars. Travis had started out with enthusiasm, but it didn't take long to realize that the cleaning project was hopeless. "There's so much stuff," he said. "All I can do is make piles of things on the tables and workbenches."

Scott barely glanced up. "That's good enough. I don't really want things put in places where I can't find them. This looks like a mess, but I know where everything is. Small piles look neater than big heaps, so do the best you can. Everything will slide back into its normal mess by next week, anyway."

Travis's mouth fell open and his arms raised in a gesture of helplessness.

Clarence caught the sign language and got up. "I need the boy to help me pick out some more activities for the little kids. We'll probably grab some lunch while we're out. Want us to bring something back?"

191

Scott shook his head without speaking, so Clarence steered Travis toward the door. Scott was cutting tiny letters spelling "McKissack" out of abalone. He had already chiseled the spaces where they would fit into the headstock. It was fine, delicate work, and Travis could see that Scott's hand was perfectly steady. He wondered how much practice it would take to get that good.

"We go through this every year," Clarence said when they were out of earshot. "He keeps putting off working on the prize guitar, then stays up every night for a week to get it finished."

"Seems like all Scott does is the guitar stuff," Travis said. "Does he have a family around here?"

"Nah. He was a foster kid from the time he was a baby. Then he got married right out of high school. But things didn't work out and they got a divorce. The wife moved somewhere out of state."

Travis waited for Clarence to say more, but that was the end of it—just enough facts to answer the question. Maybe he wasn't a gossip after all.

They had rounded the first curve when Travis remembered something. "Wait, Clarence, can we go back? I want to have the guitar with me in case we have a chance to go see Mom."

Clarence pointed behind his seat with his thumb. "I'm way ahead of you. I put it in first thing this morning. We can't stay long, but even twenty minutes will do her some good."

They drove to the next town and Clarence stopped at a general store. They found a ring-toss set and two six-packs of bubble-blowing liquid along with some fancy blowers. Then Clarence led Travis to the back of the store where jeans were stacked in cubicles lined up across the wall.

"See if you can find your size here. Then pick up a couple of those T-shirts from the sale table."

The last thing Travis was thinking about was clothes. He turned away from the shelf. "I already have jeans and a couple of shirts. Why do I need more? Especially two shirts."

Clarence steered him over to the jeans again. "I don't want to hurt your feelings, but those duds of yours are getting a little gamy. At least now you'll have a spare set to wear while your others are in the wash. And the shirts are two for the price of one so you're only cheating yourself if you only get one."

"But I still don't have any money."

"So when's your birthday?"

"Not until December."

"Close enough." Clarence pulled two shirts from the sale table and poked them at Travis's chest. "Happy Birthday."

"I'm not wearing pink and purple."

"Then you pick. Find your size and meet me at the cash register so I can pay for them." Clarence headed for the front of the store, then turned. "Pick out a pair of sneakers for yourself, too. You can't be around all those power tools with your toes hanging out."

When Travis got to the cash register, Clarence had socks

and underwear for him, too. Travis thanked Clarence for the clothes, but he planned to pay him back when he got some money. After Clarence bought the clothes, Travis went to the dressing room to put on the jeans and one of the new shirts so he'd look good when he saw his mother.

On the drive to the nursing home, the fingers of Travis's right hand nervously scratched the guitar-picking pattern on the leg of his stiff jeans. This was the first new pair he'd ever worn. Mom had always bought their clothes from garage sales and the church rummage sale. Travis was embarrassed to ask Clarence if even the old soft jeans started out this way, but since he had run his hand over a number of pairs in the stacks, and found them all to be the same, he figured these would eventually become limp and comfortable.

Clarence glanced over at him. "Still practicing, huh? I heard you last night doing 'Flow Gently Sweet Afton.' Sounded pretty good. That's one of my favorite songs."

"Mom's, too," Travis said. "And it's slower than the fox song, so maybe she can get all the words." He stopped practicing long enough to rub his neck where the tag sewn into the back of the shirt itched. He had never owned any clothes that still had tags in them. He had always longed for new clothes instead of secondhand, but who knew they would have annoying things like scratchy little neck tags?

"Now don't be expecting miracles when you play for your mother," Clarence said.

"I'm not, but each time we come, she'll get a little better. Besides, she's going to flip out when she sees the guitar."

Travis had his hand on the door handle long before Clarence seesawed his way to a stop in a parking space. "See you in there, Clarence!" he called as he jumped out of the truck. He reached behind the seat, slipping into slow motion as he carefully maneuvered the guitar around the seat back, then between the truck and the car that Clarence had parked too close to. Travis ran for the front door, not stopping at the reception desk but heading right for the sunroom. Sure enough, he spotted his mother in the same back corner where she had been a couple of days ago.

He rushed across the room, his heart pounding. Would she actually sing this time? "Hey, Mom," Travis said when he got close to her. "Look what I brought today."

Remembering that he needed to be sitting, Travis grabbed a folding chair with his one free hand and set it up in front of his mother. "I've been practicing. I have a surprise for you. Wait till you hear."

Travis saw Clarence coming in the far end of the room, so he went over and grabbed a chair for him, too. Then he put the guitar strap over his head and adjusted it on his shoulder. "You're gonna love this one, Mom." Travis strummed the opening chords, then broke into fingerpicking. He was a little nervous at first, so he made a couple of mistakes, but then he got into the rhythm of it. He still had to watch his fingers, but he glanced up to see Mom's reaction. She was leaning way over to the right in her wheelchair, her head almost resting on her shoulder. Her eyes were open, though, so she was awake and listening.

Travis sped up a little. He had been playing slowly to get every note right, but maybe Mom would be more impressed if he tried to make his fingers fly over the strings, the way Clarence could do it. Travis could feel his tongue running back and forth across his upper lip with the effort of concentration. He couldn't even play this pattern slowly a few days ago. Surely Mom would understand what an accomplishment this was, her being a guitar player and all.

He finished with a flourish. "Want to sing it with me this time, Mom?"

He felt Clarence's hand on his shoulder. "Talk to her a little bit, Travis. Give her some time to wake up before you play again."

Travis looked at his mother. She was still leaning over in the same position, and when he looked at her eyes, he realized they were totally unfocused. What had they done to her? "Mom! Can you even hear me?" He handed off the guitar to Clarence and grabbed Mom's good hand, which caused her to slip even more to the side. She still showed no signs of recognition, or even knowing that anybody else was in the room.

"C'mon, Mom. You gotta wake up." Travis got behind his mother's wheelchair, grasped her shoulders, and tried to pull her to an erect sitting position, but her feet dropped off the footrest. She slid down, ripping open the Velcro fastener on the cloth band that was supposed to hold her in the chair. Travis lost his grip on her and Clarence tried to put down the guitar and catch her from the front, but he was too late to keep her from landing on the floor in a heap.

"What's going on here?" A woman in a pink uniform—a

different aide from the one they had seen before—was coming toward them. "What are you doing to Jennifer? How did you get in here?" She turned and shouted toward the door. "Jim! I need help in the sunroom!"

A big guy in a white uniform was there in seconds. He picked Mom up and set her down in the chair, her head flopping around like a rag doll's. Her robe had pulled open, showing her nightie underneath. Travis knew that his mother would be mortified to be exposed like that. He tried to pull her robe closed, but Jim pushed his hand aside, and slapped the cloth band around her. He pulled it so tight, Travis worried that she wouldn't be able to breathe.

"Stop treating my mother like that!" Travis yelled, grabbing Jim's arm. "Why do you have her so doped up? She's practically unconscious."

"Calm down, kid," Jim said. "Your mother doesn't sense what's going on."

Travis was furious. "Well, I can see what's going on. Where's her doctor? I want to talk to him."

"Lots of luck with that," Jim said. "He barely gets in here once a month to sign prescriptions."

"What's the doctor's name?" Clarence asked. "We'll look him up, ask if he can cut down on her medications."

"You'll be wasting your time," Jim said. "Jennifer has been pretty agitated for the last couple of days so they had to increase her meds to keep her calm."

That did it. Travis couldn't stand any more. "Her name is Geneva!" he yelled. "Can't anybody here get that through their stupid heads?" Travis wanted to lunge at Jim and push him to the floor, but he stopped himself just short of that, only bumping both fists into Jim's massive chest. This was Dad's temper in him, and he fought against it. No way he wanted to be anything like his father.

Though Travis had little more effect than a mouse attacking an elephant, he had done enough to make Jim mad. The aide grabbed the back of Travis's shirt. "Okay, buddy, you just got yourself thrown out of here." He propelled Travis across the room, through the lobby, and dumped him outside the front entrance. "And don't be showing your face around here again because I'm going to write up this incident and it will be on your mother's record."

Shortly after Jim disappeared inside, Clarence came through the door and helped Travis to his feet. "No matter how mad you are," he said, brushing some leaves off the back of Travis's new shirt, "it's usually better to keep your mouth shut. But you probably knew that, right?"

CHAPTER 18

When they got back into the truck, Travis felt so awful, he couldn't concentrate on anything but his own stupidity. How could he help his mother now if he couldn't even get in to see her? What he had done would be on Mom's medical record. Would that keep Dad and June from visiting her, if by some miracle Dad decided to come here? Travis needed somebody to help him get through to these people. Clarence wasn't the one to do it because he hadn't been any help in the nursing home just now. He was a nice guy, but in their eyes, he was just an old man with no power.

"There must be somebody who can help Mom," Travis said. "If only there was another doctor." He wasn't really talking to Clarence, but he got an answer he didn't expect.

"Well, sure, there's Doc Weston," Clarence said. "He's a friend of mine. I'm pretty sure he'd have some ideas about what to do. I'll give him a call when we get back to the work-shop, see if he can meet us tonight for dinner."

"You know a doctor? Why didn't you tell me that before?"

"Didn't cross my mind until you said that. I think of Doc more as a friend. I forget he's a doctor."

"But how come you're friends with a doctor anyway?" Travis asked, thinking that doctors were so important, they probably didn't need friends—especially ordinary guys like Clarence.

"That's the good thing about fishing," Clarence said. "You get to know all kinds of people—rich, poor, some real educated like Doc, and some who can barely read. I've learned from almost all of them. Doc and I have been friends since before he went off to medical school."

That was the good thing about Clarence, Travis thought. He was genuinely interested in everybody. Some bait shop guys probably sold their fishing stuff and didn't care who bought it, but Travis could picture Clarence getting into a conversation with every customer who came into the place.

That night at the diner, they sat at their usual table. "We should go ahead and order," Clarence said. "Doc will get here when he can." The two of them ate their chicken potpies in silence, both lost in their own thoughts as they chewed. Travis couldn't decide whether to get excited about Clarence's doctor friend or not. Doc Weston could be the answer to Mom's problems or he could turn out to be a dud. Travis didn't want to plunge into the depths of disappointment again, so he wrapped himself with a cloak of skepticism, just to be safe.

Clarence was chasing his last piece of crust around the plate with his fork when he looked up and called out to a man who had come in the door, "Hey, Doc, we're over here."

"Good to see you, Clarence," Doc said. "The fish don't bite near so well since I can't get those fat night crawlers of yours."

"Travis, this is my friend, Doc Weston. He's the best doctor around—even makes house calls to the patients who can't get to his office. Nobody does that anymore."

Travis had been expecting to see a geezer, somebody Clarence's age. But instead, Doc looked younger than Scott. He wore jeans and a threadbare plaid flannel shirt that could have been older than Clarence. If Travis hadn't known he was a doctor, he couldn't have guessed it from his looks. So far, that was a plus in Travis's eyes.

Doc Weston grabbed a chair from another table, turned it around backward, and straddled it. "Clarence is used to telling fish stories. He exaggerates." The two men talked for a couple of minutes about fishing and where the crappies were biting this time of year. Travis didn't like fish to begin with, but he'd have to be minutes away from starving to death before he'd eat something called a crappie.

Doc finally turned to Travis. "So Clarence told me a little bit about your mother, but can you fill me in on the details? When was her accident?"

Okay, Travis was going to give this guy the benefit of the doubt. He thought back, counting the weeks at home since the accident, then the days on the road since he ran away. He was surprised to find he had only been on his own for six days. It felt more like a month. "I think Mom's accident was about five weeks ago. She went into a skid and rolled over in her truck. Her head smashed through the side window. They said it was a good thing she had her seat belt on or she probably would have been thrown out of the truck and killed."

Doc nodded. "I wish more of my patients would wear seat belts. It's the only thing a person can do that will pretty much guarantee that they'll live longer. So did you see your mother in the hospital? Did she know you?" Doc had a quiet way about him and was listening intently to every word. Travis allowed himself to feel a little hopeful.

"When we visited her in the hospital, she couldn't talk right," Travis said. "I'm pretty sure she still knew us, though. Her hair was all shaved off, and she had lots of stitches in her scalp. She was wide awake. Now she's in a real dump where they have her so doped up, she's practically unconscious— Peaceful Mountain Nursing Home."

"Peaceful Mountain is a chronic-care facility for people who aren't expected to improve," Doc said, "so the staff isn't trained to handle somebody who needs rehabilitation. It was the wrong placement for your mother. She probably fell through the cracks. It does happen, especially if the patient doesn't have an advocate."

"What's an advocate?" Clarence asked.

Travis had almost forgotten Clarence was there but was

glad for the question because he was embarrassed to ask what an advocate was.

"It's someone to watch out for them," Doc said. "Maybe a spouse, a social worker, or the patient's doctor. Do you have a family doctor, Travis?"

"No. We went to a clinic for shots and stuff. And I saw a doctor in the hospital once when I broke my arm, but no, not a regular doctor."

Doc had been taking some notes on a little pad. "So your mother hasn't had any physical, occupational, or speech therapy, as far as you know?"

"I don't know what she had at the hospital," Travis said. "But I don't think she's had anything at Peaceful Mountain. They don't care about her. They can't even get her name right!"

"Well, you care about your mother," Doc said, "and you're trying to get help for her, so that's good. If you give me a little more information, I'll see what I can find out." He slid the pen and pad across the table to Travis. "Write down your mother's name, your father's name, and a number where I can reach him."

Travis tried to stall. The more people who knew about Dad and the home situation, the bigger chance the family would get split up. "Dad won't even visit her," Travis said. "If you need him to approve anything, he'll tell you to go jump in a lake."

Doc smiled. "It won't be the first time somebody told me to do that."

Travis took the pen. In spite of his worries, he'd have to

trust Doc to get help for Mom. He took a deep breath and wrote down the information. He was still afraid to hope something good could come of this. "My mother is never going to get back to normal, is she?"

"I don't know," Doc said. "I can't even make an educated guess until I see her and read through her records. But five weeks isn't long for recovery from a head injury. Almost anything is possible. I'll let you know what I find out."

Almost anything is possible. Travis grabbed those words and stored them in the back of his mind.

Things were so busy at the workshop, the time went by quickly the next day, and the morning after that. Travis was dying to go visit Mom, but Clarence said they should wait to hear what Doc had found out before they went back.

Scott had sprayed the contest guitar with some sort of varnish the day before, which had brought out all the beauty of the wood, but now he was going over it with sandpaper.

"Why are you doing that?" Travis asked. "It looked so beautiful. Won't sandpaper ruin it?"

Scott shook his head and kept sanding. "Nope. This takes out all the imperfections in the sealer spray. Later today I'll do the finish spray and tomorrow I'll be sanding that."

Travis couldn't imagine what imperfections Scott was talking about. The guitar sure looked perfect to him.

That afternoon, Doc showed up with news about Mom. "Okay, Travis, here's what's going on. I worked through some red tape so I can supervise your mother's care. After I cleared things with the doctor from the nursing home, I went and looked at her records and found that her meds were increased after your first visit."

Travis was stunned. "But why would they do that? She was much better that day. By the end of that visit, she was trying to sing with me."

"I know," Doc said. "Look, here's what I think happened. Your mother was excited about your visit and was trying to tell one of the staff about it, but she couldn't make herself understood because of the aphasia."

"What's that?" Clarence had moved in next to Travis to hear what Doc had to say. "Is that what keeps her from talking?"

"It's a result of the head injury," Doc said. "Her brain knows what she wants to say, but she can't get the words out. It's extremely frustrating, especially if the people around her don't have the time to figure out what she means. I think your mother got upset, and the aide took that as agitated behavior, so they upped the dose on her medication."

"They were punishing her?" Travis slammed his hand down on the workbench, raising a cloud of fine sawdust. "That's not fair! Mom can't help it if she can't talk!"

"I know it seems to you that they were punishing your mother, Travis. The problem is that the staff members at Peaceful Mountain are used to taking care of very old people who don't do much but sleep all day so when they get somebody like your mother, they don't know how to handle her. They see every outburst as a sign that a patient needs more sedation."

Travis's heart sank. "If she gets excited when I visit her, does that mean I should stay away?"

"No, just the opposite. I want you and Clarence to visit her and take your guitars to get her singing. I've cut out the medication that was making her unresponsive. She should be alert when you see her next."

"Well, that's great, but can't you just get her out of that place?" Travis asked. "You said she should be getting some kind of therapy." He knew he had to tell Doc the whole truth because he was feeling guilty about it. "Besides, I . . . um . . . kind of lost my temper last time I was there and the aide said he was going to write up a report to keep me from coming back."

"I talked to the people in charge," Doc said, "so you won't have any trouble getting in to visit. As a matter of fact, I've written an order that specifically states that you and Clarence are a part of your mother's therapy. Since music was so important in her life before, we may be able to use it to help bring her back. You knew that instinctively, Travis, so you were already on the right track."

It made Travis feel good that he had thought of using music to reach his mom. And he was grateful that she had a doctor on her side now. Maybe things would start looking up. Travis could hardly wait to get to the nursing home that afternoon. But they had errands to run first. Clarence had to go to the park where the festival would be held and make sure the electrician was setting up the new wiring for lights and the sound system on the outdoor stage. Travis got up on the stage and looked out over the huge sloping lawn where the audience would be sitting for the concert. He wondered what it would be like to play for so many people. But right now, there was only one person he wanted to play for.

After what seemed like hours, with Clarence checking every blasted electrical switch and outlet, he was finally ready to go, and they headed for Peaceful Mountain.

"Even though Doc has talked to the nursing home staff," Clarence said, "it probably wouldn't hurt to apologize to that aide you pushed."

That made Travis mad. "The guy had it coming to him. I didn't like the way he shoved Mom back into her chair." Travis watched for familiar landmarks to tell him they were getting close to Peaceful Mountain. So far, nothing but trees.

"Well," Clarence said, "maybe he didn't like the way you dropped your mother on the floor. Either way, I think you'd be smart to be extra polite. That's a good way to make sure your mom is treated well." Even though Travis was angry at the people at Peaceful Mountain, he knew Clarence was right.

"There it is!" Travis said, realizing that they had approached the nursing home from the opposite direction this time.

When they got inside, Travis gave his name to the receptionist instead of rushing through the lobby to the sunroom. She wasn't all that friendly. "Oh, it's you," she said.

Travis forced himself to smile at her. "Yes, ma'am. I hope you're having a real nice day."

He spotted Jim, the aide, down the hall, so he went to see him before going to the sunroom. "I'm sorry I lost my temper with you the other day, sir." Travis almost choked on the

207

word *sir*, but he smiled and held out his hand. He felt phony being nice to these people, but he had to do it for Mom.

Jim looked surprised, then took Travis's hand and shook it. "Okay. No problem, buddy."

When Travis turned, he saw Clarence grinning by the front entrance. The old man gave him a thumbs-up.

Travis took a deep breath, went into the sunroom, and found his mother. Doc had been right—she was more alert, and her eyes focused on him right away. "Hi, Mom," he said, giving her a hug, and he felt her hug him back with her good arm.

He set up the chairs for himself and Clarence. Then he pulled out his guitar. "Want to sing with me, Mom?"

She smiled and nodded enthusiastically, but still had no words. As he played and sang "Flow Gently Sweet Afton," she moved her head back and forth in time to the music and started humming the tune. When he finished, she slapped her good hand against her bad one to applaud. "May!" she said, pointing to the guitar. "P-p-may."

Travis was thrilled that Mom was trying to talk, but he didn't know what she wanted to say. He'd have to puzzle it out fast because he didn't want her getting upset.

She made a strumming motion with her left hand.

"Play? You want me to play something else?"

She nodded again. "May. May. Zing."

May. May. Zing. The words spiraled through Travis's brain, but he couldn't make any sense of them.

"'Amazing Grace?'" Clarence offered.

Mom pointed at Clarence and smiled, nodding vigorously.

Travis was annoyed that he hadn't figured that out himself. He might have gotten it in a few seconds if Clarence hadn't butted in. Travis started in playing and singing. Mom joined in with, *"Maze . . . zing gray . . . sweee . . ."*

"Yes!" Travis shouted. "Mom, you're doing it. You're singing!"

Mom had tears running down her cheeks. She lost the beginning of the next line but came in loud and clear with "now I seeeeee."

The aide from the first day came over. "Well, I never. . . . Geneva, you go, girl."

Travis was so flustered he couldn't remember the second verse, so they did the first one again and Mom filled in more words this time. Travis thought her voice was beginning to sound more like it had before the accident—stronger and sweeter. But he was alarmed when they finished and she slumped back, fanning herself with her good hand.

"Are you tired, Mom?" Travis asked.

She nodded, giving him a weak, one-sided smile.

Travis squeezed her good hand. "That's okay, Mom. But you did great." He turned to the aide. "Didn't she do great?"

"She sure did," the aide said. "Geneva, you'll give concerts for us one of these days."

Mom ducked her head, but Travis could tell she was pleased. He couldn't understand why she wasn't talking, though. If she could sing words, why couldn't she say them?

Mom pointed to the guitar and did a shrugging motion, still "speaking" in charades.

"You want to do another song, Mom?" he asked.

She shook her head. "Wha . . . where?"

Suddenly he realized she was asking why he didn't have 3-G's guitar.

"Your old guitar?" he asked.

Mom nodded.

"It needs to be repaired," he said. And that wasn't really a lie. He just couldn't tell her the whole truth. Not yet.

CHAPTER 19

In the next week, the days blurred by like the cars in a fast-moving freight train. Clarence and Travis only found time for the nursing home twice, but Mom had been awake and glad to see them both times. Even though she was getting better at singing the song lyrics, Travis was disappointed that she still wasn't talking. He couldn't understand why she could do one and not the other. When Doc Weston stopped by the workshop in the middle of the week, Travis asked him about that.

"Give it time," Doc said. "You're definitely making a difference with your mother. The fact that she's even trying to speak is a big change from the way she was before."

"But Mom sings the words perfectly in some songs," Travis said. "Why can't she do that when she tries to talk?"

"It's complicated, Travis. Those song lyrics are stored in her brain as automatic speech. Finding the right words to carry on a real conversation is a separate process. You sing a lot. Don't you ever find yourself thinking about something entirely different from the lyrics while you're singing?"

"Yeah, I've done that." Travis thought of the times he sang to entertain the little kids when his mind wasn't on the words of the song at all.

"Then you know what I mean," Doc said. "And to complicate things, no two brain injuries are exactly alike. Recovery times are different, too. So keep singing with your mother. I know you're helping her."

Those words were too vague to make Travis feel better. He wanted Doc to give him an actual date when his mother would be back to normal, even though he knew that wasn't possible. It was easier to wait for something if you knew exactly when it was going to happen.

The day before the festival, Clarence dropped Travis at the workshop and went off to check on some last-minute contest details. Travis could hear guitar music before he opened the door.

When he got inside, he saw Scott playing the prize guitar for the contest. Scott was so lost in the music, he didn't notice Travis until the end of the song.

"The guitar sounds great," Travis said. He felt a little embarrassed, as if he had been eavesdropping on a private conversation.

Scott lightly touched each of the strings at the twelfth fret, setting off a series of bell-like harmonics. "I just strung her up. It's always exciting to hear a guitar for the first time. I think of it as giving the tree a voice, you know what I mean?"

Travis shrugged. "I guess so."

"Wait, I'll show you something." Scott got up and pulled a piece of paper from the bulletin board. "I could never put it into words, but a luthier friend of mine named Bernie Lehmann wrote a poem that says it all. Here, take a look." He handed the paper to Travis.

SOTTO VOCE

Relying on vicissitudes
Of wind and water
And fertile soil.

To wait beneath the snows
Enough warmth
Enough light
Just enough
To grow.

Three generations pass
The saw, the kiln, the plane.
With care and practiced hands
Resins become resonant.

The luthier listens to the tree
And the tree sings.

B. LEHMANN

Travis was stopped right off by the title. "Sotto Voce"? What the heck was that?

Scott must have seen his confusion. "The title means

speaking or singing in a quiet voice, but never mind that. Read the rest of it."

Travis could feel Scott's eyes on him as he scanned the poem. The word *vicissitudes* did him in on the first line. That made it even harder to understand the rest of it. This felt like those reading-comprehension tests where he worried so much about answering the questions at the end, the words swam in front of his eyes like a whirlpool. Only here it wasn't a grade he was working for. He didn't want to disappoint Scott by not grasping the poem that obviously meant a lot to him.

"You don't get it, do you?" Scott asked finally.

"I flunked the poetry unit in English," Travis admitted. "Sorry."

Scott nodded. "That's okay. I've never been much for poems myself, but this one is different. Remember I told you about how important the top wood of the guitar is?"

"Yeah, sure. You said it's Adirondack spruce."

"That's right, and in order for that spruce tree to grow on this land, a seed from a red spruce cone had to drop into the right kind of soil and get enough water to start growing in the first place. That probably happened a hundred years ago."

Travis looked at the poem again. "Yeah, I see where it says that."

"Good. Then the spindly seedling had to survive drought in summer and crushing snow in winter," Scott continued, "and it had to be in a spot where the light wasn't all blocked off by taller trees. And when it got big, it had to live through windstorms, and ice storms, and people wanting to cut it

214

down to make junk like packing crates. It's all luck, you know? This tree was cut by a guy who made guitars. He had it quarter-sawn and kiln-dried so the resins in the wood cured and became more resonant with each year."

Travis nodded, really understanding this time. The thought that the wood for this beautiful guitar could have ended up as a crummy packing crate was a real eye opener.

"Okay," Scott said, "now this is the best part because Bernie Lehmann loves building guitars more than anybody I know. The luthier has the job—no, it's more like the privilege—of coaxing that wood into becoming a guitar. He planes it as thin as possible, then carves away just enough of the braces to let the top vibrate." Scott fingered an E chord and played a slow arpeggio. Each note shimmered in the air a long time.

"Listen to that," Scott whispered. "That's the voice of a tree."

Travis did listen, and felt chills on the back of his neck.

That was the last quiet moment in the workshop, because a few minutes later, two guys from West Virginia came in, then a young woman from Tennesee, all guitar players arriving for the contest. Scott greeted them like old friends, and they passed the contest guitar around, everybody marveling at how beautiful it was. Travis could tell by the few bars of music each one played that this contest was going to be nothing short of amazing.

Travis went off into a corner and read the poem again. He had always thought poetry was for girls or sissies, but now he could see that a poem was a way to say something better than you could with ordinary words—something that meant a lot to you. He had seen how Scott enjoyed the work of making a guitar, but now he understood there was more to it than creating something that looked beautiful. Scott knew there was a voice trapped inside that wood, and it took a lot of time and skill to let it out. Travis thought about his mother, and how maybe if he could be patient, he'd find the voice trapped inside of her.

There were people in and out of the workshop all day, so Travis spent most of his time making coffee and washing out mugs. The front porch had become an informal stage where people would jam, putting together pickup bands, then re-grouping in other combinations. He sat on the front step and listened every chance he got. Two sisters played mandolins and sang, sounding a lot like June and Mom. Mom always said there was a special thing that happened when people who were related to each other sang harmony—something about their vocal cords being so similar that they vibrated together. Boy, would she ever love to hear this. The more he thought about it, the more he wanted to make that happen.

Travis went into the workshop and found Clarence. "Hey, Clarence. I just had a great idea. Can we go pick up Mom at the nursing home tomorrow and bring her to the festival?"

"You're jumping the gun, Travis. She hasn't even been let out for a short ride. You're talking about a whole day with a lot of confusion. It would wear her out."

"She wouldn't have to stay all day," Travis said. "We could bring her over to see part of it."

Clarence put up his hands. "Whoa, Travis. I can't. I have too many things to do at the festival to be running off. I have to be there first thing in the morning, then there's the kiddie activities, the contest, and the Adirondack Jam concert, not to mention the—"

Travis interrupted his line of excuses. "Okay, okay! I get it. Sorry I asked." Travis stormed outside and went behind the workshop, the only place he could be alone. Clarence, of all people, should understand how important this was to Mom. Doc said hearing the two of them play at the nursing home was therapy. Wouldn't coming to the festival be even better?

Travis felt helpless. If this awful thing had to happen to Mom, why couldn't it have been when he was old enough to drive? He could have his own car and pick her up to take her anywhere he wanted. He wouldn't have to rely on anybody to get around.

But wait, he knew somebody else with a car. Without stopping to think it over, he ran back into the workshop and grabbed the phone. Dad answered on the first ring—too fast for Travis to lose his nerve.

"Dad, you have to bring Mom to the music festival. She'd love it. And even if she gets too tired to stay the whole day, you could let her see part of it."

There was a moment's silence. Then, "What in the Sam Hill are you talking about?"

Travis's words came out in a rush. "It's a music festival with a guitar contest. It's in a park on Route 4 outside of Cuyler. The festival starts at nine, but the contest part isn't until ten thirty. That would give you plenty of time to get Mom from the nursing home." Travis paused for a second to let Dad say something, then plunged ahead. "Maybe you should call them first and let them know you're coming. Or, no, wait! Maybe you should call Doc Weston so he lets them know that it's part of Mom's therapy."

"You have this all figured out, don't you?" Dad said. "You think you can give me orders and I'll run right out and do what you say."

It was no use. Dad wasn't going to listen to him. Travis gave it one last try, speaking quietly this time. "Dad, I know you're mad at me, but do it for Mom . . . please?"

There was silence on the other end of the line. Travis waited a full minute before he hung up. But that was the end of it. He couldn't count on Dad for anything anymore.

"The coffee pot's empty," Scott called from across the room.

"I'm on it," Travis said. He dumped the grounds, rinsed out the pot, and poured water into the reservoir. Then he went out to the porch to listen to more guitar picking. He was going to enjoy every moment of this festival. No way Dad could take that away from him. Travis felt bad about Mom missing all this, but he'd get her here next year.

That night the Chicken Diner was packed, mostly with people Travis had never seen before. He and Clarence had to take a small table in the back corner instead of their usual spot. "You think all these people are going to be in the contest?" Travis asked.

"I'd wager they're here for the festival, all right," Clarence said. "But there will only be twenty contestants."

"Twenty? Why didn't more people sign up?"

"Oh, we got more applications than ever this year," Clarence said. "Close to a hundred, I think. But on the deadline date last month, we put all of the applications in a big box and picked twenty at random. So those are the contestants. Then we picked ten as alternates. We sent them each a letter so they'd know to practice their three-minute song."

"But if you pick them at random, you don't know how good they are."

"That's right. And we do get a few duds each year—people who have an overrated opinion of their own playing. But if we just let the really good guitarists in, we'd have the same top players every year. This way we always get some surprises, both good and bad."

Ralphene came over with their meals. She didn't even bother to take their orders anymore because she knew Travis would take the daily special right along with Clarence. Tonight was fish fry—one of Travis's favorites.

"You all set for tomorrow, Ralphene?" Clarence asked.

"I sure am. I made all the plans, and I have extra help to cover for me at the festival."

Clarence nodded. "That's good. See you there."

"What does Ralphene have to do with the festival?" Travis asked after Ralphene had gone on to another table.

"She and Arno are putting on the main meal at noon.

It's become such a big deal, they decided not to open the diner on festival day this year. Most everybody will be over at the park, anyway."

The parking lot was already half full when Travis and Clarence arrived the next morning. Travis walked around and counted license plates from fourteen different states. Most were from New England and the southeast, and a few from as far away as the midwest. He looked around, hoping against hope to see Dad's station wagon, but it wasn't there.

The big expanse of sloping field was fast filling with lawn chairs. People gathered in small groups, either listening to one person play, or playing in small groups. Travis listened to two men and a woman on guitar, mandolin, and banjo. He was sure they were a professional band, but after they finished the song, the banjo player said, "Hey, that was cool. What else do you both know? How about 'Cripple Creek'?" Travis couldn't believe that their polished performance was just jamming. It sounded like something they had practiced for months.

Travis's first job was to get the cow painting area set up for the little kids. That was off to the side, way behind the stage. He wondered if he'd be stuck there all day. If so, he wouldn't be able to see anything. Then he heard somebody testing the sound system and the music came through fine. At least he'd be able to hear.

People started dropping off little kids, and Travis had them fill out name tags that he tied to their wrists. One kid complained, saying he was too old for the baby tags. "No tag, no cow painting," Travis said. The kid gave in.

Maybe because he was used to entertaining Roy and Earleen, Travis didn't have any trouble getting the kids interested in painting. He had three kids set up with paints, a brush, and an apron to cover their clothes, when he heard Scott announcing the start of the contest. From then on, Travis gave enough attention to the kids to keep them from painting each other, but his main focus was the music. The first two players sounded great, but the third one was a dud. Travis figured even he could play circles around whoever that was.

A couple more families arrived so Travis missed some songs while he got the kids squared away with name tags, paints, and cows. Then he had to smooth over a squabble between two little girls who wanted the one can of purple paint at the same time. He solved that problem by moving the cows next to each other so that they could share.

When things had quieted down enough to hear the music again, there was a guitar that sounded amazing. Travis wondered if the musician already had one of Scott's guitars. It didn't seem fair that he might win another one. About halfway through the contest, a woman came over. "I'll take over for you here, Travis. You ought to be where you can watch the contest."

He wanted to leap at the chance, but this was supposed to be his job. "That's okay. I'm being paid to do this."

"No, Scott's orders," she said. "He wants you to see the contest."

"Okay, thanks!" Travis ran out to the front and found a spot off to the left side. From that angle he could watch the contestants' fingers as they played—at least the right-handed ones. He looked around for the judges, then realized that they must be sitting where the contestants were out of their line of sight. When Clarence told him about the blind contest, Travis had pictured the players behind a screen, but this was more interesting for the audience.

As they got to contestant number eighteen, Clarence found Travis. "After this, there's a ten-minute intermission while we get ready for the Adirondack Jam concert," he whispered. "We'll get them tuned onstage, so come right on up and help with that." Clarence pulled an electronic tuner out of his pocket and handed it to him. "We have to work fast because the Jam concert is the filler while the judges figure out the top five finalists."

Travis watched the last three players. They were all good. As a matter of fact, with the exception of two average players and that one really bad one, he hadn't heard anybody who didn't deserve to win. He sure wouldn't want to be a judge.

As soon as the last guitarist left the stage, Travis saw the Jam kids start to take their places. He went onstage with his tuner and began checking out the kids with guitars. Buddy and Clarence were making the rounds of the fiddles, mandolins, and banjos. One girl said, "You sure are lucky," as she handed Travis her guitar.

"Why's that?"

"Being Scott's helper and all. He's such a nice man. Is he teaching you how to make guitars?"

Travis watched the needle as he brought an A string into tune. "No, he just hired me to help with the festival. I've been watching him build the contest prize guitar, though."

She smiled at him. "Scott is the best. Like I said, you sure are lucky." Travis had to agree with her on that. This was a hundred times better than working with Verl, or being yelled at by Dad all the time.

Clarence came over with a guitar. "Here, tune this up, will you?"

"Okay, who's it for?"

"You," Clarence said. "A couple of the guitar kids didn't show up so we need you to beef up that section."

"But I don't know the music."

"Sure you do. We're doing 'Angelina Baker,' 'Golden Slippers,' and finishing up with 'Turkey in the Straw' with solos, the way we did at rehearsal. You know those songs, don't you?"

"I guess so."

"I know so," Clarence said. "You'll be fine. Take that empty chair up front."

Travis didn't have time to think about what was happening because as soon as he took his seat, Scott started "Angelina Baker." At first Travis was nervous playing in front of so many people, but it didn't take long before he forgot about being scared and fell into the music. By the time they were halfway through "Golden Slippers," he felt relaxed enough to look at the audience.

Even though the place was packed, people were still coming in. That was the good thing about having the festival

223

outdoors. There were no regular seats. People just kept squeezing in more lawn chairs. They finished another song and Scott was at the mike, telling people about the Adirondack Jam project, and thanking the people who had been helping him with it. He had Clarence and Buddy stand up and take a bow from their spot in the front row. Then Scott thanked the music teachers from the different schools and they stood up from points all around the audience. That's when Travis noticed a woman pushing a wheelchair. He saw Clarence get up and lead them to a spot on the side of the front row. Travis couldn't believe his eyes. It was Ralphene and Mom!

Before he could get that thought through his head, Scott said, "I want to thank a young man who was a big help getting ready for this whole festival, my assistant, Travis Tacey. Take a bow, Travis." Travis banged his guitar against a mike as he stood up, so a loud bonking sound rang out over the audience. Ralphene waved at him. But how did Mom get here? And what was she doing with Ralphene? They didn't even know each other.

Travis didn't have time to think anymore about it because Scott was starting "Turkey in the Straw." This was the song where different kids took solos. First came the fiddle solo, then the next verse was the mandolin. Everybody played during the choruses. It sounded great. Scott pointed to each soloist while another kid was playing, giving them a heads-up that they were next. Then he'd call out their name over the mike when it was time to start playing. The whole band had to vamp a minute after each one to wait for the applause to die down.

Travis knew that the guitar solo was next. He looked around the stage but didn't see the kid who had played it in the rehearsal. How could the kid not show up when everybody was counting on him to play? Travis was wondering if Scott had a backup plan, when the kid next to him said, "Hey, Travis. You're up next." Sure enough, Scott's eyes were on him. Travis shook his head. This was ridiculous. He hadn't practiced the solo.

"Now on guitar, Travis Tacey," Scott said into the mike. Luckily Travis's fingers knew what they were doing, because his brain was numb. When he started playing, he realized that Clarence had him sitting in a chair where the mike was right in front of the guitar. Had he and Scott planned this all along? He could hear his solo spreading out over the audience. This was the most amazing thing he had ever felt. He couldn't believe that the music he heard was coming from him. He even put in a little flourish at the end that he had never done before. Everybody clapped and cheered when he finished. Then a few more solos, a couple more choruses, and the Adirondack Jam concert was over. Travis couldn't wait to get down into the audience to see his mother.

"You were wonderful, Travis," Ralphene said. "I didn't know you were going to have a solo."

"I was a last-minute replacement," Travis said, hugging his mother. "I'm so glad you got here, Mom. Wait till you hear the contest finalists. You're gonna be blown away."

Mom shook her head and poked him in the chest with her good hand. "You," she said, then made a thumbs-up sign.

"Aw, I'm nothing, Mom. Wait till you hear the people in the contest. Hey, how did you get here, anyway?"

"Clarence said you gave him the idea to get your mother here, so he planned the whole thing to surprise you," Ralphene said. "Doc said we should come for only half a day, so we figured it would be best to come for the end of the contest to hear the finalists and the winner. Your mother and I have had a nice time, haven't we, Geneva?"

"Sure," Mom said. She pointed at Ralphene and grinned. "Friend." Travis couldn't remember Mom ever having a friend. Her whole life had been nothing but work and the family.

Scott was making an announcement about the contest finalists. "Our top five have been picked for the play-off. Numbers 4, 7, 13, 14, and 19. Same as before, the judges are in a place where they can hear the contestants but not see them, so don't get excited and call out any names, because we want to keep this fair. It's all about the playing, not the person. And remember, no applause until all the players have finished."

The first contestant took the stage. He was so good that Travis had to practically sit on his hands to keep from clapping when the song ended. The next guy was a teenager, probably not much older than Travis, but he was incredibly good, too. Every time Travis glanced at Mom, she was smiling. She was loving this. Travis leaned over to her. "Isn't this about the best thing you ever heard, Mom? Aren't these guys amazing?"

"Yah," she said with a huge smile on her face.

The next contestant was a girl, and she was even better than the first guy. Mom liked that. She gave Travis a thumbs-up.

"Only two more to go," he said.

Travis looked around at the audience. Every inch of space was filled with lawn chairs and people sitting on the ground, even up both of the side slopes. It made him nuts to think that this festival had been going on for years and he'd never even heard of it. While he was sitting up in the woods, probably doing nothing, he had been missing out on the best guitar playing he could imagine. But no more. He was going to get to the festival every year from now on. And he'd make sure Mom and the other kids got there, too.

The next contestant was starting to play. It was that wonderful mellow guitar Travis had heard when he was helping the kids with the cow paintings. He had been sure it was one of Scott's instruments, but when he turned toward the stage, he was surprised to see that the guitar was old and beat-up. Travis looked at the guy playing it and his heart almost stopped beating because it was him—no cowboy hat, but it was Cowboy! He'd know that face anywhere. And he had 3-G's guitar.

CHAPTER 20

Travis ran over to Scott, who was standing by the side of the stage. "That's the guy who stole my guitar. That's my guitar he's playing."

Scott put his hand on Travis's shoulder and whispered, "Shhh. Keep it down, Travis. You sure about that?"

"Positive. It's him, Scott. I know it," he whispered back.

"Okay, hold on. Let him finish. We'll sort this out after the contest."

It killed Travis to stand there through a three-minute song while Cowboy played 3-G's guitar. He didn't even care if he sounded better than anybody else. The guy was a thief and Travis was going to make him pay for what he had done.

The guy finished and started leaving the stage. "Stop him!" Travis yelled. "Don't let him get away!" As he ran, Travis saw Cowboy duck around behind the stage.

No way he was getting away this time. Travis heard Scott say, "Contestant number nineteen" into the mike.

"Hey, you. Stop!" Travis yelled. He heard the next contestant begin playing.

A guy wearing a name tag that said FESTIVAL VOLUNTEER grabbed him. "Hey, kid, be quiet. There's a contest going on."

"But that guy stole my guitar. He's getting away."

The volunteer started pushing him to the side—the opposite direction from where Cowboy had been heading. Travis craned his neck to see around him, but he didn't spot Cowboy anywhere. He looked toward the parking lot. Was he headed for his truck?

The last player finished and the audience broke into applause. Scott told the audience a band called Timber Creek would be playing while the judges decided on the winner of the contest. As soon as the band started playing, Scott ran over to Travis. "All right, let's get this thing settled. Where is that guy?"

"He went behind the stage, but I don't see him anymore."

"We'll find him. He won't take off before we announce the winner. He has too much at stake." Sure enough, they found Cowboy talking to a couple of other contestants.

"I need to have a word with you," Scott said.

When Cowboy saw Travis, his face got red, but he flashed a fake smile. "Sure. What's up?"

"You've got my guitar," Travis said. "That's what's up."

Cowboy laughed. "Sorry, kid. This guitar has been in my family for generations. You can see how old it is."

"Can you prove it's yours?" Scott asked.

Cowboy snorted. "What, you want me to show you a sales slip from a hundred years ago? You can't prove it's *not*

229

mine. It's my word against the kid's, and I'll bring in my brothers and about ten cousins who'll say they've seen this guitar all of their lives."

"I can do the same thing. My mom is out front. She'll tell you it's ours. I'll go get her."

Travis ran out to find Mom and Ralphene. He got there between the band's songs so they had a minute to talk before the music started up again. "Your mother is upset about something," Ralphene said. "I'm not sure what it is. She keeps pointing to the stage."

"It's 3-G's guitar, right, Mom? You saw it, too?"

Mom nodded her head so hard she knocked herself off balance in the chair.

Travis squatted down in front of her. "Look, I didn't tell you this before, but I did a stupid thing. I hitched a ride with that guy and he stole 3-G's guitar."

Mom's eyes got wide, then she scowled. She was struggling to say something.

"I know, Mom, you always said it was dangerous. I shouldn't have done it. But forget that for now. The guy is claiming that the guitar belongs to him. Try to calm down so you can tell Scott it's your guitar, okay? Hang on, we're taking a fast ride."

He maneuvered the wheelchair around some people who were standing by the side of the stage. Scott was still talking to Cowboy, who looked a little worried until he saw that Travis's mother was in a wheelchair. Mom was leaning way over in her chair and looked harmless. It took both Ralphene and Travis to get her straightened up.

"Mrs. Tacey," Scott said, "we need you to settle a little dispute. This man swears that the guitar he's holding has been in his family for years."

Mom shook her head. "Neh. Neh."

Cowboy laughed. "This is your big witness? She can't even talk, for Pete's sake."

Mom reached forward, trying to grab 3-G's guitar. Ralphene had to keep her from falling. "Mine!" Mom said, as clear as anything.

The judges were starting to announce the contest winners. "I've had enough of this foolishness," Cowboy said. "I gotta get out front."

"That's fine," Scott said. "Leave that guitar with me. I'll hold it until we get this settled."

"Oh, sure. You're going to side with the kid. I'll never get it back." Cowboy started to walk off, but Clarence appeared out of nowhere and stopped him. That must have taken Cowboy by surprise because he didn't offer any resistance to Clarence taking the guitar out of his hands. "Scott's a man of his word," Clarence said. "If the guitar is yours, you'll get it back. Now go out onstage with the other contestants."

Travis took the guitar from Clarence. It felt so good to hold it again, he almost cried. He looked it over. There was still a big crack in the back. "I can't believe he didn't get it repaired," Travis said. "It's a wonder it didn't fall apart."

Scott ran his finger over the crack. "So you know for sure this is yours?"

"Absolutely," Travis said. He told Scott about falling when he was chased by the dog. "The crack in the back got bigger, and hitting the pavement made this little dent on the side."

Scott took the guitar and turned it over. "This is all fixable. The guitar has an amazing tone in spite of the damage. But if that guy brings in people to lie for him, we may have a problem. Of course I believe you, but one thing I've learned is that good people aren't always the ones who win."

The judge making the contest announcements said, "Now we're down to our two finalists. Fifteen-year-old Jason Deitrich and Sam Harris."

Scott shook his head. "See what I mean?"

"Is that him?" Travis asked. "His name's Sam Harris?"

"That's him."

"He can't win your guitar and get to keep 3-G Eli's guitar, too," Travis said. "It's not fair."

All of a sudden, Mom was trying to say something. She motioned for Scott to hand her the guitar. He put it gently in her lap, then she did a circling motion with her hand, showing him that she wanted it turned over. She rubbed her finger across the thick part of the neck where it joined the body. "Eli!" she said.

Travis looked closely where she was pointing. "I think there are letters carved there. It's hard to see them."

"Eli," Mom said again.

Scott took the guitar and turned it so the sunlight hit the letters. "It looks like E. D."

"That's 3-G Eli," Travis said. "Eli Dunning, right, Mom?"

"Yes!" Mom said.

Travis heard the announcer again. "And the winner of a

genuine Scott McKissack guitar is . . ." He left a dramatic pause, the way they do on TV shows.

"Come on," Clarence said, handing Scott the prize guitar. "We have to get out there." Travis followed them. The audience cheered when Scott walked onstage, carrying his prize guitar.

The judge continued. "The winner is Sam Harris." Travis's heart sank. He couldn't bear the thought of Scott's beautiful guitar going to that dishonest creep.

Cowboy pushed the young kid aside and strutted to the front of the stage, taking bow after bow as the crowd cheered. Travis had to hold himself back from running out there and knocking him off the edge.

When the yelling and whistling calmed down, Scott went to the mike. "Making the prize guitar means a lot to me because I know it's going to go to some deserving guitar player who has honed his craft to perfection, the same as I keep working to make my guitars better and better. Every year I look forward to the moment when I can hand the winner his or her new guitar."

There was more cheering at that. Cowboy looked over at Travis and sneered. Travis couldn't believe it. Scott was going to let that jerk walk off with the prize. He didn't really have a choice. After all, the guy had won it. Cowboy had come over to stand by Scott and was reaching out for the guitar.

"But this year is a little different," Scott said. "We're going to have one more test for our winner. Clarence, would you give Mr. Harris the guitar he played in the contest?"

Clarence handed Cowboy 3-G's guitar. Travis hated to see him hold it again. What if he made a break for it? He could reach his truck in the parking lot before anybody sensed what was happening.

"The luthier who made this guitar put his initials on it," Scott said. "Mr. Harris, can you show me those initials and tell me who the guitar maker is?"

Cowboy looked inside the guitar, where the name of the luthier would usually be. Then he said, "Nobody knows who made this old thing. Besides, who cares? I won't be playing it now that I have my new McKissack." He grinned at the audience, pumped the air with his fist, and they cheered.

"Well, that's not exactly the case," Scott said. "We do know who made the guitar. The initials E. D. are carved into the neck. Travis, you want to tell the people what that stands for?"

Travis went to the mike. "My great-great-great-grandfather Eli Dunning made that guitar." It was weird to hear his voice amplified by the sound system. The crowd had grown silent. Travis took a deep breath. "That guitar has been in our family for generations. Sam Harris stole it from me." His words echoed across the field. A low grumbling sound went through the audience.

Scott stepped up to the mike. "So I figure playing on a stolen guitar is a clear disqualification," Scott said, his voice booming over the rumbling of the crowd. "And I'm pleased to present the prize guitar to a very talented young player— first runner-up, Jason Deitrich."

"What a rip-off!" Cowboy shouted. "You can keep your crappy old guitar!"

At first, Travis thought he was talking about the contest prize. Then he watched in disbelief as Cowboy raised 3-G's guitar over his head with both hands and threw it full force at the floor.

"Noooo!" Travis dove for the guitar, trying to break its fall, but he wasn't fast enough. The guitar hit the stage with a loud bang like an explosion. The back flew off the body and fractured as it made its own hard landing. Travis bent over the exposed guts of the instrument, catching the faint odor of ancient pipe smoke, as if the ghost of 3-G Eli Dunning had suddenly been released. Travis couldn't believe he had let this happen. If he had moved a split second earlier, he might have broken the guitar's fall. Travis sat up and saw Cowboy jump off the stage and run for the parking lot. Three men from the audience got up to go after him. In this crowd, stealing a guitar was serious business, but destroying one was unthinkable. The men cornered Cowboy by the parking lot, and Travis saw a state trooper run toward them. Sam Harris was going to be arrested, but it didn't really matter anymore. The damage was done.

Things happened fast after that, but to Travis it was like watching a movie. He could see in the distance as the trooper handcuffed Cowboy and locked him in his squad car. Then he watched as the trooper drove the car right up to the side of the stage. Scott sent Buddy out to keep the crowd entertained while the trooper came over to ask questions.

The first question was to Travis's mother. "You're absolutely sure that this guitar belongs to your family, ma'am?"

"Yes." Mom was sobbing, but she managed to say, "Mine!" loud and clear.

"Scott, how much did you say that guitar was worth?" the trooper asked.

Travis was stunned by Scott's answer. "I'd say at least a thousand dollars. Guitars that old are rare, and this one had a better sound than anything I've heard in a long time."

The trooper closed his notebook. "Good. In New York State, that makes it a felony. Harris will be doing some jail time for this."

That didn't come close to making up for what Cowboy had done to the guitar or the expression of sadness Travis saw on his mother's face. "I'm so sorry about the guitar, Mom. But maybe Scott can get it playing again. I've seen him take instruments that looked like scraps of junk and make them good as new." That wasn't exactly true, but Travis wanted to give his mother some hope that he didn't feel himself.

"You look tired, Geneva," Ralphene said. "Are you ready to head back?"

Mom nodded and Ralphene started pushing her wheelchair toward the parking lot.

"Let me do that," Travis said. He pushed the chair all the way up the slope, then helped his mother get into Ralphene's car. "Clarence and I will come over to see you soon."

Mom pointed at Travis. "P-p-proud," she said, then reached out and squeezed his hand.

"Me, too, Mom. I'm proud of you." He closed her door, then watched until Ralphene drove out of sight.

CHAPTER 21

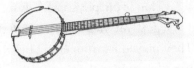

As Travis walked back down toward the stage, the audience was applauding Buddy's last song. Then Scott went back to the microphone. "That was Buddy Hubert—best mandolin player in ten counties. Now I'm sure you're all eager to hear our contest winner, Jason Deitrich, play a few songs on his new guitar."

Jason took his place in the spotlight. For a young kid, he sure knew how to play. Travis told himself that he'd practice like mad and enter the contest next year. His playing had already improved with the few lessons Clarence had given him. No telling what he could accomplish in a year.

Then Travis remembered that his guitar was just pieces of wood wrapped in an old blanket. It gave him a weird feeling to know that he had been carrying around a thousand dollars' worth of guitar on his back. If he'd known that, he would have sold the guitar and used the money to get his mother into a better hospital. But it didn't matter now. All he had was kindling, just like Dad said, way back when he had tried to smash it.

Travis barely heard the three bands that played after Jason. Then, just as the sun was starting to set, turning the sky orange and the clouds purple, somebody announced that the last act of the festival was a band called the Copper Bottom Boys. They played a fast opening lick and the crowd went nuts. Travis turned his attention on the stage and saw Scott on guitar, Clarence on banjo, and Buddy on mandolin, all wearing cowboy hats. They launched into one song after another, never pausing in between, passing the lead around, and playing so fast their fingers were a blur. The audience shrieked and whistled after each solo, finally clapping in time to the music, picking up the pace to a frenzy. Clarence whipped out a white handkerchief, mopped his forehead, then waved it like a flag of surrender before jumping back into the song with a big grin on his face. Travis was surprised to see what a showman the old man was. The Copper Bottom Boys got a rousing standing ovation. The excitement of their performance gave Travis a temporary break from his anguish over 3-G's guitar, but as soon as the applause died out, the heavy feeling weighed him down again.

It was dark by the time Scott and Clarence could break loose from all the people who crowded around to talk with them. Then Scott said, "Let's go back to the shop. I want to take a look at your guitar, Travis."

"Can't that wait until morning?" Clarence asked. "I'm beat. I need to go home and hit the sack."

Scott put his hand on Clarence's shoulder. "Go ahead,

Clarence. You've put in a long day. I'll drop Travis at your place later."

Scott loaded his guitar and some other instruments into his truck and they started off. They drove along in silence for a few miles, then Scott looked over at Travis. "You did a nice job with that guitar solo."

Travis snorted. "So when did you and Clarence decide I was going to play the solo?"

"As soon as we realized we didn't have a guitar soloist."

"Yeah? When was that?"

Scott grinned but kept looking straight ahead. "This past Thursday."

Travis slapped the seat. "I knew it! Why didn't you ask me ahead of time? Why couldn't you give me time to practice?"

"Well, first off, you did fine without practice. I knew you would. You have a good ear for improvisation. And more important, if I had asked you to play the solo, would you have agreed to do it?"

"Of course not. You know I can't play in front of strangers."

"Seems like you did fine with that tonight. Wasn't so bad, was it?"

Travis slid down in the seat. "It would have been better if I had practiced."

"But you wouldn't have practiced because you didn't want to do it. So Clarence and I had to trick you into playing in front of a big audience, and now you can do it any time you want."

"Yeah, I guess." Travis tried to picture himself playing

on that stage. Had that really been him? Maybe being in the spotlight wasn't so bad after all.

Scott took off the cowboy hat he'd worn for the Copper Bottom Boys act and threw it behind the seat. "We got more excitement than we bargained for tonight. I can't believe that Harris guy was stupid enough to show up with your stolen guitar. He sure didn't expect to run into you."

Travis shrugged. "Yeah, well, he probably figured even if he did, it was his word against a dumb kid."

"I liked the way you stood up to him, Travis. That took guts—even more guts than playing a guitar solo."

Scott and Travis were both silent for the rest of the ride. Travis wasn't sure he wanted to see the guitar again. He had a strong suspicion that the damage was beyond repair.

The workshop seemed strange with no people in it. Scott laid the blanket bundle on the workbench and gently uncovered the carcass of the guitar. This was the first time Travis had a really good look at it. The thing that shocked him was the neck, which was split away from the body but still tethered to it by a loose tangle of strings. "What happened? The neck was attached before."

"When the back broke off, the neck didn't have enough support," Scott said. "Those strings can pull with about a hundred pounds of pressure on the neck. I should have loosened the tension right when it happened, but in all the confusion, I didn't think."

"It's not your fault," Travis said. He looked at what was left of the guitar. It reminded him of a Canada goose he had once found dead at the side of the road, its long, graceful neck splayed out at a painful angle against the pavement. He had the same sick feeling now as he'd had then. To Travis, that guitar was as much a living thing as that bird, and his heart broke to see it silenced and still.

Scott carefully lined up the pieces of the back, but there were several gaps where wood had splintered away.

"You can't fix that, can you?" Travis asked.

"Can't say for sure, but the back isn't the most important part." Scott swept the slack strings away from the guitar's top and let out a low whistle. "This is one beautiful piece of Adirondack. That's why it sounded so good even with a cracked back. You just can't get wood like this anymore." Travis could see the look of admiration in Scott's face as he ran his fingers over the fine grain. "I might be able to use this top on a new guitar."

"Would you patch the place where the wood is almost worn through?" Travis asked.

"No, that's part of its history—years of people playing it. You don't mess with something like that." Scott checked over the neck. "This is still in pretty good shape, so I can use it. That would make it feel the same to play it."

"So it would be sort of like 3-G's guitar only with new parts?" Travis asked.

"Could be." Scott gathered up the pieces and wrapped them in the blanket again. "I want to study how this guitar was put together, then take it real slow with the repair. But I think I can make this tree sing again."

Travis knew it wouldn't be his guitar anymore because he could never afford to buy it from Scott. Besides, he didn't deserve to own it. He had let it get stolen in the first place. But it made him feel better to think that 3-G's guitar could still make music for somebody.

The next day, people were still coming in and out of the workshop, and there were so many pickup bands playing on the front porch, it was almost as good as the festival itself. But Travis could barely swallow around the lump in his throat, because now that everything was over, his job here was finished. And there was no reason for Clarence to let him stay at his house anymore, either. As much as the old guy had bugged him at first, Travis had begun to think of Clarence as family—sort of a crazy grandpa.

There hadn't been many days in his life that Travis wanted to last forever, but this was one of them. He would be perfectly content to sit here frozen in time, watching, listening, or picking and singing whenever somebody invited the onlookers to join in. This was home to him, where everybody shared his passion for guitars and music. But Travis knew he was heading for a showdown, because when Clarence and Scott found out he was only fourteen—and that was bound to happen soon—they'd both be so mad that he lied, they'd kick him out for sure.

Travis had to go inside to make a new pot of coffee about every half hour. Buddy finally came in with a package of paper cups. "These will save you from having to wash out all the mugs."

"Thanks, Buddy," Travis said. "We didn't have enough mugs anyway. People were taking turns. Hey, your band sounded really great last night. Where did the name Copper Bottom Boys come from?"

Buddy tapped a saucepan on the shelf over the sink. "You're looking at it right here. This is what we used to heat coffee water in. It's all tarnished now, but when it was new, the bottom was bright copper. When we needed a name for our first gig, we looked around the shop for ideas and that was the first thing we laid eyes on."

"You named your band after an old pot?"

Buddy laughed. "Sounds kind of silly, don't it? But the name has a nice ring to it, so it stuck."

Travis looked toward the door and saw Doc Weston making his way through the people in the shop. Doc patted Buddy on the back. "The Copper Bottom Boys were in fine form last night, Buddy."

"Thanks, Doc. It was a good festival all the way around. More people than ever. What brings you here this morning?"

"I need to discuss something with Travis," Doc said. "How about we go out back where we can have a little peace and quiet?"

"Okay." As Travis followed Doc outside, thoughts raced through his head. Was this about Mom? Did she get too upset about what had happened to the guitar? Or was Travis going to be exposed for lying about his age? Doc knew too much about the family. He could have figured it out.

Doc sat on the grass and leaned against the wall of the shop, motioning for Travis to join him.

Travis eased himself down on the ground. "Is this about Mom? Did she get too tired at the festival?"

"I was a little concerned about that," Doc said. "So I went over to check on her this morning. She's fine, but worried about you. We're trying to come up with a plan. You're not too wild about going back home, right?"

That took Travis by surprise. Doc and Mom had been making plans for him? "No, I'd rather stay here. But now that the festival is over . . . well, I don't know where I'll go."

"You're thinking of going on the run again." Doc said it as a statement rather than a question.

"No. Why would I do that?" Travis was beginning to feel uncomfortable. Doc was a lot younger than Clarence or even Scott. He seemed sharper, harder to fool.

"We need some straight talk now," Doc said. "For starters, I know that you're only fourteen."

Travis hunkered down. This is where it all hits the fan, he thought. But maybe there was time to head off disaster. "You didn't tell Scott or Clarence, did you?"

"No, I didn't have to. Clarence had you pegged all along. Scott and I thought you were fifteen." Doc smiled. "We each lost a five-dollar bet to Clarence. Just so you know, nobody bought your story about being sixteen."

They knew all along? Travis was really thrown off his guard now.

"Anyway," Doc continued, "we have to bring in Social Services if we're making any permanent arrangements for you, because you're a minor."

"No! There's no reason for that. I'll just go back home and everything will be fine."

"I've talked with your mother, Travis. She's worried about

the other kids. She knows your father isn't helping, and June can't handle everything alone, so we have to contact Social Services even if you decide to go back home."

Travis jumped to his feet. "But they'll split all the kids apart. Earleen will be scared to death and Roy is already so mad and hurt—"

"Sit down!" Doc barked. Travis did, reluctantly. Part of him wanted to take off on his bike, but what good would that do? Doc already knew where he lived. They'd find the kids.

Doc held up his hands. "Now relax. Nobody's getting split up. I promised your mother that. I want to arrange for someone to be there to take care of your little brothers and sister during the day so you and June can go to summer school to catch up on what you missed."

"You've been talking about this behind my back?" Whoever heard of a doctor who got all involved in people's lives?

"Listen to the rest of it before you get all bent out of shape," Doc said. "Ralphene and Arno have been foster parents, so they're already approved by the system. If you decide you can't live at home, they could be your temporary foster family, and since Clarence lives right next door, you could probably stay with him. Your mother likes the plan, but her goal is for all of you to be together eventually, when she's well enough to go home."

"Is that even possible?" Travis asked. "Will she ever get well enough for that?"

"Well, here's the other thing I told your mother this morning. We're moving her to a rehabilitation center as soon as the insurance approval goes through. It's a little closer to your home, so your dad and the kids can visit."

Travis raised an eyebrow. "Lots of luck with that."

"Give your father the benefit of the doubt, Travis. I've talked more with him on the phone. I have to admit he was pretty stubborn at first, but he's shown signs of coming around."

"So how soon can Mom get into this—what's it called?"

"The Lucas Regional Rehabilitation and Sports Medicine Facility," Doc said. "It has a good reputation and your mother won't be sitting around in a wheelchair with a bunch of old people there. With any luck she'll be moved today or tomorrow."

"Wow, that's fast." That name sounded a whole lot better to Travis than Peaceful Mountain, but it struck him funny that Mom—who probably hadn't kicked or thrown a ball since she was in high school—would be in a sports medicine place. "How long do you think she'll have to stay there?"

Doc Weston gave Travis a pat on the shoulder. "Let's not worry about her discharge date before she even gets in there. These things take time, but she's young and a hard worker. I think another six months with real treatment might . . . well, no promises, but I'm quite optimistic about her."

That was the best news Travis had heard in a long time. More than he'd dared hope for.

CHAPTER 22

The next few days were filled with small chores left over from the festival. "Putting the festival to bed" is what Scott called it. They all went back to the park on Monday to make sure everything was left the way they had found it. Then there were thank-you notes to be sent out to all the bands who played and all the people who entered the contest.

Clarence hadn't said anything about the plan for Travis to live with him, so Travis didn't mention it. He'd keep busy and wait until the old man brought up the subject himself. A few Adirondack Jam instruments hadn't fared too well being lugged around, so they came into the workshop for minor repairs. When Travis put away a damaged mandolin, he saw the bundled remains of 3-G's guitar up on the top shelf. It felt like a punch in the gut. He'd gone over that night a hundred times in his head, kicking himself for not being fast enough to catch that guitar before it splintered on the stage.

Travis had hoped to go to the nursing home on Tuesday afternoon, but Clarence got a call at the workshop that changed everything. Clarence was smiling when he came over to the worktable where Travis was restringing a guitar. "That was Doc with some good news."

Travis looked up. "About Mom?"

"Yep. He says she was transferred to the rehabilitation center this morning."

"Really?" Travis put down the guitar. "Can we go over there right now?"

"Well, Doc says they'll be doing a lot of testing and evaluating with her for the first couple of days. So we shouldn't go over there until Thursday—give her a little time to settle in."

On Wednesday night, Clarence and Travis had their usual chicken potpie dinner. All Travis could talk about was Doc's report that Mom loved the rehab center and was doing very well.

"We'll go visit your mother tomorrow," Clarence said. "I'd like to see this fancy new place Doc got her into."

"Me, too," Travis said. In spite of the fact that he couldn't wait to see Mom in her new surroundings, something nagged at him. "Hey, Clarence, would you mind driving me over to visit my family first? I'd like to know how my brothers and sisters are doing. Then I can tell Mom about them."

"No, of course I wouldn't mind." Clarence took some mashed potatoes on his fork and swished them around in the chicken gravy. "I think it's a great idea. There's nothing important to do at the workshop, so we can go first thing in the morning."

When Travis went to bed that night, he started wondering

if he had made the right decision. He was worried about the kids—especially Roy—but the truth was that he didn't really want to go back to his old life. He had seen how it could be when people liked and respected him. He didn't want things to go back to the way they were, with Dad putting him down all the time.

Travis tossed and turned half the night, then decided to make the best of it. Going home to visit didn't commit him to staying there. And no matter what he decided to do, he needed to see his brothers and sisters to make sure they were all right.

The next morning Travis spent the first half hour of the ride convinced that the visit would go well, but his confidence dissolved as soon as Clarence's truck started climbing the last hill before home. The only way Travis had been able to stay away from his family was to put them out of his mind. Now he dreaded their reaction to him.

When they pulled into the driveway, Dad's station wagon was there. Okay, he'd have to face Dad sooner or later. Might as well get it over with right away. As they got out of the truck and walked up to the trailer, the fragrance of the red spruce brought back so many memories of happier family times, it made Travis weak in the knees. He started to go for the doorknob, but Clarence stopped him. "Better knock. You've been away for a while." That thought hit Travis hard. This really wasn't home anymore. His knock was softer than he expected, as if part of him didn't want anyone inside to hear.

June was the one who came to the door. Lester was on

her hip, chewing on the handle of a spoon. June's face lit up when her eyes landed on Travis. She grabbed him in a one-armed bear hug. Lester grunted, squished between them. "Oh, Travis, it's so good to see you!"

Travis hugged her back, trying not to cry. He looked over her shoulder and saw Earleen running toward them, her arms outstretched. He was surprised by the feelings that hit him. Every cell in his body remembered that this was home. When Earleen hugged him at knee level, he turned to scoop her up.

"Travis, you came home!" Earleen squealed, planting a peanut-buttery kiss on his cheek. Then she got bashful, twisting away so she wasn't looking at him. As soon as he set her down, she ran out of the room. Then she turned and peeked at him from around the doorjamb—a safer distance to get used to him again, Travis figured.

"I'm sorry," June said, looking beyond Travis and reaching out her free hand. "You must be Clarence Alcorn. Travis told me about you. Please have a seat. Can I get you something? Coffee, maybe?"

Earleen had slipped back into the room and was clinging to June's legs now. Lester dropped the spoon and June retrieved it, then reached over to brush Earleen's hair from her eyes. Seeing June handle two kids at once without even thinking about it made Travis realize how far Mom was from being able to come home and take care of the family.

Travis was startled by the thwack of the screen door. Dad stepped inside but stopped instead of coming all the way into the room. He was only a dark silhouette against the bright sunshine outdoors, so Travis couldn't see his face. Was he smiling—glad to see Travis? Or was he going to yell and kick him out again? Travis felt unsteady, as if he were balancing on the edge of a cliff.

Then Dad moved—came toward him, not smiling, but not yelling, either. "You've grown some."

Travis doubted that. He'd been away only a few weeks. He didn't know what to say, so he shrugged, stuffing his hands into the pockets of his still-stiff jeans.

Dad glanced over at Clarence. "Are you going to introduce me to your friend, Travis?"

"Yeah, um, sure. This is Clarence Alcorn. He's been letting me stay with him while I've been . . ." He couldn't think of how to say it. While I've been what? While I've been a runaway? While I've been kicked out? While I've been starting my new life?

Clarence reached out to shake Dad's hand. "While he's been helping us with the music festival. Nice to meet you, Mr. Tacey."

"Yeah, right," Travis mumbled. "I was working for Clarence and Scott."

Dad raised his eyebrows. "Ah, so you got him to work, huh? I never had much luck convincing Travis to do that."

Travis felt his temper rising. Dad had some nerve accusing *him* of not working. He looked at the floor, letting his hair slide forward to hide the fact that he couldn't help scowling. June must have sensed his discomfort. "Travis, Roy's out back. Why don't you go say hello to him?"

Travis was grateful for an excuse to escape. He found

Roy making roads in the backyard dirt pile. Travis squatted down and held out his arms. "Hey, buddy. How's it going?"

Roy glanced up but didn't move or speak. He turned his attention to his dump truck, pulling the lever to plunk a load of dirt in the middle of his road. Travis could see Roy's anger in his stiff back, and the way his lips tightened, pulling down at the corners. June had been wrong about making Travis leave without a word. He should have said good-bye, especially to Roy, who seemed to be hurt more than any of them by Mom's accident. Roy was ignoring him now, making little vrooming noises under his breath as the dump truck drove off for another load.

Travis would have to win him over. He moved closer, pushing a toy road grader over the mound, smoothing it out. Roy grabbed the grader from Travis, tossed it out of his reach, and scooped another pile of dirt onto the road with his hands.

Travis tried again. "Nice layout you're building here. Needs some trees, though." He picked up some twigs and poked them into the dirt along the road. "We used to build whole forests together this way, remember?"

Roy plucked out the twig trees and flung them over his shoulder, still not looking up.

Travis sat back, giving up on the road game. "I know you're mad at me for leaving, Roy. It wasn't my idea, but I had to go."

Roy stayed silent for several minutes, then looked up at Travis through slitted eyes. "Did you come back for good?"

"I don't know."

Roy turned away. "Mom never came back. She's dead."

Travis put his arm around Roy's skinny shoulders. "Aw, come on, buddy. Mom's not dead. She's okay. I've seen her."

Roy shook off Travis's arm and moved to the other side of the dirt pile beyond his reach. Travis decided to sit tight and let Roy get used to him again.

Roy had added more dirt to the top of his mountain now and was moving the road grader in stiff chopping motions, carving a path that started at the peak and took a winding course down the steep slope. As Travis watched, he saw in Roy the tough little seven-year-old kid he had been in that emergency room years ago when he had broken his arm—gritting his teeth, trying with all of his might not to cry.

Travis took another stab at bringing his little brother around. "Hey, Roy. Mom sang with me the other day. Remember how she used to play guitar and sing to us?"

Roy frowned and hacked harder at the dirt, but Travis could tell he was listening. Roy's motor noises got a little louder, but not enough to drown out Travis's voice.

"Mom's hair has grown back in. Remember her pretty hair?"

Roy twisted around and found the pickup truck—the last thing that Travis had carved for him. He put it at the top of the mountain and started it down the road. "Neeeeeerrr!" Roy made a high whining noise as he skidded the truck down around the sharp curves. He was crying now, leaving a smear of mud on his cheek as he made a quick swipe at his tears. When Roy suddenly turned the truck over, making it tumble down the mountainside, Travis realized what he was doing.

By the time Travis got to him, Roy was pounding the

truck into the dirt with his toy shovel—pounding it over and over until only the roof showed above the dirt. Travis struggled to wrap his arms around Roy. "Hey, hey, it's okay." Travis got his little brother's arms pinned down, but Roy still thrashed his head back and forth. "Listen to me, buddy. Mom didn't die in that accident." Roy gradually stopped fighting. He was still tense, hands balled into fists, but he was paying attention.

"Mom was hurt bad," Travis whispered, "but she's getting better. I know because I've seen her."

Roy leaned in close to Travis's side. "Is it our real mom? The one we had before the hospital?"

"Yes, our real mom." Travis released his grip and rubbed Roy's rigid little back.

"Is she coming back home?" Roy's lower lip quivered, and then his face crumpled again. "Is she?" He put his arms around Travis and squeezed hard, pressing his head into Travis's chest.

"Well, she can't come back right away. She needs to get better first. But as soon as she—"

Roy suddenly pushed away and stood in front of Travis. "I don't believe you. You're lying again. You're always lying." He ran into the house, the screen door clapping shut behind him.

Travis couldn't make himself follow. Instead, he headed for the woods, toward the cabin. Roy had looked up to him before. Now the kid didn't believe a word he said. This family was a total wreck, and Travis had no idea how to put it back together. Why should he even try? He could have a good life now, living with Clarence, working with Scott, filling his spare time with guitars.

As he walked over the soft spruce-needled ground, Travis waited for the tension to fall away like it always had before. But the hurt stayed with him this time, making a tight knot in his throat. How he'd missed this place. But it seemed different now. Or maybe he was different. He stopped halfway to the cabin and looked back toward the house.

When he was Roy's age, he had had Mom to soothe his wounds. And Dad, in spite of his faults, had been a pretty decent father back then. Roy didn't have either one of them. He and Earleen and Lester might as well be orphans. Travis knew it would be a long time before Mom came home. What would happen to Roy in the meantime?

Travis headed for the house, picking up speed as he got closer to the door. Dad, Clarence, and June were sitting around the table drinking coffee and talking when Travis got inside.

"Roy came in here," Travis said. "Where did he go?"

June shrugged. "He just ran through. Maybe he went to his room."

"Roy's a mess!" Travis cried. "Has anybody even noticed that?"

"That kid is turning into a wimp," Dad said. "He needs to grow up, that's all."

Travis couldn't hold it in any longer. "A wimp! He's seven years old and he thinks his mother is dead. That poor little kid doesn't know what hit him."

June's eyes were wide. "I've tried to comfort him, but it's hard taking care of all three kids."

"This isn't about you, June. It's not your job to hold the family together."

Dad got up from the table. "You saying it's my job? That what you're trying to get at?"

Travis wanted to back away from his father, but he stood his ground. He wasn't fighting for himself. He had to be the voice for the younger kids, and for his mother. "Yeah, Dad, I'm talking about you."

June moved in behind Travis and took his arm. "This isn't going to solve anything," she whispered.

"Well, keeping quiet sure hasn't helped." Travis was shaking so hard, he could barely get the words out, but he was the only one who could say this. "Mom is doing everything she can to get better. She's going to be coming back one of these days, and we need to have a family for her to come home to. Dad, you have to go out and get a decent job."

June gasped and took a firm grip on his shoulder, pulling him back. "Travis, stop!"

"So I haven't been a perfect father." Dad jutted out his chin. "You think this has been easy for me? My whole life fell apart when your mother had that accident."

Travis glanced at Clarence. The old man nodded ever so slightly, giving him the encouragement he needed to keep going. "Our lives fell apart, too, Dad. Every last one of us." He stared straight into his father's eyes, hoping that the trembling he felt in his gut didn't show on the outside. If Dad kicked him out again, there would be no coming back, even for a visit. Travis knew that.

Dad held eye contact for a long moment. Travis could see his jaw muscles clench and unclench a couple of times. Then Dad blinked, looked away, and went back to sit at the table. "Okay, I didn't want to say anything until I knew for sure." He took a deep breath and let it out slowly, his shoulders sagging. "But I think I might be able to get a cook's job with a new inn that's opening up in a couple of weeks."

June slipped into the chair beside him. "That's really wonderful."

Dad kept his head down. "They want somebody from two through the late dinner hour, so maybe I could watch the kids in the morning. June, you could go to summer school and still be home in time to take over for me."

Travis wasn't convinced that Dad would really get the job, but he was willing to give him the benefit of the doubt. "I could help out with the kids." Not seeing any response from his father, he added, "If you don't want me here, that's okay. I have a place to go."

"If Travis goes away again, I'm going with him." They all turned to look at the hallway. Roy stood there with his arms folded, tears tracking crooked lines down the dirt on his face.

"Travis is always welcome here." Dad stood and reached out his hand. Just as Travis started to shake it, Dad switched gears and grabbed Travis in an awkward hug. Travis couldn't remember the last time Dad had hugged him. It made him so uncomfortable, he gave his father a couple of tentative pats on the back, then broke away and went to Roy, squatting down to whisper in his ear, "I'll make a promise to you, Roy. I'll come home to stay, if you start believing what I tell you about Mom. Deal?"

Roy nodded, his face solemn. "I guess," he said. "But you have to tell me the truth."

"I will," Travis said. "I always have, buddy. Always."

Travis heard a chair scrape as Clarence stood up. "Well, thanks for the coffee, folks, but I need to head back home. Nice to meet Travis's whole family."

There was a lot of hand-shaking all around, then Travis followed Clarence to his truck. He longed for the life that Clarence and Scott had mapped out for him, but he knew what he had to do. "Look, Clarence. I hope you don't mind, but I can't go back with you. I have a lot of stuff to take care of here, okay?"

Clarence pulled a duffel bag from behind the seat. "I think I packed up all your belongings. If you're missing anything, give me a call and I'll bring it over."

"You have my stuff?" Travis took the bag. "How did you know I'd be staying?"

Clarence shrugged. "I didn't, but I was hoping it would work out for you. I can see that you're needed here. The younger kids really look up to you."

"I ran out on them," Travis said. "I'm surprised they want anything to do with me."

"Don't beat yourself up about that," Clarence said. "You had no choice back then. Just remember if things go sour again, you definitely have a place to go. Oh, and one other thing. . . ." He reached farther behind the seat and pulled out a guitar case. "Thought you might need this. It's a loaner to practice on until you and Scott build your new guitar together. Gotta keep your skills up."

"Thanks." Travis took the case. "But I'll never have enough money to buy a guitar from Scott."

"Sure you will. You'll earn it by doing chores at the shop. Which reminds me . . ." Clarence dug down into his pocket and pulled out a folded-up envelope. "Scott told me to give you this and it almost slipped my mind. It's your pay for all the work you did."

The envelope felt thick. "Wow, thanks."

"Don't thank me. You earned it."

"Well, thanks for everything else, too, Clarence. I mean for taking me in. You didn't have to do that. I was nobody to you."

"No, you weren't, but Scott told you that I'm always taking in strays." He smiled. "I hit the jackpot this time. You made life interesting. And getting back to that guitar, Scott is dying to hear what your old Adirondack top sounds like. You can work with him on building it, and it'll be yours when you finish. That's what Scott and I did when we built mine. I couldn't afford his fancy prices, either."

"It would be Mom's guitar," Travis said.

"That's even better." Clarence got in his truck and rolled down the window. "I was talking with your father while you were outside. He seems to be coming around. I think I talked him into visiting your mother."

"Really? That's amazing."

259

"I thought you'd like that." He started the engine, then leaned out of the truck window again. "If you want, I can come pick you up next Saturday so you and Scott can get started on that guitar. You're welcome to stay the weekend at my place."

"That would be great!"

Clarence smacked the side of the truck and grinned. "It's settled, then." He revved the engine. "See you Saturday."

Travis grabbed the door handle. "Wait, Clarence! Can you do me a favor right now?"

"Sure. What is it?"

"Can we take my little brother over to visit Mom? He needs to see her with his own eyes."

"Sure, go get him," Clarence said. "But clean him up a little. You don't want the kid scaring your mother."

Travis picked up his stuff and ran toward the house. His family was still a mess, but he was beginning to see how to mend the cracks that had split them apart. "Hey, Roy, come here!" he called through the screen. "Do I ever have a surprise for you!"

Go Fish!

GOFISH

MJ AUCH

What did you want to be when you grew up?
A ballerina, an artist, or a veterinarian.

When did you realize you wanted to be a writer?
I had always thought of myself as an artist until I took a weeklong writer's workshop with Natalie Babbitt. When she said she discovered she could paint better pictures with words than paint, that struck a chord with me, and I've been writing ever since.

What was your worst subject in school?
Algebra.

What was your first job?
Designing fabric prints for men's pajamas in the Empire State Building—but only on the fifth floor.

How did you celebrate publishing your first book?
After two years of rejection, I sold my first two novels to two different publishers in the same week. I don't remember any specific celebration, other than being deliriously happy!

Where do you write your books?
I use a laptop, so I can write anywhere. One of my favorite places is on a train, because watching the scenery pass by seems to kick my brain into creative mode. I also like to write on our front porch when weather permits.

Which of your characters is most like you?
There's a little of me in all of my main characters. They all carry my value system and sense of justice.

When you finish a book, who reads it first?
Members of my two critique groups hear the book as I'm writing it. We're lucky to have some wonderful children's writers in our area. Each group meets once a month and we all drive up to an hour to get together. I get valuable early input from writers I respect and trust—Tedd Arnold, Patience Brewster, Bruce Coville, Kathy Coville, Cynthia DeFelice, Alice DeLaCroix, Marsha Hayles, Robin Pulver, and Vivian Vande Velde. The main person I count on is my editor, Christy Ottaviano, who pushes me to take the story far beyond the point I could go alone.

Are you a morning person or a night owl?
I'm a little of each, so I probably don't get enough sleep. I try to write every day when I first wake up, as long as it's after 5 AM. Then I have a tendency to fall asleep watching late-night TV. I guess that makes morning my more productive time.

What's your idea of the best meal ever?
Any meal eaten with good friends.

Which do you like better: cats or dogs?
I was raised with cats as a child, and although I still enjoy them, it has been dogs that have captured my heart. Our last

three dogs have been rescues. It gives me and my husband, Herm, great pleasure to take in a dog that has had a tough life.

What do you value most in your friends?
Two things. First is honesty. I don't like people who play mind games. I like to know straight out what they're thinking. It's hard to have any kind of relationship when people don't tell the truth.

Second but equal is a sense of humor. I admit to being a humor snob. I like people who are spontaneously funny. I'm lucky to have a large group of friends who fall into that category. There is always humor crackling around the room when we get together.

What makes you laugh out loud?
Spontaneous funny conversations with friends. Spending time with genuinely humorous people gives me much more pleasure than so-called professional comedians.

What's your favorite song?
I love playing and singing old jazz standards. Some of my favorites are "Moonlight in Vermont," "A Nightingale Sang in Berkeley Square," and "A Foggy Day in London Town."

What are you most afraid of?
Fire, which was probably what drove me to write *Ashes of Roses*.

What time of the year do you like best?
Fall, especially in the Northeast. It's the one season that doesn't last long enough. I never tire of the reds, golds, and brilliant oranges of the fall foliage.

If you were stranded on a desert island, who would you want for company?
My husband. He's my best friend and soul mate.

If you could travel in time, where would you go?
I'm happy with the years my life has spanned so far. I grew up in simpler times, back in the forties and fifties, and now I get to experience the amazing technological advances we have today. There are many earlier periods that interest me, but I wouldn't want to visit them because of the discomfort factor. They'd be smelly and buggy!

What's the best advice you have ever received about writing?
Don't talk about writing. Just sit down and do it.

What do you want readers to remember about your books?
I hope that they carry the characters with them for a long time and consider them to be friends.

What would you do if you ever stopped writing?
There are lots of other things I enjoy doing. Music is a big part of my life. I love singing three- or four-part harmony. If I weren't a writer, I'd probably be a backup singer. I also enjoy playing string instruments—guitar, banjo, mandolin, and fiddle. I'm not very good at any of these, but I love the challenge of trying to get better.

Other hobbies include designing and sewing clothes. I do this mostly for myself, although I made most of the costumes for our daughter's medieval wedding, and it's fun sewing the costumes for the chickens in our picture books.

I wish I had the time for some serious, non-book-related painting. I was an art major in college, and love doing abstract oils on large canvases.

What do you like best about yourself?
The fact that I'm honest. It gets me in trouble sometimes. I try to be tactful, but I always tell the truth. I think it makes me a friend who can be trusted.

What is your worst habit?
Procrastination. I'd be a lot more productive if I could keep myself from going off on tangents instead of staying focused.

What do you consider to be your greatest accomplishment?
I don't know how much credit I can take for this, but Herm and I raised two wonderful and talented children. They're now both artists in their own right—Kat, a freelance graphic and magazine designer, and Ian, an interactive and motion graphics designer working in advertising. They both have turned into genuinely good human beings.

What do you wish you could do better?
Everything! I love to learn new things, so I'm always working on something—right now it's playing jazz guitar—but I'm always frustrated that I don't progress as fast as I'd like.

What would your readers be most surprised to learn about you?
That I hated history in school. All they had us do was memorize dates of battles. That's why I like to write historical fiction, so I can make a period from the past come to life.

Twelve-year-old Basil's been associating numbers with colors since he was a kid. His gift (or curse) has turned him into somewhat of a loner, but everything changes when he meets Tenzie, the pushy new girl with similar freakisms. When Basil's world falls apart, Tenzie may be the only person who can help him put it back together again.

Meet Basil and Tenzie in
ONE + ONE = BLUE

CHAPTER 1

I'm the biggest loser in the seventh-grade class at Calvin Marshall Middle School. So far, nobody has challenged my position. My class was supposed to be the stars in the lower school this year. Then a notice came around in August that said they were changing everything around because of overcrowding. The lower school would be kindergarten through sixth, and seventh grade would move up to the new middle school with grades eight and nine. My grandmother homeschooled me my whole life until this year, so grade levels didn't mean much to me. Besides, for a bottom-feeder like me, the reorganization was no problem. The lowest point is a secure position—it never changes. But for kids like Joel Mack, the class jock, or Ashleigh Gianelli, the class beauty, missing out on a year of ruling the lower school and dropping to the lowest rung on the middle school ladder was a big shock. Joel, who probably towered over just about everybody in his old school, looks like a fourth-grader here. And Ashleigh is pretty, but she can't compare to the ninth-grade gorgeous girls. Some of them could be in the movies. Honest. I'm not kidding.

I figured out right away that lunch can be the worst period of the day because where you sit says a lot about how important you are. Not a worry for me. Right at the beginning of the school year, I staked out a claim at a small table—actually a desk—in the back corner of the cafeteria, where I could observe what was going on. From my vantage point, I've been watching how the other kids formed groups. It took a couple of weeks for the table arrangements to shake out—three grade levels of every category—the gorgeous girls, the brainiacs, the techno-nerds, the jocks, and the kids who think they've hit the jackpot when they get a D plus.

Well, that's sort of a bottom group, and my grades could qualify me for that table. I'm not like them, though, because I'm smart everywhere but in school.

When it was just Gram and me doing lessons together, there were no other kids to compare myself to. We would have long, interesting discussions about whatever subject I was studying. Gram made me feel like I was some kind of a genius. Then the first few tests in public school put me pretty much on the bottom of the pile. I didn't want to upset Gram by telling her how bad my grades were, but I knew she would find out when the first report cards went home.

To make things worse, most of the kids in my class had been together since kindergarten, and I didn't know any of them. Having a name like Basil Feeney didn't help me fit in, either. My mother, Carly, named me after an herb. It was the main ingredient in her favorite sauce—pesto—so things could have been a lot worse. Carly dumped me with my grandmother when I was five and ran off to Hollywood to become a star.

I might have been able to overcome the bad grades and the no-friends thing if it hadn't been for my freakism. I was even starting to make one friend, Jason Ferris. Jason and I sat next to each other in most of our classes because our last names started with the same letter. We weren't exactly best buddies, but he was the closest thing I'd ever had to a kid friend. For a couple of weeks, Jason and I got along pretty well. I even started sitting with him at a real lunch table once in a while.

Then came the day we were supposed to be correcting each other's math review worksheets. Jason read the problem out loud. "One jar holds 635 marbles, and another jar has 463 marbles. If you put them all together, how many marbles would you have?" He looked up from the paper. "You said 798. It's supposed to be 1,098."

"That's because of three and six both being yellow," I explained. "I get them mixed up a lot. Don't you?"

Jason dipped his chin and peered at me over his glasses.

I should have realized something was wrong, but like an idiot I kept going. "Same thing with one and zero both being white. I mean, there are so many colors. Why couldn't each number get a different one?" This seemed so logical to me. For as long as I could remember, every time I saw a number, it had a color for me. And every time I saw a color that was the exact shade of one of my numbers, it would make me think of that number. It was as normal as breathing, which was why I couldn't understand the look I was getting from Jason.

He sat staring at me, but didn't have to answer because the bell rang and we went to lunch. At least Jason did. He grabbed his lunch bag and was in line by the door before I could stand up. We weren't allowed to cut ahead, so I didn't see him until I got into the cafeteria. By the time I got my milk, Jason was sitting at a table that was full, so I retreated to my desk-table in the back corner.

I saw Jason talking to the kids around him, then they all laughed. He turned and pointed at me, and they all looked at me and laughed again. I was pretty sure he was talking about me, but I didn't understand what was happening until we got in line to go back to class. The kid in front of me—I think his name was Max—said, "My eight is orange. What color is yours?"

So different people had different colors for their numbers? Was that the reason Jason acted so weird? "Eight is sort of a dark blue-purple," I said. "Orange is five for me."

The kids around us started laughing. When I got on the bus for the trip home, I could tell that everybody knew about my numbers / colors freakism. And for the first time in my life, I realized this wasn't a normal thing that everybody had. I could hear comments coming from all over the bus. By the time we got to my stop, I was convinced I was the only person in the world who saw numbers as colors and colors as numbers.

Gram knew I was bummed the minute I came through the door. "Have a bad day, Basil?" She could read me like a book.

"Yeah, I guess."

"Tell me about it. It always helps me to talk about a problem."

I was just about to open my mouth when she said, "As long as it's not a math problem. You know how bad I am at that."

Of course she would think I was having trouble with one of my subjects. That's when I realized that I'd never talked about my colors / numbers thing with her. I had probably thought about colors when we were doing math worksheets, but I couldn't remember ever saying anything out loud. Why would I? It was as much a part of me as breathing, and I thought everybody had it. But now I knew I was the odd one. How would Gram feel if I hit her with the fact that her grandson was an all-out freak? So I didn't tell her.

That's when I stopped trying to make friends in school—not that I'd ever had any real friends. I never saw that many kids when I was homeschooled. Once in a while, Gram and I would get together with the homeschooled kids in Broxburg for something like a fossil field trip to Craig's Creek. There were lots of other get-togethers, but I really hated them. I don't think Gram was too wild about them either, because she never forced me to go. Our friends were all adults, older ones like Gram, who didn't have kids my age.

Giving up on having friends really hadn't been my decision anyway. Kids started making fun of other things about me, like my rooster-tail cowlick and my nose, which takes a slight left turn halfway down my face. Everybody thought I was too weird to hang out with. So from then on, I settled into my position as class loser, and I kept the numbers / colors freakism to myself. I kept everything to myself.

CHAPTER 2

It was the first Monday in October when I walked into the cafeteria and knew right away—my class loser title was at risk. There was a girl sitting at my desk-table who could have been the poster girl for Sunny Daze Thrift Shop. I know this for sure, because I'm their poster boy.

I plopped my milk and lunch bag on the table. "This is my spot," I said.

She looked up at me through glasses that had tiny plastic flowers glued all around the openings. I say openings, because there wasn't any glass in them. "There's plenty of room," she said. "Pull up a chair."

She was inviting me to sit at my own table? I stood

there staring, but that didn't seem to bother her. She was busy picking slices of radish out of what looked like a cream cheese sandwich. "I'm Tenzie Verplank," she said. When I didn't move, she got up and grabbed a chair from the techno-nerd table and plopped it down across from her. "Sit. Stay," she ordered, the way you'd talk to a Labrador retriever.

If I went anywhere else, I'd have to deal with a whole table of strangers, so I did what she said. Our knees bumped together as soon as I sat down. I pulled my chair back. I was facing the wall, which made me uneasy. I'd had enough experience with people slapping "kick me" signs between my shoulder blades to know you never sit with your back to the room. Now the only thing I had to look at was Tenzie.

I concentrated on my lunch. This was a good day—thin slices of roast beef wrapped around pieces of avocado, red and yellow pepper sticks with cucumber dip, and almond cookies with cranberries. Gram says it's important to have lots of color in every meal to make it interesting. Some of the lunches she comes up with could be framed and hung on the wall.

"How come you sit here alone?" Tenzie asked. "No friends?"

"I don't see any friends sitting with you," I said.

"We just moved here," she shot back. "What's your excuse?"

Her eyes were drilling a hole into my forehead. It wasn't that they were unusual looking like green or violet. They were dirty bathwater gray. It was the way she looked out of them, not shy and off to the side like you expect from a new kid.

"You got a name?" she asked.

"Basil."

"Basil like in pesto?" she asked.

I glared at her. "Just Basil."

We sat there chewing and ignoring each other for a few minutes. Well, I was ignoring her, but I could feel her staring at me. When she started radish-picking the other half of her sandwich, I sneaked another look at her. I don't know anything about girls' clothes, but I was pretty sure hers wouldn't cut it at the gorgeous girls' table. She had on this big flowy dress thing, and Tenzie's skinny arms hung out of the short puffy sleeves like the clapper on a cowbell. The dress was a wild print of blue and orange flowers, the exact colors for my two and five. The flowers practically vibrated in front of my eyes, making it hard for me to look away.

Tenzie took the last bite of her sandwich, wrapped the rejected radishes, and got up. "I'm sitting here tomorrow," she said. "See you then, Pesto." As soon as she left, I slipped into my regular seat, but it didn't feel the same now that my safe loser's spot had been invaded.

I spent the rest of the lunch period watching Ashleigh Gianelli study the eighth-grade popular girls' table. The older girls all had hair that was straight and shiny and swung forward when they looked down. Ashleigh must have tried to straighten hers out, but in the steamy heat of the cafeteria, it was starting to curl up again on one side. I thought she looked better with curly hair, even if it wasn't swingy, but what did I know? No matter how much gel goop I used in the morning to plaster down my cowlick, it always broke loose by the time the bus arrived at the school.

When I got to my next class—math—I noticed a bright flash of two and five. Tenzie was sitting in the desk in front of mine. She looked over her shoulder. "Hey, Pesto, you following me around?"

I slid down in my seat, hoping nobody had heard what she called me.

Mrs. Lowe was writing multiplication problems on

the board. "We're going to try something different today," she said. "I'm giving you a chance to show off your multiplication facts. When I call on you, stand up by your desk and solve the problem out loud." She said this like she was doing us a favor. This should have been easy for me, because Gram started teaching me multiplication tables a few years ago. When I looked at the problems on the board now, the colors all ran together. Maybe it was because I was scared to stand up in front of the class to answer.

Mrs. Lowe started by calling on a kid in the first row. Before I could get the numbers into my head, the kid had solved the problem and was back in his seat. Then Mrs. Lowe called on the girl behind him. She was taking a little longer to figure out the problem.

I looked at the clock, trying to estimate how long it would take to get to me. Maybe my turn wouldn't come until tomorrow, and I was pretty sure I felt a bad cold coming on. I coughed. Yep, I could feel those little cold germs multiplying in my throat right now, building whole colonies of misery. I'd have to stay home for sure.

Mrs. Lowe called on the third girl in the fourth row. She was skipping people! Not fair! I coughed again, hoping I could bring the cold on faster and go to the nurse. But my plan backfired. My cough caught Mrs. Lowe's attention. I started chanting in my head. *Don't call on me. Don't call on me.* As Mrs. Lowe raised her hand to point at me, I felt my stomach form a fist around Gram's colorful lunch. Maybe I could throw up right now.

"Basil," she said, "you try this problem."

I tried to focus on the numbers. Thirty-eight times nine. Nine! When Gram and I practiced the multiplication tables at home, I always burned out by the sevens, and Gram never pushed me to go further because she was as confused as me.

I stood up. Mrs. Lowe was tapping the eight and the nine, back and forth. Back and forth. It was almost hypnotizing, watching the chalk bounce from one number to the other. Purple, brown, purple, brown. "Come on, Basil. Eight times nine. You know this."

The purple eight and brown nine danced in front of my eyes, and then the blue two and orange five of Tenzie's dress joined them, flashing in and out. What were the numbers was I supposed to be multiplying? Four times eight? No, there was a nine. A brown nine. Tenzie's blue two and orange five merged and made brown. "Two plus five is nine," I blurted out. There was an explosion of laughter. I wanted to be invisible again.

The kid next to me snorted and slapped his desk. "You kill me, Pesto." He had heard the name.

"Concentrate, Basil. We're doing multiplication now," Mrs. Lowe said with that fake-patient voice teachers get when they don't want people to know they think you're stupid. "What's eight times nine, Basil?"

Tenzie covered her mouth and leaned back. "Seventy-two," she whispered.

"Seventy-two," I said, and sat down, relieved to have the ordeal over.

But it wasn't over. Everybody was laughing again. Did Tenzie slip me the wrong answer?

"That's right, but you're not finished, Basil," Mrs. Lowe said. "Stand up and do the rest." She was bouncing that piece of chalk again. "Three times nine."

"Twenty-seven," Tenzie whispered. As I parroted the answer, I thought about how seventy-two was green and blue, and twenty-seven was blue first, then green.

"Basil, stay with me here." Mrs. Lowe was saying something about how we had to carry over the seven to the twenty-seven. Tenzie whispered the final answer. "Three hundred and forty-two," I repeated after her.

"Very nice work, Basil." Mrs. Lowe had a maybe-this-kid-isn't-a-total-moron-after-all look on her face.

I could already feel the danger of being a nonloser. Now I'd have to live up to the reputation of giving a right answer. "Or maybe it's three hundred and fifty-four," I said, slipping into my seat. The pressure of high expectations slipped from my shoulders and fractured on the floor around me.

Tenzie turned in her seat and gave me a puzzled look.

I just smiled and shrugged. Tenzie was no threat to my loser status or my desk in the cafeteria. She'd be sitting with the eccentric brainiacs in no time. There were a lot of open spots at that table. She'd fit right in.